ATOMIC SEA

Amazon Reviews

"I loved this book... it's a clever story about thoughtful, caring people from different backgrounds (there's even a love story or two woven into it) thrown into an unexpectedly terrifying and violent political situation, and how they deal with it with humor and ingenuity."

"Brilliant! Every chapter holds a twist you can't see coming. Fast moving and worth the reading ride."

"Took me a couple of days to get into it, but hit the halfway point and could. not. put. it. down. Great read. Sort of this weird mix of thriller style action, contrasted really strongly with the down to earth Australian thing. Also, the protagonist is female and in her forties - she's not James Bond, not bullet-proof. Completely relatable. And in a world where there's a lot of men with a lot of guns, it was a perspective I found pretty enjoyable! Giving this five stars."

"Atomic Sea is a novel I loved from start to finish. With so many twists and turns one could be fooled into thinking this is a straight up action thriller (and it certainly feels like it is in some parts - in a great way), but what sets Atomic Sea apart from others is the wonderful beating heart of its delightful, intelligent cast of characters who must face very relatable and human challenges amidst all the carnage around them."

ATOMIC SEA

C. M. LANCE

SEA
BOOKS
PRESS
seabooks.net

Print ISBN 978-0-6489851-0-5
Ebook ISBN 978-0-9872113-9-2

Published by Seabooks Press
seabooks.net

To my IPv6 comrades
Tony Hill, Kevin Karp and Michael Biber

It's one of the more common modern forms of doublethink ... to allow that of course the universe we experience is a mental construct rather than an objective reality, and then to turn right around and insist that some currently popular features of that mental construct—the deadness, mindlessness, and meaninglessness of the cosmos, for example—are objectively real truths, while features of mental constructs that our culture doesn't encourage—the presence of life, mind, and meaning in the nonhuman cosmos, for instance—are just plain wrong.

John Michael Greer

Contents

PART I. BROOME
Prologue   1
1. Worm Turning   2
2. Minister Iceberg   12
3. My Cousins   26
4. At the Jetty   38
5. The Glowing Powder   48
6. Contamination   63
7. The Pink-Orange Device   72
8. Cliffs of Minyirr   86

PART II. WALMADAN
9. Mutations   94
10. A Bewildering World   103
11. The Eerie Warship   112
12. The Sunset Gala   125
13. The Ambassador Weeps   138
14. A Dome of Golden Light   148
15. Sanctuary   156
16. Cyclone Cyril   166

PART III. MURUJUGA
17. Operation Sparrow   179
18. Red-Black Rocks   192
19. A Green Gully   205
20. Return of the Blue Boat   218
21. The Tinny   230
22. An Unfortunate Turn of Events   244
23. Ancient Hands   254
24. Reality   264

Thank You, Readers   268
About the Author   269
Acknowledgements   269
Other Books   270

PART I. BROOME

Prologue

The blue wooden boat drifts.

The sea is still, the waves are slow ripples. The hull rolls just enough for a steel drum to softly clang one way, then the other, between the mast and the side of the old Asian fishing boat, someone's hard-scrabble livelihood.

Yet those on board do not have the look of labourers: they were once plump men with soft hands. The man in the cabin leans forward on the table, his head on his arms. The other one lies on the deck, fingers over his eyes as if wiping away tears.

I'd like to imagine a shower of rain had swept in to cool him, to mingle with his tears and offer him a final drink, to ease him through that agony of vomiting and voiding and weeping burns. I hope it rained and gave him a moment of comfort, but I don't expect it did.

Then in the dimness I notice a heap of white powder beside him and the hair on my scalp lifts.

The powder is glimmering with a soft blue light.

Simon whispers, 'Is that shit *glowing*?'

'Oh fuck,' I say, backing away, my voice shaking. 'We've got to get out of here!'

Was it only three days ago I thought my life dull?

1. Worm Turning

Jessie's plane has already landed when I get to the airport. The terminal is just a large, airy shed and from the door I can see my sister waiting by the conveyor belt, wearing a black T-shirt and jeans, a backpack over one shoulder, her long hair up in a pony-tail. A magenta and orange pony-tail.

She grabs a suitcase and comes towards me grinning. We hug and I take the bag.

'Wow, Jess. Kitchen sink?'

'Didn't know what to bring.'

'Well, you only need the minimum. Can't you feel the heat?'

Just then we emerge from the terminal and she gasps. 'Holy hell, Lena, it was only six degrees in Melbourne.'

'Welcome to Broome, little sister. I doubt it's ever hit six degrees here.' I grin. 'But the hair suits.'

'Did it especially for Broome—orange, purple, pink—appropriate, yes?'

I laugh. '*Perfect*. Welcome, little sister.' We drive out of the parking lot and I put the air-conditioning on full blast and say, 'Now, the hotel's not far. Let's get you registered then we can sort things out.'

'Things?'

'This evening, the welcome event. A tour of Worm Turning with nibbles and refreshments. You don't have to come if you don't want to, but I got you a ticket—'

'Do we get Chernobyl champagne and Fukushima finger-food?'

'Oh God, Jess, don't say things like that at the conference. Except to me of course.'

'Okay. Hey—food, wine and a big hole in the ground. Who could ask for more?'

It's the first time we've met in nearly a year. I work in Sydney, Jessie in Melbourne, so my conference here in north-west Australia was a great excuse for a holiday together. The rather nice hotel, with its pool set in a swathe of green above teal-blue Roebuck Bay, doesn't hurt either.

While Jess unpacks I return to the endless last-minute tasks of the committee. Event organisers are handling the registrations so I mainly run around sorting out mislaid presentations and soothing ruffled feathers. Finally everything seems to be on track for tomorrow, so I go back to my room for a shower and change into my new grey linen sheath.

But the dress that seemed so smart in Sydney appears drab in colourful Broome. I try to do something with my hair, pulling it up into a bun then letting it hang to my shoulders. It used to be red-gold when I was young but now? Mousey brown at best. It looks dull. I look dull. My life is dull.

I sit down with a sigh.

Jess knocks and I let her in. She glances at my dress. 'Haven't you got anything more festive than that, Lena?'

She's changed into black jeans and a silk tank top, set off by scarlet lips, dark eyebrows and cheekbones like cut glass. And the orange and magenta hair.

'You should bloody talk,' I say. 'Haven't you got a single garment that isn't black, Jessie?'

She grins. 'Not a one.'

We gather with the others at the front of the hotel and take our seats in a luxury bus. I nod at my fellow committee members and a few friends, surprised at how many people are strangers but, after all, this is an inter-disciplinary conference, with geologists, biologists, physicists and even the odd economist.

Arnold, the committee chair, checks everyone on his list is present, then the doors close with a whoosh and the bus departs. We head out on a road going north.

Jess and I settle back and catch up with the latest on friends and family. She's my baby half-sister: my parents divorced when I was ten, and when I was twenty Dad married Suyin and had Jess. I've always adored her.

She works for one of the massive Internet companies, the consistently cool one she says. She doesn't even have to leave her beautiful apartment in central Melbourne to go to work either, they do everything remotely. Once I teased her about holding meetings via hologram and she said, 'Next year.' I don't think she was joking.

We pass through a landscape of orange-dust pindan and small gum trees, the indigo sky above blending with a hazy lavender horizon. The scrub isn't the dry grey-brown I'm used to seeing around Sydney either: here it glows with lime, emerald and silvery jade.

After a couple of days in the Kimberley I'm still not used to the vividness of the landscape, the rich blues of the sea and the rust-reds of the soil. Even Jess, usually unimpressed by nature, keeps turning around to stare.

The road isn't sealed but it's wide and glides smoothly beneath us, and we reach the Worm Turning plant in less than an hour. At a big T-junction we drive onto a sealed road with beautifully landscaped verges and sculptures scattered among the flowering shrubs.

After a short time I see enormous steel gates ahead of us, guarded by a surprisingly large cluster of soldiers in black. In a clearing to one side is a little camp of tents and chairs with a fireplace in the middle.

The bus slows. Suddenly there's a group of people running along beside us. They're yelling and waving placards reading *Our Land Not Yours, No Nuclear Plant, Stop Digging in Sacred Ground!* Some of the protesters are silver-haired Sea Rovers but most are Aboriginal.

In Sydney I know only two Indigenous people—a girl from Wagga doing a doctorate and a boy from Redfern in my honours class. They're handsome brown kids, bright as buttons, my grandfather Mike would have said. But these people are dark-skinned, their faces plain, passionate, furious.

The bus stops for a moment at the gates and I realise a large white-haired man outside is gazing at me. Our eyes meet and I can't turn away. He nods thoughtfully as if he knows me.

Then he smiles, a glorious open smile illuminated by his long white beard, and I can't help but return it. What a lovely man—why on earth would I think 'plain'?

With a roar of acceleration the bus rushes through the gates. Looking back, Jess and I can see the soldiers pushing into the group, swinging their weapons viciously at the outnumbered protesters. We turn to each other, horrified.

'Wow. That's overkill for some bits of cardboard,' she says.

I nod, thinking of the bearded man and his lovely smile.

We drive quickly along a road bordered with manicured bushes, then turn right into a large car park and halt. We emerge in the afternoon heat and are met by three tour guides, the leader a young, cool-faced woman.Our beefy bus driver greets her and takes her aside, murmuring.

She turns back to us. 'Ladies and gentlemen, welcome to Geo-Garrod's new plant, Worm Turning,' she says. 'Our apologies for that little unpleasantness at the gates. Professional agitators that's all. We'd like to point out that this land was acquired legally, via compensation to the traditional landholders.'

'So what *was* it about, then?' says Jess. Sometimes I wish she'd let other people ask the awkward questions.

'There's always a disgruntled few,' says the woman, shrugging. 'Didn't get their share I expect. Now we'd like you all to climb aboard for the tour.'

Three small buses painted in the crimson and green of Geo-Garrod Ltd are waiting for us. Jess and I are towards the end of the queue, so when we get on our bus we have to take separate seats.

I'm beside a pleasant-looking young man—well, most people seem young to me now I've passed fifty. He's lanky and bearded, with curly brown hair and a long sensitive face.

I nod hullo and say, 'Lena Whalen,' and he replies, 'Matthew Rossi.'

'And what's your interest in the conference, Matthew?'

'Um,' he says, rubbing his forehead with his hands, and I realise he's upset.

'Are you okay?'

'Oh, bit appalled at what just happened at the gates,' he says. 'Those people are friends of mine.'

'Yes, that was horrible. Do the soldiers always pile into them so aggressively?'

'Often enough.'

The bus doors shut and we start driving past the main building, around to the rear of the plant. It's a startlingly modern complex, with curved red and olive-green steel shapes along the facade that seem to echo the surrounding landscape.

'The guide said the agreement for this land was legal,' I say tentatively.

'Well, she would say that, wouldn't she?' Matthew laughs softly. 'But no. They paid some opportunists for their signatures—all blacks look the same to them after all. But they keep refusing to talk to the *real* custodians of this land, those people outside the gates.'

'Isn't there some tribunal they can appeal to?'

'Are you kidding? No, the Sea Rovers lawyers have done what they can but so far ...' He turns and smiles wryly at me. 'You're not from around here, obviously.'

'Sydney.'

'Ah. Well, things are different here in the west. A lot of people would just love it if this state separated completely from Australia. They hate land rights law—any Commonwealth law—and they think they'd all get rich if they could do whatever they liked.'

'What?'

'Western Australia's closer to Asia than the eastern states. It's always had a secessionist streak but the mining roller-coaster has really brought the crazies out to play.'

'I had no idea.'

'Now there's only a couple of independents stopping the politicians from giving it a go. God knows what would happen if ...' Matthew shrugs. 'Anyway. Sorry to be depressing.'

The guide taps the microphone and says, 'Welcome, ladies and gentleman. Here you see Worm Turning's innovative new nuclear reprocessing plant, many times smaller than similar facilities due to Geo-Garrod's patented technologies. The plant has already received international awards for its engineering and architecture.'

At the rear of the building we drive past a massive open structure full of loading docks and railway lines. It's as dramatic and attractive as the front.

'To your left is where the plant will receive used nuclear fuel from all over the world. After undergoing Geo-Garrod's revolutionary new treatment, valuable radioactive material will be extracted and returned to its owners. The waste will be encased in inert material and disposed of in the famous Wormhole.'

The bus turns away and we drive along a sealed road through bushland. A double railway line leads from the plant, running beside the road.

Matthew says, 'So what brings you to the conference, Lena?'

'I was press-ganged onto the organising committee—I work in medical nuclear physics. What about you?'

'Geology. Recently relocated to Broome from a lab in Perth.'

'Nice change,' I say. 'Why did you make the move?'

'Oh, I wouldn't stop pointing out that the structure of this region isn't quite as Geo-Garrod claims. Unfortunately my lab was in the running for a big contract from Geo-Garrod and once they got rid of me they landed it.'

I'm surprised he's so matter of fact. 'That must have been a bit ... rough.'

'Turned out for the best,' he says. 'I've set up a small local consultancy now. Family here, too.' His sensitive face is still and I wonder if there's more to it than that.

After a kilometre or so we halt in a car park and get out. We climb a flight of stairs onto a timber platform and I see Jessie through the small crowd and wave. She smiles and goes back to showing something on a mobile to a young man, who seems more interested in gazing at her smooth brown shoulders.

Our guide says proudly, arms outstretched, 'Ladies and gentlemen, Worm Turning's famous Wormhole.'

I move to the railing and look forward and gasp, like everyone around me.

I'd always assumed the Wormhole was some sort of ordinary mine, but it's a vast, open-cut, wound in the earth. Railway lines spiral several times around the sides then pass into a tunnel at the bottom and disappear.

'The excavation is half a kilometre deep,' says the guide. 'And below the surface is a maze of tunnels spreading down a further half kilometre, where the waste will be permanently stored.'

'My goodness, *marvellous*,' says Arnold, the committee chair, his bushy white eyebrows almost meeting his hairline.

'Sales of mineral sands from the excavation have helped fund the plant and mining will continue for some time yet, however the initial phase is complete. The Wormhole is now ready to begin storing nuclear waste and it's large enough to do so for a long time into the future.'

'When do operations begin?' asks someone in the crowd.

'After the grand gala opening next week.'

I stare at the structure, astonished by its sheer scale.

'Amazing, yes?' says Matthew quietly beside me.

'Not at all as I'd pictured.' I look at him, curious. 'But you don't like it.'

'No. Something's wrong with the whole thing and it could be dangerous.'

'To whom?'

'All of us. They've systematically lied—'

'Dude!' A plump young man in a black T-shirt slaps him on the shoulder. 'Didn't think you'd have the nerve to turn up. Man, you're a glutton for punishment.'

'I think I'll just go and see my sister,' I say, and slip away through the crowd. Matthew Rossi seems like a sweet guy but it sounds as if he's got a bit of a chip on his shoulder.

I move to the railing again. What an enormous hole, all that soil—mineral sands, I think the guide said—dug up, shipped away and sold. And that was just a precursor to the main event, the revolutionary new reprocessing plant.

I turn and contemplate the red and green steel building in the distance. What an audacious scheme.

The conference welcome event is held in a vast reception foyer at the front of the plant. They serve us exquisite canapés and what may be the best champagne I've ever tasted. I chat to people I know and get introduced to dozens I don't.

It's all a bit of a blur after the second glass, but very pleasantly so. As always, Jess is perfectly at home chatting to a bunch of techies.

Later, when we leave the plant, I tense as our bus passes through the now floodlit gates. The ominous soldiers are still there and as the lights glitter on their insignias I realise they're American military, not Australian.

The protesters are back in their camp—I see moving shadows against the flickering fire—and I hope they're all right, especially after the pounding they took today. From what Matthew said they have good reason to protest.

Jessie has fallen asleep on my shoulder, tired after the flight from Melbourne. I brush my cheek against my sister's hair for a moment and smile to myself, content to be with her again.

Non-technical people find her difficult. She asks awkward questions and finds it hard to bother with people who can't keep up with her crystalline intellect. She's in her thirties now and I worry she won't find the right sort of guy to settle down with, someone who'll love her and let her be her own slightly eccentric self.

But then, who does get to find that special guy? I sigh.

Street lights are now flashing past the windows and we're turning into the brightly-lit hotel car park. I shake Jess gently and say, 'We're back.'

The doors whoosh open and we stumble out of the air-conditioned bus into the hot, humid evening. Arnold calls out, 'Don't forget, everyone, nine a.m. start on the *dot* tomorrow.'

People say goodnight or wander off to the bar overlooking the bay, but I've eaten canapés enough for a four-course meal and Jess says she has too.

We briefly consider the prospect of a swim in the turquoise pool but decide it's time to crash out instead. It's been a long day.

2. Minister Iceberg

I hold up the card showing zero minutes remaining but the speaker ignores me. I stand and go to one side of the stage with his gift, hoping he'll take the hint.

'Let me just revisit ...' he says.

God, I hate chairing at conferences.

'I'm afraid we'll have to cut it short here Dr Wilson, we've run out of time,' I interrupt. 'I'm sure anyone with questions will take them up with you at morning tea. Would you all please thank Dr Wilson for that very interesting presentation.'

I give him his gift (a bottle of local wine) and start clapping, and the audience follows without obvious enthusiasm.

The man I call Dr Tedious sits back in his seat with a cross expression. From earlier talks I know his question would just be the usual dick-waving, so it doesn't bother me to end the session now. We're ten minutes over time as it is and delightful coffee scents are wafting in from the foyer.

At the break I stand quietly in the background and gaze at the attendees—mainly men of course. Occasionally I meet another female scientist, but as a woman in my field I'm usually pretty lonely.

I've done my best to learn the matey tribal customs over the years, and most of the time I fit in. Roughly. Every now and then it's painfully brought to my attention I never really can.

After the break my chairing duties are over, so I'm able to

relax and listen to the talks. I sit not far from the auditorium door—never know when a discreet departure might be welcome, especially if the jargon gets excessive.

I check my program for the session and see the first presenter is the young man I met yesterday, Dr Matthew Rossi speaking on *Geomorphology of the Dampier Peninsula: a New Perspective.*

Lanky Matthew takes the stage. After the usual problem with his slides—I think, come on support folk, does this have to happen every single time?—he settles in and gives a calm, efficient talk. It's something about structures deep in the land, unrecognised instability, unusual minerals.

I don't follow the details, but alerted by his words yesterday I realise he seems to be proposing something unwelcome to the mood of the audience. The geologists in particular don't seem very happy. I know many are employed by Geo-Garrod, and I wonder what's making them so cranky.

It doesn't sound like revolutionary stuff to me, but then what do I know about the geomorphology of the Dampier Peninsula?

Matthew finishes. 'I'm happy to take questions.' Excellent speaker I note, ended well within his allotted time.

The chair points at one of the raised hands and someone says, 'Look, Matthew, you've been trotting this out at the last few conferences and I just don't see how you can defend it any more. Surely the work of something something indicates something?' (I'm paraphrasing here.)

'Dave, they're not looking at this model, criticisms have focused on the older model.'

'A lot of good results have come out of that one,' someone interjects from the floor.

'One at a time, please,' calls the chair.

A new speaker stands. 'We all know the recent model has major flaws. You can't base predictions on that.'

'It's not based on the discredited section of the recent model,' says the young man patiently. 'This is the latest extended model.'

There are a couple of groans of contempt from the audience, and the chair says, 'Thank you Dr Rossi, for that most interesting presentation,' and gives him his speaker's gift. There's a scattering of applause.

Matthew leaves the stage, head down. Poor guy. Science is brutal.

After lunch it's time for my own presentation, an overview to bring the non-physicists up to speed. Although I've spoken many times it's always a bit nerve-racking, but soon I settle in.

The good stuff first: the atom is your friend. Radiation for medical imaging, scanning, diagnosis, treatment. Reactors to heat steam, drive turbines, create power.

Then the not so good: nuclear waste, accidents, fallout. Rotting old plants nobody wants, shiny new ones too close to fault zones. Exposure, survival rates, promising treatments.

I talk about the Hiroshima and Nagasaki children, the Chernobyl kids, the Fukushima babies, and the whole new generation from Hanford yet to come: always the children. I don't emphasise the fact there's not much anyone can do when particles, fast and invisible, overwhelm living tissue.

Finally here, Worm Turning. The new plant to relieve the pressure of all that nuclear waste which so urgently needs reprocessing after the Hanford *incident*. (That's the term the spin doctors prefer to *disaster*, but I'm not sure even that comes close—perhaps mega-something might work?)

I close the talk by simply saying Worm Turning seems like a good idea. The audience approves and I get away with just a minor intellectual mauling from Dr Tedious.

Afterwards I get a cup of tea and sit on a balcony overlooking Roebuck Bay, and wonder how there could be so many shades of blue-green in that water.

Teal on the horizon, turquoise closer in, jade and aquamarine near the shore, and hues without names that recall gemstones and stained glass. So beautiful.

In the auditorium some economist is extolling the benefits of the nuclear industry but suddenly I can't cope with the buzzwords. I sigh and find myself puzzling how I got to this low point in my life.

Jessie's mum Suyin worked in medical physics and the subject fascinated me. Radiation in medicine was invaluable and life-saving in so many ways, and as a research student I loved the intellectual puzzles of my studies.

But research requires a focus on statistics rather than people and that abstraction insulated me for a long time.

Then in the nineties I went to work with a humanitarian group supporting the Chernobyl children, the thousands of kids suffering with radiation-induced cancers. After that I couldn't regard people as an abstraction any more.

It damaged me professionally, of course: now I'm stuck at the middle levels of academia and know I'll go no further. I don't have the right attitude, you see.

My hair flutters in the warm breeze and the reflection in the glass catches my eye. I wonder how others see me—a confident organiser who stands in an auditorium and tells eminent scientists what to do? An academic who speaks with calm authority on complex subjects? A quiet woman who moves unnoticed in the background of other people's lives?

Max used to say I reminded him of confident, lovely Meryl Streep. I doubt anyone would think that today.

Jess doesn't attend the talks because she's got teleconfs with Beijing and Tokyo, but that evening, as I'm dressing for the conference dinner, I tell her about Matthew Rossi's words at the Wormhole, and the odd atmosphere in his presentation today.

She's vaguely interested, but as it doesn't involve computing she doesn't really care. She's wearing some black slinky thing with a cutaway back. I search my luggage for something that might make me feel slightly attractive, with zero result, and put on a brown dress.

'Lena, what *is* this?' says Jess. 'Brown? You used to wear such pretty things. You're still not grieving for that creep *Max*? You've got to get out and find someone new.'

Drawing on my eyeliner, I shrug, which is something of a mistake.

'I'd like to, but so far ...'

'Well, tonight's your lucky night, I bet,' says Jess confidently.

She is so wrong.

The dining room is bedecked with flowers, a jazz quartet softly playing. Jess and I are a few minutes late, which is unfortunate as everyone else has managed to find seats with their friends.

The only table with spare places is the boring one with the committee and official guests. And pariahs, I note, seeing Matthew sitting awkwardly alone.

I sit down between him and a man with a shaven head, and Jess sits on his other side. Across the table is the chair of the committee, Arnold, with his busy white eyebrows. The waiter pours us wine.

Arnold says, 'Lena, we've had marvellous news—the Minister will be able to join us this evening after all!'

Oh damn, I think. I was hoping to avoid her.

'Now do let me introduce everyone,' says Arnold. 'Glenn Garrod, this is Dr Lena Whalen from our organising committee.'

I look up in surprise. The shaven-head man is the notorious owner of the Geo-Garrod plant? He's in his sixties, more attractive than he appears on TV, his eyes friendly, his shoulders solid in an open-necked shirt.

'And Dr Matthew Rossi—' Matthew nods.

'And ...?' asks Arnold.

'Oh, sorry,' I say. 'My sister, Jessie Whalen—Professor Arnold Sanders, chair of the committee.'

Arnold's eyebrows go up. 'Sister?'

I explain. 'My father remarried. We're half-sisters.'

With his usual tactlessness Arnold's eyebrows remain up.

Jess says, 'My mother was Chinese, Dr Sanders, that's why.'

'Indeed, yes of course.'

People arrive and mill around at the door.

'Arnold, I think they're here,' I say. He leaps up and goes to greet them, and my heart thuds.

Hell. Oh, *hell* to the thousandth power of hell.

Arnold proudly escorts two people to the table. 'Everyone, let me introduce the Honourable Alise Berg, Minister for the Industrial Environment, and her new chief of staff, Brigadier Max Leopard.'

My stomach clenches.

Greetings, handshakes. Alise is wearing a blue silk suit that looks both professional and exquisite. Her platinum hair shimmers to her shoulders, her heart-shaped face is so perfect

I want to slap her.

She's on charm automatic until she sees me. 'Good *heavens*, Lena. It's certainly been a while. You're looking ...'

'Hello, Ice. Yes it has. How's James?'

'Fine,' she says coolly. 'And I'm sure you have *so* much to talk about with Max—' She waves her hand at her new chief of staff.

'Hello, Max. See you've moved up in the world,' I say lightly, feeling sick.

'Dr Whalen.' He nods stiffly, his eyes looking past me.

Jess stares at him with loathing.

'Don't tell me you're *still* cross with each other,' says Alise. 'You'll be able to get that divorce soon enough.' She smiles sweetly. 'We must all move on.'

Thankfully they do.

I take a swig of wine. *God*, I hadn't expected—

Glenn Garrod murmurs, 'You've clearly met the Minister before.'

'Um, Ice? Yes, did our doctorates at the same time. But she dropped out, preferred politics instead.' (And my first sweetheart, James. That still stung.)

'Ice? Ah, Ice Berg.' He's amused. 'And the Brigadier?'

I take another swig. 'My ex-husband, or soon to be. I'd heard he was promoted but didn't realise it was onto the Minister's staff.'

Max Leopard? If he'd been named Alpha Male he couldn't have been more butch, with his severely handsome face and his mysterious past. Too late I realised the only mystery was his compulsive lying.

Thank heavens I never changed my name to his as he'd

wanted. *Lena Leopard*? Great stripper name.

'You're a nuclear physicist, Lena, I believe?' says Garrod.

'Oh? Yes, but not your sort, I'm on the medical, human exposure side of things. Fuel reprocessing's way out of my league.'

He leans towards me with the full force of his famous charm. 'Don't be modest, I read your latest paper in the Journal of Physics. It was excellent.'

'Thank you, Glenn. Surprised anyone's read it.'

'I made certain I was across everyone's specialities before agreeing to speak. Don't want to be drawn and quartered tomorrow.'

I grin ruefully. 'There'll always be someone who won't like what you say.'

'Half the country in my case.'

'Wasn't it sixty-seven percent in that last survey?'

'Ouch. Let's not be too precise here.' Garrod looks at me, eyebrows raised. 'You're one of the sixty-seven percent?'

'As a scientist I must always assume the best advice is being followed.' I'm a little flustered by his proximity but it's easy to take refuge in formality, my second nature. 'It's odd putting a plant in such a remote part of the country, but at least it's safely isolated. And it's certainly needed—the levels of unsafe nuclear waste are just appalling.'

'And of course, you've got to agree our disposal technique is a first,' he says.

'Yes. Rather neat, that—almost a closed loop. Very impressive, at least from the limited data you've released about it.'

'Commercial secrecy must take precedence over scientific openness,' he says, smiling. 'But I can promise you our plant does exactly what we've said it does.'

'Well, it's desperately needed, so congratulations on the innovation. We had a tour of the grounds yesterday and it really was impressive.'

Garrod nods, pleased. He leans down and takes something from a briefcase.

'If you'd be interested in attending the opening ceremony next week, Lena, I'd be delighted to see you there. Invitations for you and a friend, with my compliments,' he says, handing me two ornate cards.

'That's very kind, Glenn. But I thought it was supposed to be a highly exclusive event,' I joke.

He grins. 'It certainly is, and damned tedious too. You might improve things a bit.'

I smile to myself as I tuck the tickets in my bag. Despite my brown dress the shroud of middle-aged invisibility hasn't quite settled over me yet.

The Minister comes back from glad-handing the room and sits down beside Garrod, demanding his attention. I'm relieved to see Max is over at another table. He's seated beside Dr Tedious and I'm not sure who to feel sorry for. Neither, I finally decide.

A man in uniform arrives and sits down beside the Minister.

'Oh, *there* you are,' says Alise, touching his arm. 'Everyone, this is Colonel Wayne Zukowski, liaison for the US government at Worm Turning.'

He's boyishly handsome with crew-cut hair, about my age I suppose. Arnold introduces us all and the entrée arrives.

I'm enjoying the food and music but realise there's a silence to one side. I'd noticed Matthew speaking to Jess earlier but she seems to have gone quiet, probably mentally working through some technical problem.

I turn to Matthew. 'I enjoyed your talk today.'

'You must have felt lonely then,' he says, amused.

'Most of it went over my head, but it sounded like an area of disagreement.'

His gaze flickers past me and I glance around too, but Glenn Garrod is deep in conversation with Minister Berg.

Matthew says quietly, 'I think they've got the geology wrong. The Dampier Peninsula isn't as stable as they claim and they've misrepresented the field analysis and—' he shakes his curly head, 'something's wrong and I don't understand it.'

I've met a few scientists convinced they alone have The Truth but he doesn't sound like one of them.

'How certain are you?' I ask.

'I've been visiting this region for years, spent months camping in the country. As a geologist I've done dozens of field trips and kept up with the latest research. And as a friend, I've sat down with the elders and listened, *really* listened—'

'Sorry?'

'The Aboriginal elders, some of the people in that protest camp. They know more about what's under the surface of this land than anyone.'

'What, compared to modern science?' I say lightly.

A look of pain comes over his face and he goes to reply but Alise's voice cuts across the table like a scalpel.

'So, Lena—how's academic life *treating* you?'

'I'm enjoying it, Ice. It's—dynamic.' I'm sick of the treadmill but I wasn't going to give her the satisfaction of knowing that.

'I was *terribly* sorry to hear about you and Max,' she says, as intimately as you can get across a dinner table full of people hanging onto your every word.

'And James?' I say. 'Pity that didn't work out. What's he doing now?'

'Oh, an embassy, somewhere,' she says tightly. Poor James—a brilliant physicist but she'd forced him into the Diplomatic Service, then dumped him.

'And Environmental Industry? Oh, sorry, Industrial Environment?' I say. 'Hard to tell one from the other, really.'

'The environment as a recreational resource is under another portfolio, as I'm sure you know *perfectly* well, Lena.' Her eyes are cool. 'It's my responsibility to deal with the harsh realities of industrial growth and economic benefit.'

'At what expense?' says Jessie suddenly. 'I thought any serious cost-benefit analysis across the entire human and environmental economy, not just political cherry-picking, gives a very different measure of those harsh realities.'

'I'm sorry,' says Alise. 'And you would be—?'

'Jess Whalen. Universal secure system interconnections.'

'My goodness, what a *big* title.'

'It's not a title, it's not even a discipline. It's what I do.'

Alise looks at me. 'Of course, *now* I remember. You have that strange blended family, don't you Lena? Your sister, yes?'

I nod, and mercifully the main course appears. We finish without further breaches of protocol, although I can see Arnold is already planning I won't be on next year's committee.

That's fine by me, there probably won't be a next year anyway. This conference is basically a one-off to reassure the public that the best minds in the country have considered the new plant at Worm Turning and given it the scientific thumbs up. Apart from Matthew Rossi, that is. Interesting.

The table is partly empty now as people circulate. Alise is charming her way around the room with Glenn Garrod at her side, and Jess has gone over to chat to a bunch of techies clustered around some device.

Wayne Zukowski nods affably at me and I say, with my helpful committee hat on, 'Are you stationed permanently at Worm Turning, Colonel?'

'For the immediate future, ma'am.' His voice is attractively deep.

'I suppose it's usually pretty quiet out there.'

'So long as the protesters keep their distance, certainly. But there's always the threat of terrorists.'

'I thought it was so remote there'd be no chance of that.'

'Beg to differ, ma'am. It's under the protection of the US Government and our agreement with your people is pollution *and* security, a world first. But this remote coast, right next to China?' He shakes his head regretfully. 'You need us and by God, we'll look after the place like it's our very own territory. We signed on the dotted line to do just that.'

'We're not precisely *right* next to China,' I say, and he smiles as if I'm joking.

'As good as.' He refills my wine glass. 'Now do tell me all about Sydney, ma'am.'

Luckily people drift back to the table before I have to sum up five million people and thirty square kilometres of civic infrastructure in a few words. Dessert is served along with more enthusiasm from Arnold, then the excruciating evening is finally over.

At least I didn't have to talk to Max, and the bigwigs are leaving after the Minister's speech tomorrow. They'll be back next week for the gala opening of Worm Turning, but with luck we won't have to meet again.

Jessie and I go to my room for a cup of tea. She flings herself down on my bed as I turn on the kettle. I think of the look of loathing she gave Max and say hesitantly, 'Did he ever try anything on with you, Jess?'

'Who, Maxie the creep? Just once. I broke his finger.'

'Good on you. He said it was from playing football.'

'Well, he wasn't going to start telling the truth any time soon, was he?'

I smile. 'Did you have a good chat with the techies?'

'Techies? I'd have got more sense out of Madame Iceberg than them. They imagine their stupid new device is advanced.'

'Isn't it?'

She rolls her eyes and says, 'Wait on, got something for you.'

She goes to her room and returns with a small cardboard box. We sit together on the bed as she opens it.

'Now this is *advanced*,' she says with satisfaction. 'I'm doing the field testing.'

As far as I can understand, Jessie's speciality is somewhere between hardware and software, devising human-scale devices with unprecedentedly secure communication capabilities (her words).

But that doesn't look anything like the contents of the box: two wrist cuffs with intricate designs in gems and coloured enamel, and two rings covered with flat blue moonstones.

'Jess, they're *gorgeous*.'

'Here, put these on.' She taps on one cuff and it opens, then she closes it around my left wrist. 'And the ring.' She slips it onto my middle finger. Both ring and cuff fit snugly but as I move my wrist the cuff flexes, the colours shimmering.

Jess puts the other cuff and ring on her own slim hand, and I say dubiously, 'Field testing?'

'Yeah. See that small green stone on the inside of your wrist? There. And the array of enamel dots above it? Watch.'

She taps several points on her own cuff. I feel a tickle against my wrist. She walks into my bathroom saying, 'Touch the green stone then hold your hand near your head.'

I do and her voice in my ear says, 'Cool, eh?'

'They're *phones*! Jess, that's brilliant!'

'No need to yell. I know they are.' She comes out of the bathroom grinning. 'Three years in design, first prototypes and now I'm testing them to destruction. I call them comcuffs.'

I kiss her in delight. 'Comcuffs! You amazing thing, show me how they work.'

'Well, I'll show you the code for opening them. The display is this small panel, and the ring has lenses for taking images, video too. Cuffs hide their data inside other network traffic, looking like a sort of digital static, invisible and untraceable.'

'Jess, I can't believe it. Dick Tracy watches, but pretty ones.'

'A bit better than that, thank you very much,' she grins. 'But listen, Lena. They're *seriously* secret.'

'Okay, secret, got it. Now show me all the magic.'

3. My Cousins

I awake at dawn, emerging from a delicious dream. I haven't touched a man for a long time and I yearn for contact: belly on belly, warmth, stubble, sweat—I groan in frustration. I want to be open, known, sated. That's what my body wants at any rate.

The rest of me says no. Trust again? Let someone come that close again? I don't think so.

I decide to go for a walk. The air is fresh and cool, the sky clear blue and gold-tinted to the east. My head clears as I stroll down the rise from the hotel to the town.

I look out to the bay, which isn't the postcard scene you might imagine, though it's still beautiful—blue-green water lapping on a muddy red shore lined with emerald mangroves. This is old Broome, not the glossy resort at Cable Beach a few kilometres away.

Near the road, half-hidden by trees, I can see a cluster of small dusty buildings, an Aboriginal community. On the town's green oval I've seen groups of dark-skinned people sitting under the trees or walking unsteadily or arguing.

The contrast could not be more brutal: my colleagues in the cool luxury of the hotel, those people with lives of such hardship. Two interlaced worlds, each of them invisible to the other.

I turn towards Dampier Terrace, facing onto the bay. It's so quiet all I can hear is a car in the distance and a couple of seagulls. I notice a display of two luggers, boats once used for pearlshell fishing, and gaze at them with interest.

This is the first time I've been to Broome, but I have an odd connection to the place—my grandfather Mike Whalen grew up here between the wars. His mother even owned one of these big wooden boats and his father used to build them.

Mike would sometimes say my eyes were the colour of Roebuck Bay and now, seeing those turquoise waters, I recognise the compliment.

I'm sure every family has its secrets, funny and sad, and Mike was ours. I didn't even meet him till I was twenty. He'd had a fling many years before with my grandmother, and to everyone's surprise—including his—it turned out he was my dad's real father.

My darling Nana would say, 'Well, it was just before I got married after all, and my husband died in the war and I didn't have the foggiest I was pregnant to Mike, oh heavens.' And then she'd blush crimson and Mike would hug her.

I grew up in a small country town where my studious dreams puzzled everyone. My parents were divorced: Mum was happy with her new partner, and Dad, well, complicated doesn't come near it.

But my grandfather, an engineering professor, was the only person I knew who understood my love of science, who understood me: and he fitted into my family as if he'd always been part of it.

Mike's death a few years ago has left me with a bizarre sense of emptiness. While I can remember he was a kind, perceptive man, there isn't any emotion with that knowledge. I simply can't feel Mike's comforting warmth any more. A psychiatrist told me this was just the result of shock and would pass with time, but even after so long it hasn't.

I wander into a side street and around the corner, past the open-air cinema where Mike used to watch black-and-white movies as a boy. I'd hoped this trip to Broome might re-awaken my sense of that dear man, and I try once again to imagine him here in this place he loved so much.

But I can't feel him here. I can't feel him anywhere.

The final day of the conference, thank heavens, but it's the big one. First up the Honourable Minister for the Industrial Environment with a long, dull version of her 'economic benefit' speech from last night. Jess was right, it's just cherry-picking, with no genuine accounting of the real cost.

Bored, I flex my wrist to make the comcuff shimmer pleasingly. Even if it wasn't a fabulous device it would still be lovely. Jessie and I have been practising talking to each other—a casual hand to the head and soft sub-vocalising, and no one else notices a thing.

Applause at last, then the next speaker, charming Glenn Garrod from last night: the owner of Geo-Garrod Ltd and instigator of this new fuel reprocessing project. He's wearing a loose tie, the sleeves of his sky-blue shirt rolled up. He looks competent, approachable.

He begins, 'You're here to discuss Worm Turning and that's a good thing. People need to know how safe it is. How environmentally smart it is. How it can protect us by reducing the tonnes of nuclear waste that threaten us all.'

He looks at the journalists in the front row. 'So, a reprocessing plant—what *is* that? Well, the world is full of ageing nuclear power stations. We're stuck with them but I'll certainly say here and now, I'm glad to see more efficient new facilities already in production.'

A scatter of applause, and a colourful slide comes up on the screen. Uranium fuel is burning tidily inside a reactor, the reactor is heating steam, the steam driving turbines, the turbines creating electricity, and the electricity making a family happy as they pick flowers and smile at each other.

I sigh. If only it were that easy.

Garrod continues smoothly. 'As we all know, nuclear fuel has a limited life and becomes waste after a few years of use. For a long time that waste was kept in vast numbers of storage drums—until recently, of course, when the shortcomings of such a scheme were discovered in the most terrible way possible.'

He grasps the podium and lowers his voice. 'Well. The Hanford Incident. We all saw the tragic news reports. And we can only pray those parts of Washington State and the Columbia River become habitable again one day.'

He wisely doesn't show a slide of what happened to the people of Hanford. Not many happy families there.

Garrod stares fiercely at the audience. 'Suddenly we found ourselves with a global crisis. Thousands of tonnes of waste urgently needed reprocessing, far beyond the capacities of existing conventional plants!'

A new slide appears, an artist's concept of the red and green factory we'd visited the other day, more glossy than the real thing and set in lush countryside rather than the Australian bush.

'The solution the world was crying out for? *Worm Turning!* Our fast, secure plant with its patented technology can take all that lethal waste and break it down, leaving just a small active source and a chunk of stable remainder. We return the source to its owners and bury the remainder on-site in our other great innovation—the *Wormhole.'*

A slide of the Wormhole at sunset appears. It looks like an abstract painting in a glamorous penthouse rather than a great wound in the earth.

Garrod spreads his hands, smiling disarmingly. 'Look, people, doing this stuff is bloody expensive. But Worm Turning pays for itself. Next to a superb source of mineral sands, we're mining it, shipping it away, recouping the expense and even making a profit to keep our shareholders happy.'

There's laughter.

He leans forward and says emphatically, 'And that stable remainder is buried deep inside the Wormhole forever and ever. It's win-win-win for all of us!'

The last slide is a graphic of ships—somehow *happy* ships—converging on Worm Turning, which is also greening the desert, saving the planet and no doubt bringing about world peace.

'And this new era starts in just a week, a week until the future begins! Thank you.' Garrod steps away from the podium to a roar of applause.

Bloody clever, I think, then see movement near the front of the auditorium. A deep voice calls out, 'You're destroying sacred ground, Garrod, breaking the serpent's back! It'll turn on you in the end!'

Garrod chuckles and returns to the microphone. 'I guess that's the real meaning of 'worm turning' but I don't think it's going to fly here. Wondered when you'd pop up, Paddy, old mate.'

I see several security guards heading down the front. They converge on a small group of Aboriginal people—a middle-aged woman, a young man and a large white-bearded man, who's the one calling out.

The guards march them to the exit near me, then stop for a

moment to listen to something on their earpieces, and I suddenly realise the white-bearded man is the protester I saw at the plant.

Our eyes meet and he nods and smiles delightfully, just as he did the other evening. The guards start pushing their captives roughly towards the exit. They pass through the doors to the foyer outside and I get up and follow them.

'That's enough,' I say. 'I'm from the committee. Leave them with me, please.'

'We're supposed to eject them,' replies one guard.

'I've got the responsibility here. Go back to the auditorium, you're needed there.'

They shrug and leave. I look at the three surprised ejectees.

'So,' I say, surprised myself, 'can I offer you a cup of tea?'

The white-bearded man laughs. 'Sure you can.'

We sit on the balcony with our tea, looking out to the bay. A new speaker is on stage so everyone else is still in the hall.

'I saw you on the bus the other night,' says the man. 'But I know you anyway.'

'I don't think so,' I say. 'I've never been to this part of the world before.'

'You got relatives around here?' asks the woman.

'Not really. My grandfather grew up in Broome, and his half-brother came back, but he died a few years ago.'

'Liam,' says the man. 'Liam Whalen. Good mate of mine.'

'That's *him*, my uncle! How on earth did you know?'

He grins. 'Not blackfella magic—just your name tag. Good painter too.'

(He certainly was. Granddad gave me some of his famous brother's paintings and I treasure them.)

'Welcome,' says the woman. 'Welcome to country, cousin.' She has friendly eyes and a dramatic silver streak down one side of her hair.

I laugh. 'I'm not really a cousin—'

The white-bearded man says, 'Yes you are, you just don't know it yet. Lena, is it? I'm Paddy Bull, this is Maggie Everett and that's Aidan Cooper.'

The young man smiles. 'Hiya, Lena.' He has dark arched eyebrows, perfect cheekbones and a silver earring.

'So what were you yelling out to Garrod in there?' I ask Paddy, to stop myself staring at beautiful Aidan.

'I told that bugger he was breaking the back of the serpent and messing with sacred ground. It'll hurt him in the end.'

'Sorry,' I say politely. 'What do you mean?'

'Look. Things I can talk about and things I can't,' Paddy's brow creases. 'But what I can say is there's a serpent deep underneath. Runs from the top of the Dampier Peninsula, past Worm Turning, past Broome to south of here. If you dig into it, interrupt it, it'll be bad for everyone. Really bad.'

'But that's ...' I can't say *superstition* to these lovely people.

'They think we're against change for the sake of it,' says Aidan, 'but it's not that.'

'Here's the man,' says Paddy. 'He'll tell you all about it.'

Lanky Matthew is coming towards us, grinning. 'I see you've met my friends, the elders. This is what I was trying to explain last night.'

Assumptions. Got to lose my big-city assumptions.

These aren't naive outback folk. Aidan is a paramedic, Maggie a primary school teacher and Paddy a drug and alcohol counsellor for his countrymen. Paddy and Maggie are clearly elders, but Aidan?

'An elder is someone with knowledge, and responsibility for

that knowledge,' Maggie explains.

We're sitting in a quiet corner in the cafe. I don't want to be interrupted by anyone from the conference as they stream out for coffee. I'm fascinated by my new companions. My 'cousins.'

'Let's put it in scientific terms, Lena,' says Matthew. 'Knowledge of this land has been passed on by Indigenous people for the last sixty thousand years or more—initiations, legends, even the stories we invaders are allowed to hear. It's not mythology. It's a code—part social structure, part natural science.'

'Okay,' I shrug. 'Codes makes sense to me.'

'The codes preserve a wealth of knowledge of geological structures above and below ground. What the elders have told me aligns precisely with research and my own observations.'

Paddy looks exasperated. 'Well of *course* it does, Matthew. Jeez.'

'There's a large aquifer, a deep subterranean watercourse the length of the Dampier Peninsula,' says Matthew in his quiet voice. 'And the Wormhole is right over the aquifer—if they break into it, the flooding will devastate the mine. Worst of all, the stored material will pollute the aquifer.'

'But why haven't their surveys found it?'

'Haven't gone deep enough, and now they won't because they're certain there's nothing to find.' He shakes his head, puzzled. 'Slow acceptance of research I can understand—but there's something else too, something very odd going on.'

'What?'

'It's a long story—'

Maggie laughs. 'I've heard all this before. My cue to go, got a class.'

'And me,' says Aidan. 'On duty soon.'

'I'll come too,' says Paddy. 'Good to meet you, Lena.'

We stand and I shake hands with these three fascinating people I met such a short time ago. I feel something I can't identify but it makes me surprisingly happy.

'See you later, cuz,' says Aidan.

Matthew and I sit down again; he's all elbows and knees. 'Cuz?' he asks.

'My grandfather came from here, and his half-brother—my great-uncle—was part Aboriginal.'

'Whalen? What, not *Liam* Whalen?'

'Yes. I had no idea that would matter so much.'

'Family's everything here. But you don't have to be family to become family.'

I laugh, then realise he's perfectly serious.

'So what's this odd thing about Worm Turning, Matthew?'

'Some background,' he says. 'Years ago a gas refinery was proposed north of here at James Price Point. The Indigenous name is Walmadan. There were massive protests. Heard of it?'

I shrug. 'No, sorry. There are so many industrial projects and protests but usually something gets worked out. Isn't that what happened?'

'No, backward and forwards for years, but bit by bit the infrastructure was built up.' He rubs his bearded chin slowly. 'Look, I'm a geologist, I *like* the idea of minerals being used for human benefit—but there's already a refinery like that in the Pilbara, and for the locals a gas plant just means ruining the valuable tourist economy.'

'So what's a gas plant got to do with Worm Turning?'

'The basic infrastructure at Walmadan was already in place when the reprocessing project burst out of the blue. The protesters were caught off guard and the whole thing got instant approval.'

'The Honourable Minister Berg, I suppose.'

He nods. 'And then of course the Americans got in on the act. Terrorists, security, the same tired old bunch of bogeymen.' He shakes his head. 'I have *never* seen a project move so fast, every legal safeguard was bypassed. Most reputable geologists can't believe it.'

'What about the ones at this conference?'

'Most of them work for Geo-Garrod.'

I'm surprised. 'I thought this was an honest review. It's not?'

'I'm the token nay-sayer, but it's a whitewash. The basic science hasn't been done and protections aren't in place, legal or social. And it's on appropriated Aboriginal land.'

'Apart from the social aspect—and come on, Matthew, it's just a bit of bush—haven't the Americans guaranteed they'll take full responsibility for security or pollution problems?'

'Yes. That's what really scares me,' he says. 'When have they ever taken responsibility for their own pollution, let alone anyone else's?'

I laugh, then stop in surprise. He's right.

'And,' Matthew says hesitantly, 'it's *not* just a bit of bush, Lena. It's stolen land, beautiful land with great importance to the Kimberley. Something's wrong with how this was done and why it was done in that particular spot.'

I say dryly, 'Okay. I agree it doesn't sound very ethical. But that's not strange in itself, just business as usual.'

'Perhaps so, but other things worry me too. They're lying about what they're digging up, for instance. You heard Garrod announce they're selling the mineral sands at a profit?'

'You don't believe him?'

He shakes his head. 'Not true. There are deposits of the stuff everywhere. There's even a worldwide glut at the moment, no reason for anyone to be paying big money.'

'So what's actually in these sands?'

'Mostly titanium and zircon. Titanium goes into paint and zircon yields zirconium.' He smiles. 'But you'd know all about that.'

I nod. 'Zirconium's used to clad nuclear fuel rods in reactors, it lets the radiation pass straight through.'

'But to get zirconium out of zircon they have to remove traces of hafnium, and that has quite the opposite action,' he says with an odd intensity.

'Yes.' I say, puzzled. 'Hafnium *absorbs* radiation so it's used to control nuclear reactions. Not much good for anything else though.'

He leans forward and says quietly. 'But what about the induced gamma emission of hafnium-178?'

I look at him in amazement and burst out laughing. 'Oh, come off it, Matthew. You don't believe that tired old urban myth, do you?'

'The US Defense Advanced Research Agency put millions into studying it.'

'DARPA puts millions into lots of things, it's their idea of loose change. And just like the imaginary hafnium bomb, they go nowhere.'

'So you don't find it strange the idea was ridiculed, the results practically buried?' Matthew says.

'No. It was absurd.'

'The Chinese and Russians don't think so. They've recently done some interesting work.'

I'm surprised. 'Really? I didn't know.'

'Doesn't get much publicity. I'll email you the papers. What's your address?'

I tell him, wondering if he does have a chip on his shoulder after all. He enters my address in his phone then looks up at my doubtful face and says, 'I'm not crazy, Lena, I promise you.'

He's a lovely young man and I'm probably being a bit hard on him. 'Matthew,' I say gently, 'This is tinfoil hat territory, you know?'

'I used to think so too,' he says. 'But look, there's something else. The data they've published for the mineral composition is completely bogus.'

'Bogus?'

'A friend of mine did the initial analysis and privately told me about it,' he says. 'Then she was suddenly transferred and given a promotion, so now she couldn't care less.'

'Good for her.'

'A lot more effective than telling her to keep quiet, true. But I went to look for myself,' Matthew says. 'I know the area and it was easy enough to get through the fence, take my own samples, do my own tests.'

'And?'

'Geo-Garrod states it's the standard yield, one or two percent. But the Wormhole mineral sands have closer to *twenty percent* hafnium. It's a stunningly rich motherlode, there's nothing else like it on the planet.'

He spreads his hands and says quietly, 'So I keep wondering who's paying that big money? Who wants this stuff so badly—and why?'

4. At the Jetty

The conference ends that evening, with lots of hand-shaking and back-slapping and promises of eternal collaboration. I help with the usual committee tasks—sorting out loose ends with the venue organisers, pulling down banners, picking up appraisal forms, gathering water-glasses—all the famous glamour of global scientific interaction.

In the night Jessie and I go out to a restaurant for dinner, and sit at a table on the veranda. The air is humid but a breeze cools us down.

Over the meal I tell her about my strange day—meeting my 'cousins' (hers as well), and Matthew's concerns. She says she likes his sequence of logic about the hafnium, but then Jess likes sequences of logic about anything.

We consider desserts. 'The apple thingy might be nice,' I say.

'Mmm. Looks a bit like your mum's speciality.'

'Oh, I got an email from her last night, I say. 'They're leaving the boat for a few weeks and having a holiday in Cairns. Should be lovely for them.'

Jess says firmly, 'Enough of all that. What about *you*, Lena?'

'Me?'

'You. Now this massive exercise in reality avoidance is over, what are you going to do?'

'Pick up the dropped threads of my research. Carry on teaching, supervising postgrads. The usual.'

'And is that what you want to do?'

'Oh, Jess, I don't *know*. My research isn't going to be as useful as I'd hoped. I've got no new ideas. I'm fed up with teaching kids who don't like learning.' I sigh. 'Why did you have to ask me such an awkward question?'

'To hear your answer.'

'Obviously.'

'So *you* could hear your answer.'

I bury my face in my hands. After a moment I say, 'I was hoping to ignore the disaster of my professional life for a week or two while we have a holiday.'

'Okay. Ignored as of now. The apple thingy does look nice.'

I gaze at her with exasperation. Literal, sweet-natured Jess.

Next morning I wake up still puzzling over Matthew's concerns about hafnium in the Wormhole sands. But I decide to worry about it later—I'm a scientist, I have to assume there's a reasonable explanation. Once again I go for an early-morning walk to the old town while the air is still cool.

I admire the glamorous jewellery shops and their displays of large creamy pearls, then notice an old jetty stretching through the mangroves on Dampier Creek. I step onto it and walk carefully out to the end, seeing tiny red crabs in the mud below scuttling away in panic at the noise of my feet.

No one else is around, but I feel safe, and oddly content.

I sit near the end of the jetty and play with the comcuff Jessie gave me, touching the buttons she said were for taking photos. It's not difficult at all.

The lens is one of the moonstones on the ring, and the images appear, wonderfully sharp, on a wide silvery gem on the inside of my wrist. Then I try to sort out the video setting, and after a few false starts I'm charmed to see a view of pink clouds moving in the morning sky.

I lean back on my arms and take a deep breath and enjoy the peaceful scene. The rust-brown mud looks richly fertile and the roots of the glossy green mangroves reach like fingers into the air. Birds flitter past and the red crabs shuffle busily between their holes.

I close my eyes and feel myself relaxing deeply. It's as if I'm sinking into the jetty, the mud, the teeming life all around me. I smile. It's a new and pleasurable sensation. A long time passes, but it doesn't seem to matter. I feel so content.

Then I hear something splashing and come alert, imagining crocodiles. But it's just a man wading through the ankle-deep water in the mangroves. Damn. I was enjoying being alone.

He sees me and waves, and I politely wave back. He comes towards me, a fishing rod over his shoulder, and I realise it's the handsome young man I met yesterday, Aidan Cooper.

'Heya, Lena,' he says, as he gets closer. 'Great morning, eh?'

'Hi, Aidan. Just beautiful. Had any luck?'

He shakes his head. 'Nah, not today.'

He splashes back towards the shore. I follow, retracing my steps on the old jetty. When we meet he says, 'Cafe up the road's just opened. Want to get coffee?'

'That'd be good.'

He puts on his sandals and we walk to an arcade with small shops, get the coffees and sit at a table on the footpath.

I can't help noticing how striking he is, especially with that rakish silver earring. The shape of his eyes and golden skin show mixed ancestry too, like a lot of people I've seen around Broome—almost more Asian and European than Aboriginal.

I say, 'Do you do much fishing?'

'Relaxation mostly. Some of my rellies think I've gone soft

and couldn't last a day in country.'

'Your relatives still hunt for food?' I ask, surprised.

He smiles. 'Yeah. Run a trekking company for rich tourists.'

'Oh.' Another stereotype bites the dust.

'Always overbooked,' says Aidan. 'Deadly food.'

'That means good, doesn't it?'

'Yeah, great, fantastic.'

'Did you grow up around here?' I ask.

'Nah—near Karratha, further south. But Mum's from Broome. Her dad was a Japanese pearlshell diver back in the day.' He laughs. 'You were just about to say it, weren't you? *You don't look Aboriginal.*'

My face goes hot. 'Sorry, would that have been offensive?'

'Depends. If you're denying someone a scholarship, say, after you've taken everything they had for generations, then yes. Honest curiosity, no.'

'Scientist, I say. 'Always curious in my case.'

'Well, being Indigenous is defined by descent, identification and community, but none are easy. Descent? No birth certificates, and families broken apart when a hundred thousand kids get stolen for the sin of being partly white.'

'But wasn't that *ages* ago?' I say.

'Only sixty years. Curious, Lena? Ever wondered how so many half-white kids got conceived in the first place? Colonisers see rape as a perk of the job. My dad's granny—' Aidan swallows. 'Well, accounts for the narrow nose.'

He takes a breath. 'Identification's hard too. Kids felt shame, alienation, getting their culture beaten out of them in those bloody institutions. Why identify with people they're told to despise? Bonds get eroded, lost, denied.'

He sips his coffee. 'So really, being accepted by community, that's pretty fundamental. When people know each other's country, grannies, aunts, great-uncles, when they know where you *fit*—that's what matters. Not what you look like.'

I nod slowly. 'Okay. Thanks, Aidan.'

He smiles. 'You'll need to be across all this family stuff, cuz. First time back home, you said. How're you finding it?'

'Broome's not my home. I'm from South Gippsland, live in Sydney. Only my granddad's family came from here.'

'Holiday, then?'

I nod.

'Ah, might surprise yourself. Hard to leave this place.'

'I have my work in Sydney,' I say. 'Interesting stuff.'

'Yeah, must be.' I think he knows I'm lying.

I clear my throat. 'And you're an ambulance paramedic?'

Aidan nods. 'Started as a volunteer then went into a training program. I really like being an ambo.'

'Can't imagine a place as peaceful as this with too many emergencies.'

'Lot of drugs and alcohol, Paddy Bull's pretty busy. Not just an Aboriginal problem, across the whole community—guess that's how it is everywhere now. But all up, yeah, this is a pretty good place to live.'

'Deadly?' I say tentatively.

Aidan grins. 'Way deadly.'

'I hope Paddy and Maggie are all right after yesterday,' I say. 'You were pretty brave taking on Geo-Garrod in public. Are they big employers around here?'

He shakes his head. 'Nah. The plant's mostly automated, which doesn't help the kids needing jobs. The Sea Rovers have helped with a couple of court challenges, but no luck. But the real problem is what the plant's doing to country. The damage is massive and soon there'll be no going back.'

He puts down his mug and leans towards me. His eyes are

amber beneath the dark arches of his brows.

'And I worry about what Matthew says. You're a physicist, Lena—what do you think about the mineral sands with all that hafnium stuff? Could they really make a bomb out of it?'

'I don't know, Aidan. It sounded plausible some years ago, but fell apart in experiments. Matthew says people are still working on it, but I expect it's like the fantasy of perpetual motion or cold fusion—realm of crackpots.'

'Whoa, bit harsh there, mate,' he says, grinning.

'Well, science is harsh, it has to be. But personally, I just hope any new sort of bomb stays as impossible as possible.' I smile at my own words. 'Dopey thing to say.'

'You need that holiday I reckon. I'm taking time off too, annual break,' he says, finishing his coffee. 'You going on that boat cruise later today? I'll be crewing—they're mates of mine.'

'Yes I am, should be nice,' I say. 'It's so lovely here.'

'But not all paradise, remember. Summer's always bloody hard work, and even though it's autumn now it's still stinking hot, hasn't rained for weeks. Then there's the tropical cyclones too, of course.'

'Cyclones? In *April*?'

'Yeah, sometimes.'

'My granddad Mike told me about a cyclone when he was a kid,' I say. 'He said boats were smashed, houses blown away. But I guess buildings are much stronger today.'

'Broome's been stupidly lucky for a long time,' he says. 'But a direct hit from a cyclone would be like an atom bomb. Not much at all would be left standing.'

'Oh.'

Aidan frowns slightly. 'Look, I'm not trying to wind you up, but keep an eye on the weather. For instance, there's a low a thousand kays north-east right now. It'll probably wander off into the Indian Ocean as usual. But if you hear it's coming closer, pay attention.'

'To something a *thousand* kilometres away?'

'Oh, yeah.'

I get back to the hotel in time for breakfast. Today we've got the end-of-conference event Aidan mentioned, a sail along the coast on an old Broome lugger.

This is for the people who aren't immediately leaving town, of course. I assume Garrod and Berg have already flown the coop and taken my rat of a husband with them.

I'm just pouring a cup of tea when I realise the rat in question is hovering at the restaurant door. I'm even more surprised when he comes over and sits at my table.

He clears his throat. 'The other evening I noticed Garrod giving you invitations to the opening of Worm Turning.'

'Yes, I'm very well, thank you, Max, so is my family. How are your parents?' I ask.

'I haven't got time for pleasantries—'

'That's true.' My throat hurts.

'Lena, listen.' His jaw tightens. 'Please.'

I'm surprised. I don't think I've ever heard him say that before. Then he ruins the effect.

'It's not a good idea for you to go. I'd rather you didn't.'

'Why not? Bad for your image? Iceberg's been taking the piss?' I'm suddenly angry. 'Get lost, Max. I'll go if I want.'

His fists clench and I remember the rage beneath the smooth surface. He says, 'You stupid bitch. I'm trying to help.'

'Yeah?' My heart's pounding.

'Look, I don't think it'll be safe. Too many interests colliding. Protesters, psycho Yanks, hyped-up security out in the middle of nowhere looking for a fight.'

'At the gala? I suspect the only danger'll be blindness from all the diamonds.' I'm suddenly puzzled. '*Psycho* Yanks? Don't you mean Iceberg's best buddies?'

He licks his lips, his eyes evasive. Here we go, I think, what crap's coming up now?

'It's just a feeling ...'

'Feeling? Christ, Max, you'll be cuddling kittens next.'

I'm furious to realise my eyes are stinging. I just wanted to get through this *bloody* conference and have a peaceful holiday. The last thing I wanted was to talk to this horrible man again.

'Look, I just don't trust that Yank terrorist bullshit,' he says bitterly. 'They don't even believe it themselves. I can't work out why they're throwing such cash at this stupid little project. They're in a depression, their own country's knee-deep in shit, it's all crumbling roads and illiterate kids. I just don't get it.'

With a shock I realise he's sincere. I say, 'Perhaps it's not such a stupid little project. They might see it as getting rid of the nuclear shit, at least.'

He scoffs. 'Lena, you and your mates might agonise about nuclear waste, but governments don't give a fuck. Despite Hanford, the longer the problem's swept under the carpet the better they like it. Exploit what they can, move on, let someone else pay for the clean-up—that's how they've always done it. What's changed?'

'The problem's so massive to me I forget most people just don't care.' I look at him. 'But do you really think it could be dangerous at such a public event?'

'The whole thing makes me uneasy and I don't know why,' he says pompously. I'm astonished to hear him admit there's something he doesn't know.

Hating myself for placating him, I say, 'Look, I'm not

desperate to go, all I want is a quiet holiday. I'll see how I feel when the time comes.' I change the subject. 'Congratulations on your new job. How's it going with Minister Berg?'

'Not easy.' He frowns. 'She's too bloody cosy with Colonel Zukowski. And she's playing both ends against the middle ... except most days I'm not even sure what the ends—or the middle—are. I just do what I'm told,' he says with a shrug.

I gaze at him for a moment. His dark hair is less perfectly trimmed than usual, there are a few wrinkles on his shirt and he seems to have mislaid his defining self-assurance. I reject a sympathetic urge and stand.

'Well. Thanks for the advice, Max. Got to go.'

As I'm changing into shorts and T-shirt for the boat trip, I think about Max's odd words. Did he mean what he said or was he simply trying to manipulate me, as so often before?

I sigh and wonder how I could ever have become involved with such a strange man, a military man. But it made a kind of sense. Granddad Mike saw me as light-hearted—and I was, when I was younger—but I was also the child of a man damaged by the Vietnam War.

Dad's rages, his silences, his bitter unhappiness hurt us all, and when my parents separated it was a relief. Later, Dad found a certain contentment after marrying Suyin, but as I grew older I knew I both loved him and feared him still.

My boyfriends were mostly blithe spirits so I managed to avoid serious commitment, and I wasn't desperate for kids—Jessie, my little half-sister, was baby enough—but in my heart I hoped it might yet happen. In my forties, I was witty, attractive, content in my world. Then I met Max.

He was charming. He seemed someone I could at last rely

upon. His mind was good, he read widely and his hinted-at exotic past fascinated me. I felt I'd found my life's partner and we spoke of having a child.

To him I think I was a challenge—a pretty woman with a brain he'd joke, as if it were an inconceivable combination. He'd always murmur my title, Dr Whalen, when introducing me. For a time I think he was proud of me.

We married after a passionate year together, and everything changed. I refused to be told what to do, even by a substitute father. He had some odd fantasy of wifely submission—well, that worked out about as well as you might imagine.

Our sex life ended. He said I was demanding, disgusting, ridiculous. There were outbursts of rage: I was proof of his own failure. Then I discovered he lied, compulsively, about everything.

If he forgot to pick up bread, none had been baked that day. If he didn't ring, his phone was out of order. If he was going somewhere for just a moment he'd disappear instead for hours, and respond with disdain if I asked where he'd been. Most painfully of all, he denied he'd ever wanted a child.

After a long time trying to cope, the confusion and sorrow overwhelmed me and I couldn't stop weeping. I found a kind psychiatrist, took medication, struggled to understand. My shrink said Max was a narcissist—lacking empathy, a liar, a fantasist—but having a name for it didn't help.

At last we separated and I began to build a new life. I tried, at any rate.

5. The Glowing Powder

Jessie is coming on the boat trip too. She says she wants to see how the comcuffs operate in sea air, but she's already mentioned they're waterproof so I think she just likes the idea of a sail. I know I do. I've never been a sailor but the few times I've boarded a boat I've felt a surprising sense of contentment.

In the small bus taking us to the port I tell Jess about my chat this morning with Aidan. She says she hopes we get to see a cyclone in action and I say I'd rather not. I don't mention Max, I want to think over his puzzling warning first.

The bus rolls onto a beach and halts. We splash enjoyably through the shallow water to an aluminium boat, a tinny. To my surprise Matthew Rossi is in charge of it.

He's not dressed for a conference today—instead he's wearing a lurid tropical shirt which Jessie gazes at in disbelief. She's in her usual black of course, a tank top and linen shorts beautifully draped on her slim frame.

Matthew starts up the engine and ferries us out in two trips to the moored lugger. Not far away is a Sea Rovers yacht, with its distinctive golden sun logo against a blue background. The silver-haired crew on board wave to us and we wave back.

Mum and her partner Mitch are Sea Rovers on a boat in Queensland, and I'm proud of them. Sea Rovers are retired high achievers who refuse to settle for a quiet life. Instead they pit lifetimes of experience in law, business or government against the juggernauts of mindless development and, judging by the hysterics of the shock jocks, they're often effective.

As we approach the lugger I see it's about twenty metres long, the bow beautifully curved like an old-fashioned clipper-ship. *Sparrow* is written in large white letters on the bronze-green hull. *Sparrow?* What an odd coincidence.

The sides of the lugger are low and part of the railing slides back, so it's just a step up to reach the deck where Aidan is waiting with a helping hand. With his silver earring and dashing looks he reminds me of a pirate, Hollywood-style.

'We'll have to stop meeting like this, cuz,' he says, smiling. 'Whoa, watch your step there,' he adds as the lugger sways and I almost fall. Jessie is ahead of me so I grab her arm for balance. Aidan looks at me with one dark eyebrow raised.

'Aidan, this is my sister Jessie. Jess, this is Aidan. He's sort of your cousin.'

Jess greets him in a surprisingly friendly way. Maybe Broome's starting to relax her at last, although Aidan's charm could well be a factor.

After everyone is aboard Matthew closes the railing and ties the tinny to the stern of the lugger—along with Aidan he's apparently part of the crew. They move around quickly, releasing and coiling ropes. The engine starts and I see a man with steel-grey hair near the rear of the boat.

Matthew moves past and I joke, 'I didn't know geologists moonlighted as sailors.'

His quick grin appears. 'The skipper's my uncle. This lugger's the main reason I like living in Broome.'

The engine rumbles and we start out to sea. The crew hoists the cream-coloured sails and they fill with wind. Matthew assembles the passengers, nine or so of us, runs carefully through a safety drill and shows us how to use our life-jackets.

He produces bottles of sunscreen and insists we all put some on. Even in April the sunlight is fierce and I'm glad of my hat.

We leave Roebuck Bay behind and motor past the rocky orange bluff of Gantheaume Point then along beautiful Cable Beach. We keep moving north near the coast for a time then turn westwards out to sea.

The skipper cuts the engine and suddenly we're coasting along under sail alone. The intense quiet is breath-taking.

The deck is timber, the deckhouses painted glossy white. Jessie and I sit on a deckhouse while Aidan tells us about the old pearling lugger, calling the boat 'she' until it begins to seem oddly right.

He says she's called a ketch because the taller of her two masts is towards the bow. The masts themselves carry large rectangular sails with tangles of ropes going in every conceivable direction.

'Come on, let's do the grand tour,' Aidan says.

We carefully clamber down the narrow steps at the stern into one of the two deckhouses. It holds a compact kitchen he calls a galley, with a table and built-in seating and ingenious little cupboards and shelves everywhere.

We climb back to the gently rolling deck and walk forwards holding onto what Aidan calls the shrouds, which sound rather funereal to me.

Near the bow is another deckhouse with solar panels on top for the boat's electrics. Below it are the bunks, a bathroom and a toilet, and Aidan shows us how to use the water pump without causing a maritime disaster.

The engine is hidden away in a cramped room running between the galley and the sleeping quarters. In the old days it would have held an air pump, Aidan tells us, for the diver in his helmet and rubber suit, searching the ocean floor for pearlshell just as his own grandfather did: a perilous life of accidents, illnesses and cyclones.

When we emerge again on deck it's almost a surprise to see the glorious blue-sky day. Then trays of delicious nibbles and plastic flutes of bubbly emerge from the galley and after a while everything seems simply perfect.

Jess and Aidan get into a light-hearted argument over some sort of technology, so I leave them to it and wander around, chatting occasionally to the other passengers. I think about the boat and tell myself no, must be a coincidence. *Sparrow* would have been a fairly common name, after all.

Matthew said earlier we might see some whales, but right now I'm charmed by the pod of dolphins diving and swimming beside the moving lugger. I tell myself they're not really smiling, but they certainly seem to be having fun.

We head further out to sea, the land just a sliver behind us now, the breeze ruffling my hair and the waves gurgling against the hull. I sit near the bow enjoying the air on my face and remembering the lovely sense of deep relaxation—so unusual for me—I'd felt this morning on the jetty.

As the boat gently rises and falls I find myself thinking about the concept of sea—in my field we talk of seas of electrons or seas of instability between islands of elements.

Here, I'm charmed to notice, the gently moving sea seems to spark off a glimmer of insight into a problem I was researching before I came to Broome, and I think, yes, that might work.

After a long, peaceful time I wander back towards the stern and say to Matthew, 'This is just amazing. Thank you so much.'

'You should thank my uncle, it's his lugger. Simon, this is Lena Whalen. Lena, Simon Rossi.'

'What a beautiful boat this is,' I say to the man at the tiller. He's wearing sunglasses so it's hard to see his expression. He grunts something that appears to be agreement.

He's tanned, strong nose, grey hair untrimmed, shoulders the sort that might be a nice place to rest a weary head. About my age too. In my small academic world, attractive men of my own vintage rarely come along and if they do they're usually partnered. Is he wearing a ring? No. Stop gawking.

'Do you think we'll see any whales?' I ask.

'Maybe,' he says.

'It's odd this boat is named *Sparrow*,' I say. 'My grandfather's mother once owned a Broome lugger called *Sparrow*. Could it be the same one?'

'Doubt it,' he replies.

His face has laughter lines, but he's not smiling. Okay.

I move away and lean against some ropes and watch the water. The wind crackles a sail.

Hell. My serenity is gone and I'm back in the endless loop of the past: Max's rejection, any man's rejection. I'm sick of it. Who cares if some stupid boat-driver doesn't like my scintillating conversation? Dickhead, I can just hear Jessie say.

I sigh. I'm not petite or skinny or adorably inept, and I refuse to pretend I don't have a mind. It's never been easy finding compatible partners and now, after the disaster of Max, it seems hopelessly daunting. Still, I must try. Enough mourning, Lena.

After a long time sitting quietly, I yawn and realise I'm tired, lulled by the boat's gentle sway. The sun is low in the sky now. As well as the dolphins I've seen two turtles and a yellow sea snake but so far, no whales. I've had some nice chats with other passengers too but now everyone is quiet, sitting around the deck lost in their own thoughts or gazing at the horizon.

I suddenly notice Matthew is speaking urgently to the skipper, Simon. He's pointing at something and I turn and see it too: a boat in the distance. It's not moving and no one is on deck.

Simon starts the engine and we motor for a time until we're closer. We slowly circle the other vessel from perhaps fifty metres away.

It's larger than the lugger and made of blue-painted wood. It has a long cabin at the stern, a single mast, and the deck rises to a sharply pointed bow.

As we come downwind of the boat everyone murmurs and exclaims as a terrible smell sweeps over us. I see Simon and Matthew exchange looks and speak quietly to each other. We motor upwind, away from the smell, and stop.

We gather around the tiller. The only sound is small waves pattering on the hull.

Simon asks, 'Do we have any doctors aboard?'

No one responds, so I say, 'I have medical experience.'

Aidan says, 'I'm an ambo, Lena, might be better—'

'No, Ade, it's important the crew stay here,' says Simon. He glances at me. 'All right. Life-jacket on and come with me.'

I pull on the lifejacket. Matthew and Aidan haul the tinny back to the side then Simon climbs down into it and I climb after him. He starts the outboard motor and says, 'I want you to steer. Can you do that?'

'Yes, of course.' Dickhead, I think as I sit beside the tiller.

Matthew hands down some heavy coils of rope which Simon piles beside him. He tells me how to engage the engine and we start. After a wiggle or two I keep us moving in a straight line. We close the distance to the other boat on slow revs as Simon carefully uncoils the rope behind us.

I'm curious. 'Why didn't you bring Aidan? An ambo would more useful than me.'

'Probably.'

He suddenly seems to notice how Neanderthal he sounds.

'Sorry. The boat needs at least two crew to sail it safely and if I'd brought Ade along and something unpleasant happens here,' he nods his head towards the blue boat, 'that'd only leave Matty to get everyone back to port.'

'Do you think something unpleasant will happen?'

'Well, you can smell it,' he says. 'You know what's there.'

I nod.

An old ladder is dangling near the bow of the blue boat. Simon climbs it then leans down and says, 'Pass me the tow-rope.'

I do so and he ties it securely to the boat, then I hand him the tinny's mooring line to fasten too. After that I climb the ladder. He steadies me as I step on board then we stand, stunned by the ghastly smell. It surrounds us like sewage. We glance at each other.

'All right?' he says, looking pale. I nod.

We move along the deck and on the far side we find the source of the smell. What was once a man is lying there, his hand on his face. Flies blanket his body, buzzing like white noise, and what they don't obscure is glistening brown and black and red.

Simon steps to the side of the boat and vomits with quiet efficiency. I do too; despite my mental preparation there's no way in the world to stop it.

'Holy Jesus—' he says. He wipes his mouth on his sleeve then pulls out a handkerchief and gives it to me to wipe mine. He takes a small camera from his pocket.

'All right. Better get some pictures before disturbing anything.'

As flashes from his camera light up the evening, I take images with Jessie's comcuff behind his back. Concentrating on which buttons I need to push helps me stop thinking about the pathetic corpse sprawled in front of me.

Between the side of the boat and the wooden mast is an open steel drum with foam padding. With the boat it rolls one way, then the other, making a soft clang each time. It looks like the packaging for several shiny metal cylinders lying near the man's body.

The cylinders are about the size of large soft drink bottles and remind me of something, but in the horror of the moment I can't think what. I can see one of them has been forced open, presumably with the hammer and chisel lying beside it.

A coarse white powder spills from an aperture in the cylinder and is scattered on the deck. The breeze lifts the lighter grains eerily every now and then and blows them against our legs. I feel uneasy. Just the ghastly situation, I think. Keep calm.

'We'd better check inside too,' says Simon with a tone of resignation.

I follow him along the side of the cabin to the stern. The steering wheel is out in the open, and in front of that is the cabin door. In the gloomy decrepit room we see a table to the left, and a man lying with his head on his arms. He too is covered in droning insects.

Another broken-open cylinder is on the table and a pile of the powder is on a small mirror, chopped finely with a razor blade.

I say, 'Were they sniffing that stuff?'

'Looks like it.'

Simon snaps photos and I discreetly take images with the cuff, but neither of us wants to stay a moment longer in that hot stinking room. We go back to the deck and I can't help but gaze at the body again.

The poor bastard's hand is over his eyes, as if he was weeping when he died out here in the pitiless heat, and I remember Aidan saying it hadn't rained a drop for weeks. In the dimness I notice a heap of white powder beside the man and suddenly the hair on my scalp lifts.

The powder is glimmering with a soft blue light.

At the same time Simon whispers, 'Is that shit *glowing*?'

'Oh fuck,' I say, backing away, my voice shaking. 'We've got to get out of here!'

I hear the clang as the boat sways, and stare towards the bow. 'Look!' I point to the steel drum, rolling against the mast, with the hazard symbol for radiation just visible on its side.

'I think this powder's caesium-137,' I say. 'I recognise the containers now—we've got to get off the boat immediately, I'm not kidding!'

'Didn't think you were.'

We turn and dash along the deck, back to the ladder. Simon helps me over the side and as I'm climbing down I stop, and with the handkerchief he gave me I take off my sandals and throw them into the water, then step into the tinny barefoot.

'You too,' I say, and before he gets in he pulls off his deck shoes and throws them away, along with the handkerchief.

He starts the engine and we roar at high speed back to the lugger. My heart is thumping in terror. I've spent my career protecting other people from radiation poisoning but had never imagined I'd have to face it myself.

I can see Simon's fierce profile against the evening light. Is he as frightened as me? Probably not. But then, he has no idea what we're up against.

I think of the coarse powder scattered around the deck, blowing onto us, and feel sick again.

We reach the lugger. Simon fastens the tinny then looks at me.

'We're contaminated, aren't we?' he says calmly.

'Yes, I think so.'

'Okay. Matthew—everyone. Keep away,' he calls. 'Move to the stern, don't come near us.'

We clamber onto the deck. Jessie yells, 'What is it, Lena? What's happened?'

'That boat's contaminated, Jess—we've got to clean ourselves off!'

'The bathroom,' says Simon. 'Come on.'

As I'm climbing down the steps of the forward cabin I yell out, 'Matthew, wash the deck down, wash everywhere we've walked.'

The bathroom is just large enough for the two of us. 'Strip,' I say, yanking my T-shirt off, my shorts, my underwear. 'Don't mess around.'

'I'm not,' he says. 'What about the camera?'

'Put it up on that ledge. Worry about it later.'

Simon turns on the shower. 'You first,' he says, undressing, and I duck under the water, rubbing soap in my hair, over my body. It is beyond irrelevant I am naked in a confined space with a naked man I don't know.

'You too, come on, I'm almost done,' I say. 'Wash out your ears, nostrils, mouth, eyes.'

There's a knock on the door. 'I've got towels and spare gear out here,' calls Matthew. 'And plastic bags for your clothes.'

'Good man,' says Simon, soaping his furry chest quickly.

'Start the engine and get us back. Radio ashore and get the emergency services alerted for a hazardous material event.'

'We should do our clothes too,' I say. 'That stuff's water soluble, we can wash out as much as possible before getting back to port.'

Kneeling side-by-side we desperately soap and squeeze our clothes. Then I open the door and drag in the bags and towels. We stuff the wet clothes into the bags then I wrap myself in a towel and give another to Simon.

I take a deep breath. 'Oh, Christ.'

My legs are suddenly weak, and I collapse onto a wooden bench along one side of the bathroom. Simon sits down heavily beside me. He shakes his head.

'What the hell just happened?'

I spread my hands in amazement. 'There's a boat out there covered in some of the most poisonous stuff in existence. And we just tiptoed through it like babes in the wood.'

'Be fair, we spent a good bit of time puking too,' he says with a quick smile like Matthew's.

I half-laugh, half-sob for a moment, then wipe my face. 'Sorry. Bit of a shock.'

I gaze at him: he's pale underneath the tan.

He leans his head back against the wall. 'Those poor bastards. Did they die from radiation?'

I nod. 'Probably. Looks like they thought the powder was a drug. Oh, Jesus.' I start shivering, trying to recall dosage levels and mortality rates, but I can't think.

Simon opens the door and pulls in a pile of clothes. 'Here,' he says, 'Sailors' vintage T-shirts and daggy trackies. Get warm.'

He drops his towel and pulls on some track pants, and I notice he has a glorious bum. I scold myself for my superficiality and look through the pile of clothes. I throw on a

T-shirt but have to stand and take off my own towel to get some track pants on. I think Simon's watching my bum out of the corner of his eye. So he's superficial too.

I pull on a woolly jumper and some thick socks, and rub my hair dry and sit down again, exhausted. Simon wraps his camera in a T-shirt then sits beside me. He gazes at me, his face still. His eyes are an odd silvery grey, fringed with dark lashes.

'Now. Before we go out to the others, tell me the truth. How bad is this, really?'

'Depends if we've breathed any in, how long we were exposed,' I say. 'I'm pretty sure it was caesium—I recognise the cylinders, the old assemblies. We've done what we can by washing it off, but ... I just don't know.'

We tow the grim blue boat behind us to the port. It's night by the time we're there and emergency vessels swarm around us, shining bright lights over everything. The other people from the lugger are ushered away in a launch, Jessie waving forlornly as they leave.

Simon gives the emergency team leader his camera, then we have to pull on protective suits before we're even allowed into another launch. We're landed on a small beach near the head of the wharf.

White-bearded Paddy Bull is there, his dark eyes concerned. He seems to know Simon well—they greet each other warmly, but of course can't shake hands. As we pull away in an ambulance I see a large military transport screech to a halt and American soldiers in black gear jump out.

Simon and I are rushed to the small regional hospital, sirens howling and lights flashing. Once there we're showered again, examined with radiation counters and injected with substances. Nurses in protective suits take blood and tissue samples and put us in beds in a special isolation ward, attached to quietly-beeping monitors. The room is large and bright and empty apart from us.

They dim the lighting so we can sleep but it's still too bright. My head is spinning. My legs and feet are hot and throbbing painfully. I look over at Simon in the other bed, a few metres away. He opens his eyes and turns his head towards me.

'You scared?' he says quietly.

'Yes.'

'Me too.' He rolls gingerly onto his side. 'But what scares me the most is why there's a boat full of high-level radioactive crap drifting around near Broome.'

'What if it had run ashore?' I say. 'It'd make the place uninhabitable for a long time. Worm Turning would be in big trouble then.'

'Funny. That's just what I was thinking.'

I gingerly lean up on one elbow. 'You don't believe the boat was going to be used to attack the plant, do you?'

'No idea. But I expect it'll be spun that way no matter what the truth is.'

'Those men looked Asian. Maybe the spin will be that they're Chinese.'

'Probably. They're the latest bunch of official baddies after all,' he says. 'But those poor bastards were just fall guys. They couldn't have known what they were carrying—they'd never have opened the cylinders otherwise.'

I lie back down with a sigh.

'What do you think will happen with my camera?' Simon asks. 'It's a bloody good one.'

'They'll try to decontaminate it,' I say. 'If they can't, it'll get concrete boots and end up in the Wormhole.'

He laughs softly. After a few moments he says, 'What was your name again?'

'Oh—Lena Whalen.'

'You remember you asked about my lugger *Sparrow*?'

'About a million years ago.'

'A Lucy Whalen from Broome owned her until the sixties, then a couple of different people rebuilt her over the years, then I bought her. So if Lucy was your grandfather's mother, sounds like it might have been her boat.'

I'm pleased. 'Yes, that was her name. Thanks, Simon.' After a few moments I say without thinking, 'Why were you bloody so unfriendly earlier, before all this happened?'

'A dickhead, you mean?'

'Some might put it that way.'

He's amused. 'Sorry. I thought you were one of the bastards who gave Matthew such a hard time at the conference. And I was obsessing about something too, so you got the professional stony face. That's what Matty calls it.'

'He's your nephew, right?'

'Yeah. Raised him after my sister died.'

'He's a nice guy. And a good scientist too. Has he told you his theories about Worm Turning?'

Simon nods slowly, his eyes worried. 'That's what I was obsessing about.'

That night it's hard to sleep. My burns throb and sting, my mind races. How on earth did I get tangled up in such bizarre, terrifying events? I sigh in the dark.

Oh, if only Mike were here to talk to. Granddad Mike, who understood all aspects of me, from the light-hearted girl to the passionate scientist. It was such a joy to share his wry jokes, to work on problems together, to gossip about the latest research.

He and Nana lived high on a South Gippsland hill, and I think longingly of our peaceful meals together on the terrace, watching the changing light on Corner Inlet waters and the deep blue peaks of Wilsons Promontory beyond.

When Max and I became involved, I realised Mike didn't like him—he knew too much about military men he said lightly— but I think he still hoped I'd found lasting happiness.

He was getting tired by then and sometimes I'd hear him gasping a little at some small effort and I'd worry. It wasn't the usual deep comforting rhythm of his breathing, something I think I'd know anywhere if I ever heard it again.

That was the start of Mike's long sad departure from our lives. But though I yearned for his wisdom during the hard days of my marriage, I'm glad he never saw how badly it turned out for me. Or what a mess I've found myself in now.

6. Contamination

Next morning our hands are red and our legs have painful blistered patches, but our vital signs are apparently vital enough and the nurses take us off the beeping monitors. Wearing protective white suits they put dressings on the burns and give us analgesics.

To pass the time we read copies of the local newspaper. The headline is Worm Turning—Boom Ahead! On page seven I find five lines on the salvage of an abandoned fishing vessel, without a word about its ghastly cargo.

I say, 'Did you notice there's almost nothing about the boat in the paper?'

'I noticed.'

'Suppressing the story?'

Simon nods. 'Reckon so.'

'So maybe they won't spin it against against the Chinese.'

Leaning against his pillows Simon shifts and winces, and looks at me. 'Weird in itself, don't you think? They usually take every opportunity they can to put the boot in.'

'Yes. Maybe they're waiting till they know more about it.'

'Never stopped them before.'

Dr Yuan, in charge of our case, visits us mid-morning in a protective suit and checks us over.

'You seem to be doing well,' she says.

'Have they tested the powder yet?' I ask.

She nods. 'Yes, definitely caesium-137. You are both extremely fortunate your exposure was so limited.'

When the nurse brings the trolley with our lunch, she's also got a bunch of the most extravagant flowers I've ever seen. 'For you, Lena,' she says, putting the vase beside my bed. 'From Glenn Garrod. The card says, *To a brave, beautiful woman, and my favourite nuclear physicist.* Lucky girl, he's stinking rich.'

After she's gone I say, 'Probably written by the florist.'

'Yeah. My florist's keen on nuclear physicists, too.'

I smile. 'We met the other night at the conference dinner. He's invited me and a friend to the grand opening at Worm Turning.'

'I wonder if we'll be out of here by then,' he says slowly. 'That's about five days away isn't it?'

'Yes. They'll monitor us for a while but if we don't get any worse they'll probably release us fairly soon. If it's going to happen, these kinds of burns usually turn bad after a few weeks, not straight away.'

'How bad?'

'Deep, weeping lesions.'

'Christ. What else could be on the menu?'

'Headache, vomiting, diarrhoea. Unconsciousness. Death.'

'Got the headache for sure. Hope that's as far as it goes.'

'Me too.' I sigh. 'All we can do is wait.'

Then a thought strikes me. 'How did Glenn Garrod know what happened last night if it's not in the papers?'

'I was wondering that too.'

In the afternoon, we see Jess and Matthew and Aidan waving to us through the glass doors to the ward. Jess discreetly indicates her comcuff. I've still got mine—the nurses couldn't remove it last night (I said I'd forgotten how) so it got decontaminated with the rest of me.

After they've gone I get up and go to the bathroom and contact Jess with the cuff.

'Are you alone, is it okay to talk?' I whisper.

'Yes,' she says. 'Lena, how are you?'

'All right for now. What happened to you lot after the ambulance took us away?'

'They ran radiation detectors over us, but we were clean so they just let us go home.'

'Oh, Jess. What a *nightmare*. And I hope I haven't damaged your cuff in all of this.'

'They said I should test it to destruction anyway.'

'I'm doing my best,' I say, and she laughs. 'But listen, I took photos with it out there on the boat. Simon took plenty too, so mine are probably just duplicates—but can I send you copies for backup?'

Jess tells me a brief sequence of enamel dots to touch, and in a few moments she says, 'Right, got them.' Her voice changes. 'Holy fuck, Lena. That's what was on the boat?'

'Oh, Jess, it was dreadful.'

'I'll store these safely, don't worry. You just get well.'

When I go back to bed, Simon asks, 'So who was that woman at the door with Matty and Ade? She was on the lugger, too.'

'My sister—half-sister—Jessie.'

'Ah, yes. I noticed the resemblance.'

'Did you?' I say, surprised. 'Most people only see she's part-Chinese and a lot younger than me.'

'Same cheekbones, same smile.'

It's quite a compliment to be compared to Jess. I say, 'She's more like my own child sometimes. She's stunningly smart, a geek genius, but often people don't understand her.'

'You haven't got kids of your own?' Simon asks.

'No. I'd have liked to,' I shrug. 'But stuff happens. Or didn't, in this case. What about you?'

'No,' he says after a moment. 'Matty's my only family.'

I try to find a comfortable position to lie in, but fail. After a time I say, 'So how did you end up in Broome with a lugger, anyway?'

'Oh—early retirement from a research job in Perth. Matty and I used to take holidays around here so it seemed like a good place to retire. And the lugger came along when I had more money than sense.'

So he used to be a researcher? That's interesting. 'What field?' I ask.

'Coastal ecology,' he says wistfully. 'But they broke up the state Environment department a few years ago, merged half of it with Alise Berg's Industrial Environment and the rest of us with bloody Recreation, for Christ's sake. And their mission statement was apparently to green-light any development, particularly if it was on the coast. After a time I couldn't hack it, had to get out.'

'Understandable.'

'But still, I like living in Broome,' he says, 'and it's even better now Matthew's here too.'

'He told me. Fired for disagreeing with Geo-Garrod.'

'Mmm. Doesn't say much about it but there was a broken engagement in Perth as well, so he really needed a change. And it's great having him around—he loves sailing, he's a big help on board.'

'Is the lugger a lot of work?'

I turn my head painfully to look at him. Not conventionally handsome—strong nose, dark eyebrows, those silvery eyes—but he's oddly nice to contemplate.

'Yeah, the work never ends. And I've done some costly modifications too.' He smiles to himself. 'But when the company's good and the wind's just right, I reckon it's got to be worth it.'

Sitting back on pillows and drinking afternoon tea I ask, 'Simon, why are you so worried about Matthew's theories anyway? Most people don't take the hafnium bomb idea seriously, it's science-fiction stuff.'

'Then who wants those high-yield minerals so badly?'

'Perhaps they don't,' I say, sipping my tea. 'Perhaps it's just a good place to put a reprocessing plant and Garrod's lying about making a profit from the Wormhole to keep the share price up.'

'That seems too elaborate. Look, there are ships from all over the world on their way to Worm Turning right now, with nuclear waste they're desperate to dispose of, especially at the low prices Garrod's charging,' says Simon, frowning. 'But he could ask a hell of a lot more and they'd still pay it, so why does he need a mine to subsidise the plant?'

'Maybe it gives him a big hole to put the processed waste in.'

'Why not just dig a hole then? And what about this bloody blue boat covered in caesium? Could that be connected to the hafnium-rich minerals?'

I shake my head. 'Unlikely. Caesium's radioactive, and those assemblies we saw on the boat used to be used to treat cancers —though not nowadays, there are better therapies.'

'And hafnium?'

'Totally different—it's not radioactive, in fact it stops nuclear activity. I don't know of any link between them.'

'Then what about a connection to the Worm Turning plant?'

He absently scrapes his thumb over his stubbled chin.

'That's a specialised setup to reprocess reactor fuel rods,' I say. 'Not for things like medical assemblies, even if someone was stupid enough to ship them in with a couple of guys who think they're full of drugs.'

'All right,' says Simon slowly. 'So the contaminated boat is probably a completely different mystery.' He shrugs. 'Perhaps it was to be some kind of attack.'

'And we were just ... wrong place, wrong time?'

He nods. 'But Worm Turning is weird enough in itself. The indecent rush to approval, the dodgy geology, the lies about hafnium levels—they're all suspicious. But what really scares me is that Matthew's the only researcher standing up and saying so, and he's making a target of himself.'

'But good science is full of people disagreeing with each other.'

Simon puts down his cup. 'This isn't good science. It's not even good business. Nothing good about it.'

That evening, while we eat our surprisingly tasty hospital dinner, Simon asks, 'I was wondering. How did you *know* that stuff was radioactive? Blue glow, dead bodies—clearly something pretty crap was going on—but you knew exactly what it was.'

I swallow some salad. 'Goiânia, 1987.'

'Goyan—?'

'A city in Brazil.'

'What happened?'

'A radiotherapy machine was accidentally abandoned. Two men were looking for scrap metal so they stole the assembly and trundled it away in a wheelbarrow. It was full of caesium-

137 and they opened it a little way.'

'Like our guys on the boat,' says Simon, cutting into his fish.

'Except they lived. One lost some fingers where he'd handled the assembly, the other an arm.'

'Ugh. Was that the end of it?'

'Oh, no. They sold it on to a scrap merchant who got his men to break it open properly. He was charmed by the glowing blue powder and showed it to family and friends. They all thought it was carnival sparkle, so they dabbed it on their skins.'

'Christ.' Simon stares at me, slowly lowering his fork.

'The wife of the scrap merchant, Gabriela, became ill. She saw others were getting sick too and got the assembly to a hospital—she saved a lot of lives.'

'How many were contaminated in the end?'

'Hundreds, some of them simply passers-by, though because they got fast treatment only four people died. But one of them was Gabriela herself, and another was her niece, who'd just played beside the pretty powder—she was only six. They were buried in lead coffins, encased in concrete.'

He sighs heavily. 'Stuff of nightmares.'

At about eight p.m. we have a visitor, Colonel Wayne Zukowski, the head of the American force protecting Worm Turning—the rather attractive man I'd met that night of the conference dinner. He's wearing a protective suit but seems relaxed.

'I'd like to officially debrief the pair of you on the contamination event,' he says. 'Separately, for accuracy.'

He takes Simon to one side of the room so I can't hear them and records him describing what happened on the blue boat. He then sits beside me.

'I hope you're feeling better now, Dr Whalen,' he says in his deep, pleasant voice. 'I was sorry to hear you'd been in such a dangerous situation. If you don't mind, please tell me what happened on that night and just what you saw yourself.'

Afterwards he says formally, 'I have been asked to express the gratitude of the United States Government to the two of you. Your alert response prevented potential disaster.'

I ask, 'Why isn't there anything in the paper about this, Colonel?'

'We don't want people to worry, ma'am. It was obviously a failed terrorist plot and we'll just have to be more vigilant in future.'

'But what if it happens again?' asks Simon.

'It won't.' The colonel is surprisingly confident.

'Where's the boat now?' I ask.

'We recovered the radioactive substance, then the vessel was taken out to sea and sunk with massive fire-power.'

'But what about the bodies? Surely there must be relatives—'

The colonel says politely, 'The terrorist remains had to be disposed of safely, ma'am.'

'Safely?' says Simon in disbelief. I'm surprised he's so vehement. 'You've just dumped a shitload of contamination in the ocean—don't you know how shallow it is off this coast?'

The colonel stands. 'It's a big ocean, Dr Rossi. We were outside the nautical limits and we do what we have to do. Sir.'

He nods at me. 'Good afternoon, ma'am.'

After he's gone, Simon and I look at each other.

'Interesting,' he says. 'He's a little older than you'd expect for that rank—may have been passed over for promotion. He won't want any problems on this posting.'

'That doesn't mean you have to be so cranky with him,' I say. 'He might be trying to do what's best.'

'Best for whom?' Simon's eyebrows are drawn. 'I really don't like the way this whole thing's being glossed over.'

'He was strangely calm, wasn't he? Anyway, better hope our stories are consistent or we'll be taken out to sea and sunk with massive fire-power too.'

Simon laughs softly. 'Now I remember why I left the army. That pigheaded certainty, no alternatives allowed.'

'You were in the army?'

'Before I did ecology, when I was young and stupid. Mainly disaster relief, despite our finely-honed homicidal skills.'

'Oh.'

Well, that's that. He might be a fellow scientist and a nice guy (with a glorious bum)—but army? I don't think so, Lena.

7. The Pink-Orange Device

The next day is quiet. I don't respond much when Simon starts conversations and after a while we doze most of the time. Good, I tell myself, it gives our bodies a chance to rest. The truth is I'm still haunted by painful memories and don't want to talk to Simon: to a military man.

Dr Yuan comes to visit us late in the afternoon. She's in a normal white coat and I say, 'That's promising. You're not suited-up.'

'We tested everything we can and you two seem clean,' she says. 'You didn't ingest anything we can measure. You only experienced dermal exposure and the burns are superficial. I don't foresee any long-term problems.'

'That's great,' says Simon. 'So when can we get out?'

'Today if you want.'

'But we've got no clothes,' I say in dismay.

'Use the ward phone, get your families to bring some in. There are papers to sign on discharge but once that's done you're free to go. The nurse will give you dressings to keep your burns healing cleanly. But please, any signs of further illness—dizziness, vomiting—contact us immediately.'

'Thank you so much,' Simon says with feeling. 'Your staff have been wonderful.'

'And the ward and decontamination facilities—they're superb,' I say. 'In fact, I don't think I've seen anything so professional anywhere.'

She smiles. 'All thanks to Geo-Garrod, of course. They fast-tracked this new wing for the hospital.'

She turns to go, then says to Simon, 'Oh, your camera, Dr Rossi. The Emergency Services gave it to us the day after you were admitted and we've successfully decontaminated it. Pick it up from the nurse when you're leaving.'

Half an hour later Jess, Aidan and Matthew are there with clothes for us—I suppose our old clothes are at the bottom of the Wormhole by now.

It's a Sunday evening and when we go through the hospital doors the road is quiet. I blink and say, 'It's all so strangely normal. I feel as if we've been away on another planet.'

'Come on, the ute's over here,' says Jess. 'We're going to Simon and Matthew's place. The guys are going to cook us something to eat and we can just relax.'

'Sounds great,' says Simon. 'Thanks, kids.'

'Kids,' says Matthew. 'I've been able to vote for fifteen years.' He looks from Simon to me. 'I'm glad you're all right. You gave us quite a scare.'

Simon's house is in the old part of Broome. It's cool and airy, with wide verandas and lattices and dark timber floors. This is the first time we've had a chance to talk properly to the others since that dreadful evening, so Simon and I tell them about everything we saw on the blue boat.

That makes us all feel fairly subdued, but then the prospect of food cheers us up. Aidan cuts vegetables and jokes with Jessie, perched on a stool at the bench, both of them slim and golden-skinned and surprisingly alike.

Matthew, in a bright tropical shirt, moves efficiently

between chopping board and stove, stir-frying something that smells wonderful. Simon and I sit quietly in armchairs sipping wine.

'Being waited on hand and foot—I could get used to this, Matty,' Simon calls out.

'Better not,' says Matthew. 'It's only because we feel sorry for you. Won't last long.'

We eat at a table on the veranda and the meal tastes even better than it smelled, then afterwards we drink coffee.

The wind suddenly rustles the trees and I see the sky is clouding over.

'Oh, I hope the lovely weather doesn't disappear,' I say.

'Yeah,' says Aidan. 'Remember that low I mentioned when we were talking about tropical cyclones?'

'You don't mean—'

'Nah. Well, it's turned into a category one, but that's pretty harmless. Out to sea about six hundred kays away and they think it'll come ashore further south. But it'll whip things up a bit here over the next week or so.'

'They've called it Cyril,' says Jess.

'Sounds almost cute,' I say.

'Don't be deceived,' says Matthew. 'We went through one, about sixteen, seventeen years ago wasn't it, Simon? I've never been so terrified—and the eye didn't even pass over Broome. I'm not certain we'd be here talking if it had.'

Simon nods. 'I've never been so scared either. Oh, except the other evening, seeing Lena's face when she realised the powder was glowing.'

'You seemed remarkably calm at the time,' I say. 'It was most reassuring.' I'm glad I'm starting to relax with him again.

'Professional stony face, remember?' he says. 'I'm good at that.' He looks around. 'Hey, where's my camera, anyway? I want to check it's all right.'

'Here,' says Matthew, getting it from a sideboard and handing it to him.

Simon turns it on, then swipes through the small bright images on the viewer. He grins and says to Aidan, 'There's the day before, getting the lugger ready and you messing round on the foremast.'

'Someone has to play the fool after all,' says Aidan, with mock dignity. 'I take my responsibility very seriously. Anyway, Matthew was being even sillier out on the bowsprit.'

'Ah, but he didn't get it on record, mate,' says Matthew, grinning. 'So it didn't happen.'

Simon swipes forwards on the camera, then back again, his smile fading.

'What is it?' I say.

He looks up at me, puzzled. 'The pictures I took on the blue boat, they're not here. But it's a digital camera, not film—radiation can't affect it, surely?'

I shake my head. 'No, the images should be there. Any from earlier in the day?'

'Yeah. I took a couple when we were sailing. There's you, up at the bow looking mysterious.'

'That's a brilliant picture of Lena,' says Jess. 'What sort of telephoto does it have?'

'Jeez, don't *ask*,' says Aidan. 'He'll be talking digital optics all night.'

'Listen, everyone,' says Matthew, his eyes serious. 'This doesn't seem right. Simon, are you sure you took photos?'

'Of course. Lena, you remember?'

'Yes, I saw the flashes.'

'So there's no possibility it didn't work?' says Matthew.

'Unlikely,' says Simon. 'I've used this camera in all sorts of conditions. It's almost unbreakable, never failed before.'

'Give it to me,' says Jess.

Simon is surprised, but hands it over. She takes a flat, almost oval object out of her backpack which doesn't look like anything I've ever seen before. It's pink and orange and iridescent where the light hits it.

'What on earth is that?' asks Matthew.

Jessie smiles. 'You may be able to buy one in a few years. It's a computer like a Formula One racer—stripped to the bare metal and not for the faint-hearted.'

She opens it and taps the keyboard lightly here and there, the camera sitting beside it. 'Okay, let's have a look at the OS.' After a moment she turns to Simon. 'Wow. I'm impressed. Nice little beast.'

Aidan looks at me, eyebrows raised.

'Operating system,' I say. 'And it takes a lot to impress Jessie.'

'Fuck,' says Jess thoughtfully. She taps the keyboard for a time, concentrating, then looks up. 'Everything from the late afternoon of that day has been deleted. And whoever did it tried to cover their tracks, changed logs and timestamps. Dickheads. Thought they could hide it.'

'You can't recover the pictures?' says Simon.

'No. In this case they didn't just delete the file handles, they actually dev-nulled the blocks.'

'Have you the slightest idea what that means?' Matthew murmurs to me.

'No,' I reply. 'But if Jess says they're gone, then they're gone.'

'But who—?' asks Aidan, bewildered.

'The hospital perhaps,' says Simon, frowning. 'Or Emergency Services? They had it for a day before the hospital.'

'Maybe someone just screwed up,' I say.

Jess shakes her head. 'No. The images have been carefully

and deliberately erased.'

'But that doesn't make any sense,' Matthew says. 'It was the only evidence of what was actually on the boat.'

I glance at my cuff and open my mouth, then realise Jess is staring at me intently. I close my mouth.

'An American colonel saw us in hospital,' says Simon. 'He said they'd taken the boat and the bodies out to sea and blown them up. So they're gone. The newspapers had no stories about it and now the pictures taken on the boat are gone, too.'

'Only you guys really know what was there,' says Aidan, his brows drawn. 'For the rest of us it's just second-hand.'

'But what about the emergency services?' I say. 'They'd have seen the bodies and the assemblies.'

'Nowadays they're subject to quite extraordinary levels of official secrecy,' says Simon slowly. 'Like the military.'

'And if it's not on the record,' says Matthew, 'it didn't happen.' His face is pale above his beard.

Simon looks at me with his silver-grey eyes and says gently, 'Yeah. That's something of a concern. Think I'll talk to a friend about this.'

He stands and goes back into the lounge. I hear him murmuring on the phone and in ten minutes or so, as we're tidying up the kitchen, there's a knock at the back door.

Simon opens it to a muscular middle-aged blond man and introduces him as Jumbo. He takes him into the lounge and I hear them talking in low voices.

Matthew says, 'That's interesting, Jumbo here in Broome—he's usually in Perth. He used to work with Simon.'

And he's ex-army too, I think. I saw enough of his mean-faced, mean-minded sort when I was married to Max. Simon and Jumbo come back to the kitchen, and Jumbo's narrowed eyes above a polite smile meet mine as he departs.

'What does your friend think?' I ask Simon as I'm putting plates away on a shelf.

He stacks some mugs in a cupboard. 'Not sure. He's going to try to find out what's going on.'

He keeps his back to me and I'm puzzled. He seems to be hiding his expression.

I go to the bathroom before we leave and in the hallway I notice a small photo. With a shock I realise it shows a young, dark-haired Simon with a pretty woman and a smiling boy.

Simon's hand, wearing a wedding ring, rests on the woman's shoulder. The boy is perhaps four years old and has Simon's unmistakeable eyes.

No kids, eh? My heart thumps. Even if they'd divorced and she lived on the other side of the world, he still had a child. Yet in the hospital he'd told me to my face that Matthew was his only family and I'd believed him. Now I recall the brief, evasive hesitation before he spoke.

Why did he lie to me? Why did he even *bother*?

But then, I think bitterly, Max's lying was often about trivia, never any rhyme or reason to it. Some people just lie, they can't help themselves. Was Simon ashamed of the divorce? Custody battle? Deadbeat dad? Whatever.

After the disaster of Max I was certain I'd never again be taken in by an attractive, deceitful man, but once more I've been a gullible fool.

Before I return to the others I slow my breathing until it's steady. *Whoever is careless with the truth in small matters cannot be trusted with important matters*, said Einstein. I don't need Einstein to tell me that.

Don't forget this, Lena. Simon Rossi lies.

Later, Simon drives Jessie and me back to the hotel.

'Contact me immediately if you're worried about anything,' he says before he leaves. 'Here's my number. I mean it.'

'All right,' I say. I don't mean it.

I'm so happy to be out of the hospital. It seems a lifetime since we went sailing on *Sparrow* but it was only three days ago. Unbelievable. I take a deep breath and the night air is deliciously warm and scented with frangipani. I'm not going to think about anything unpleasant right now, I tell myself firmly.

When I open my door the room is stuffy and I say to Jess, 'I've done nothing but lie around for days. I'm going for a quick swim in the pool before bed—want to come?'

'Okay. You go ahead, I'll be there in a min. Just have to check something.'

I pull on my swimsuit and grab a towel. I feel the plasters on my legs and remember the nurse said they were waterproof. I go through the gate to the pool, which is sparkling beneath a cluster of tropical palms. A few people are splashing around in the water, while over to one side a small crowd is chattering near the brightly-lit bar.

It's such a lovely night, the breeze humid and warm. I can see the nearly full moon between clouds high in the sky. The pool glows with blue underwater lights which makes my heart jump for a moment, reminding me of the deadly powder on the boat. Don't think about it now I tell myself. Just relax.

I wrap my room key in the towel and ease into the warm water from the shallow end. My burns sting just for a moment then I paddle out to the middle of the pool and float on my back, content.

I watch the moon passing behind the scattered clouds. The noise from the bar is just a distant buzz. Even with my ears under water I hear a child start to wail. Its parents collect their towels, toys and child and finally leave. Now there's only one or two others left in the pool, quietly enjoying the warm night like me.

The clouds remind me of the cyclone Aidan mentioned—tropical cyclone Cyril—and I smile at the name. A category one, he'd said. Interesting, I think, looking at the sky. That cloud's moving pretty fast for something pushed by a storm six hundred kilometres away.

I hear a couple of people chatting to each other, then splashing and getting out. I wonder where Jessie is. It always takes her longer than she expects to 'check something.' I'm floating serenely near the side where the noise from the bar is quieter, blocked by the edge of the pool.

My mind drifts back to the morning a few days ago when I'd felt so unusually and delightfully content, relaxing on the jetty in the early morning sunlight. What a lot of strange things had happened since then.

I hear a splash as someone dives in and think, good, Jessie's here now. And suddenly I can't think at all.

My mouth and nose are full of water and someone's pushing me under. My eyes are open and I can see the eerie blue lights and bubbles swirling around me.

I twist and somehow get to the surface, gasping air. I see a man reaching out to push me down again, a young red-faced man with muscles and tattoos.

I kick at him and catch him, I hope, in the groin. He grunts then leaps through the water at me again, grabbing my shoulders and forcing me beneath the water. I bite viciously at one of his wrists and he lets go.

I kick again, backwards, and find I'm hard up against the edge of the pool. He comes at me and I can't get away. One of his wrists is bloody. I can hear someone yelling, 'Fire, help, fire!' I think, that's silly, it's water not fire.

The man draws back his fist and snarls, 'Cunt!' and punches the side of my face and shoves me under again. I kick, I claw at his hands, I try to bite but he's relentless.

Bubbles and foam are swirling, my chest is bursting, I'm desperate to breathe. I can't help myself, I gasp and feel agony in my nose, throat, chest. The blue lights start to fade.

And suddenly someone's lifting me and I break free of the surface and I'm coughing and retching but oh God I'm in the air! Jessie is beside me in the water, anguish on her face. A man is holding me up, calling, 'You all right, love? Can you hear me?'

Over his shoulder I see my attacker struggling with two other men near the gate. He violently breaks free and runs away into the darkness.

Someone wraps me in a blanket and leads me, my legs unsteady, to a chair. The paramedics come and give me oxygen and a policewoman takes my statement and Jessie's too. It was her crying out, 'Fire!'

'People will come and help if they think there's a fire,' she says calmly. 'But sometimes they hold back if they think there's violence.'

The policewoman gives her a curious look and says, 'Seems to have worked, I guess.' She takes statements from the few who saw the young man but they're confused and incoherent. Finally they all leave and I limp back to my room with Jess.

I can see in the mirror I've got a purple-red mark on my right cheek. Jess looks at it and says, 'That's good, he's a left-hander. Easier to identify.'

'Jess, it's *not bloody good*. I came to Broome for a conference and a holiday. What the hell is going on?' I'm still trembling uncontrollably.

She pats my shoulder, then sits on my bed and lightly touches her comcuff.

'I'm calling Simon,' she says.

'It's almost midnight, too late. Call him tomorrow.'

She shakes her head; she can be impossibly stubborn. He answers almost immediately, so I suppose he hasn't gone to bed yet either.

'Some muscle-bound dickwit just tried to drown Lena in the pool. Left-hander. (Pause.) No, she's all right, bit bruised. (Pause.) Okay.'

She touches the cuff again and looks up. 'He'll be here in a minute.'

I put my head in my hands. 'Oh, Jess. I don't want him here now. I feel like shit.'

'He's seen you looking worse, Lena.'

'Not funny.'

We wrap ourselves in bathrobes and sit down. I look at her. 'Why do you think this happened? Surely it's all coincidence ...'

'Don't know. But Simon knows more, I'm certain of it.'

Jess can be awkward in some situations, but when she's not under pressure she's stunningly clear-sighted about people. She says it depends on whether or not her catecholamine hormones have overwhelmed her analytic brain. I'm not arguing.

'Why do you think that?'

'He wasn't surprised when I called just now,' says Jess. 'And when we discovered the camera images had been wiped he was angry but not shocked.'

I think back. Yes. Unlike the rest of us he wasn't surprised it had happened. Why not?

Simon arrives. He sits down beside me on the couch and gently touches my bruise.

'I agree with Jess,' he says. 'The dickwit's definitely a left-hander. Do you remember anything else about him?'

'The tattoo on his neck was a stars-and-stripes flag. Common enough but I think he had an American accent too.'

'What did he say?'

'Only one word. He called me—cunt. But it wasn't nasal like an Australian would say it, it was more, I don't know, American.'

Jessie tries it out, straight-faced, in a range of accents. 'Carnt, curnt, c'nt, cornt, coont, cuunt.'

'That last one wasn't any dialect known to humankind, Jessie,' I say. Suddenly it's all too crazy and we burst out giggling.

'It's all right,' I tell Simon, gasping, 'Jessie's a programmer, she speaks many languages,' which sets us both off again.

After a time I sigh and push back my hair, and say, 'Sorry. I think we're a bit hysterical.'

'Yes. It's been a rough few days,' says Simon.

I look at him. 'It has. And that's something I want to ask you about: you don't seem very shocked by any of this.'

'In case you hadn't noticed we seem to be in the middle of some very strange happenings. Why should I be surprised there's more?'

'No,' says Jess. 'Come on. You can do better than *that*, Simon.'

He laughs grimly. 'You're right. Actually, there's been a shitstorm at my place too and it's a long way from being funny. I'm probably a bit hysterical too.'

'What's happened?' I ask.

'After I dropped you off, Aidan left and Matty went to bed. I sat up for a while then fell asleep on the couch, but woke hearing a noise in the kitchen. I was about to turn on the lights and charge right in but something made me stop. And then I smelled gas.'

He rubs his face with both hands. 'I found a small torch and checked the kitchen. The gas burners were fully open and if I'd switched on the lights the spark could have triggered an explosion.'

I feel sick.

'I shut off the gas and aired the kitchen, shaking like a fool. The back door was unlocked but it often is. I was about to come up here and check you were all right when Jessie rang. So you see why I wasn't all that surprised you'd been attacked too.'

'But *why*?' says Jess, furiously. 'It's unbelievable.'

'Because we're the last of the evidence,' I say slowly. 'Simon and me. The boat's gone and so are Simon's pictures. There's just us now.'

'No,' says Jess decisively. 'Not all the evidence.'

'You have more?' he asks, suddenly alert.

'Yeah. Listen, I know you're still bullshitting us about something, Simon, I know it. So when you decide to trust us with whatever you're hiding, then I'll tell you about the evidence we've got.'

He hesitates, then shrugs. 'I can see why you might think I'm hiding things, Jess, but not everything in my life is relevant here. You'll have to believe me on that.'

He glances at me. 'There's something else I want to talk to you about, Lena, but let's leave it till tomorrow. And it might be a good idea if you sleep in Jessie's room tonight, just in case.'

'Yes, think I will. And you lock all your doors and windows, too.'

Later, I'm restless on the other bed in Jessie's room. Glowing blue bubbles haunt me as soon as I close my eyes. I keep seeing the man's fist coming towards me, the rage in his face. I've never been attacked in my life, this is awful, *appalling*.

Combined with the dreadful few days in hospital, the nightmare of the blue boat ... I toss and turn, trying to forget for long enough to fall asleep ... and finally drift off.

8. Cliffs of Minyirr

Next morning I look at my bleary eyes and purple cheekbone and lank hair in the mirror. I sit down on the bed and moan, 'I'm a wreck. A boring, tragic wreck.'

Jess is sipping coffee in her bed, looking like a model for some fabulous magazine, her coloured hair spilling over her slim brown shoulders. She gazes at me and says, 'Wow, you are too. Poor Lena.'

She puts her cup down and sits up, cross-legged. 'Hey, I've got a plan—let's go shopping and take you to the hairdresser. Let's have a nice, easy day.'

'Someone just tried to murder me,' I say darkly. 'What if they do it again with a curling iron?'

Jess looks at me patiently. 'I think that dude'd be pretty obvious in a hair salon.'

I sigh and think, for heaven's sake, we're on holiday. 'All right, we'll do it,' I say. 'It's broad daylight after all.'

'I'll ring Simon and tell him where we're going first.'

I groan. 'Do you *have* to?'

'Yes. We should keep in touch.'

I shower and as we're getting ready I say, 'I think I'll get the things from my room so all my stuff's in one place.'

I unlock my door and collect my sensible conference outfits hanging in the cupboard and check the bathroom. The housekeeper has already been in so it's all tidy. I carry my clothes into Jessie's room and hang them up.

When we're leaving, Jess says, 'Just thought of something. Open your door again.'

I do so and she runs her fingers through her long ponytail. She closes a couple of loose hairs between the door and the jamb.

'Saw it in a movie,' she says. 'If they've fallen down next time we look we'll know someone's been in. I'll do the same with my room too.'

'Oh, Jess. This is insane. I'm starting to wonder if we're being paranoid. Maybe that awful man was just some random psycho who hates women.'

'Yeah, and maybe his mate turned on the gas at Simon's place because he hates men too. Don't think so, Lena.'

We drive to Chinatown, the small shopping area of old Broome. Jess says, 'Hair first. Here's a place.'

I sit in the chair and the young hairdresser asks what I want done. The back of my neck is hot and sweaty. I look at the limp dangling strands and say, 'Chop it all off, I'm sick of it. Give me something short, sort of light and fluffy all over. And a rinse to lift the colour.'

In just two hours I'm looking in the mirror again, amazed. Based on my vague request the hairdresser has done a fantastic job.

Wisps around my face soften the bruising and my layered chin-length hair is light and wavy. The colour is reddish-gold, bright and shiny. My eyes look enormous and my neck twice as long. I've had a manicure too and the nails on my fingers and toes are now a silvery rose.

Jess and I drink coffee in an open-air cafe full of young

backpackers. It's the same street I'd walked along just days ago, thinking about Mike, with palm trees down the middle and the old picture theatre on one side. Around us are scruffy tourist-traps and glittery jewellers, and cars moving past slowly in the hot air.

'You look brilliant, Lena,' says Jess. 'Wow, my ideas are good. And here, while you were being pampered I bought you a few things.'

She shows me quickly what's in the bags. She knows my size so I expect they'll fit but I'm shocked. 'I can't wear those, Jess. They're way too ... I don't know, bright, flimsy. Young,' I say, with a sigh.

She looks at me, her head to one side, exasperated and laughing. 'You're such a doofus, Lena. Come on, let's go back to the hotel and you can try them on at least.'

The day is humid and hazy and it's a relief to get back inside the air-conditioned unit. I spread out the clothes Jess bought for me on a bed. They're a revelation—for someone who only ever wears black, she has a wonderful sense of colour.

I try them on. Soft greens and blues bring out turquoise lights in my eyes, festive corals and golds echo my hair and put a glow in my cheeks. There are two tops with deep necklines that look great with my new hair, some shorts, trim jeans and a long fluttery dress, all in those delicious colours.

I stop saying 'Jess, I couldn't possibly wear this,' and after a while just start admiring myself. Eventually I fling myself down on a bed and laugh.

'You are the most amazing person in the world. I'd never in a million years have looked at these! But they're gorgeous. You're a genius.'

'And note how well everything goes with your comcuff,' she says.

My cuff is so light I've almost forgotten I'm wearing it. I look down and see she's right. The colours of the gemstones and enamel harmonise beautifully with the clothes.

'I do love colour,' says Jess. 'It's just not for me.'

I get up and kiss her. 'Thank you, my brilliant little sister, what a great way to start forgetting this awful week. Oh, and I must pay you back for all this. What did it cost?'

'Nothing. I've hired you as head program tester for the cuffs. It's on expenses.'

'You can't,' I say. 'That's nepotism.'

She shakes her head. 'No, seriously, we've already done some valuable testing, Lena. And under a bunch of extreme conditions, too, radiation, decontamination, swimming-pool chemicals, just for a start.'

'High-pressure submersion too, don't forget. Guess you don't get that to order in your Melbourne apartment.'

Jess and I get lunch from room service then I doze for half an hour while she catches up with email. When I wake up I lie blinking for a few moments, trying to remember what it is that's niggling me. I put on my new shorts and a pretty top and go to boil the kettle for a cup of tea, then suddenly realise.

'Jess, we didn't notice if the hairs in your door had fallen down or not!'

We go to the door and they're lying on the floor. We look at each other in dismay.

'That could have happened when we came back from shopping,' says Jess. 'I didn't even think to look—'

'Me neither. But let's check my door.'

We go out into the humid afternoon, the sky over-clouded, the breeze hot. There's just one other room between Jessie's and mine and there are low bushes between us and the parking lot where I've left my hire car.

We reach my room. The door is shut, innocuous and anonymous, but Jessie's long pink hairs are lying on the ground, half-draped over the sill. Jess gasps. I feel a cold chill on my scalp.

I say, 'Someone's been—'

Jess grabs my hand and whispers, 'Come back,' and yanks me towards her room. I stumble off-balance and say, 'Slow down—' and there's a popping noise.

A brick explodes where my head was an instant before.

Jess and I look around in shock. In the parking lot a vehicle is revving its engine. A young red-faced man is leaning out, glaring at us, holding up something metallic.

'*Run!*' yells Jess and we run.

I hear more popping noises and feel fragments of exploding bricks. A moment later we're back in Jessie's room, slamming and locking the door.

She taps at her cuff, at the same time calling out, 'Get away from the door, Lena!'

I move back shaking, and hear a screech of high-speed acceleration. I carefully peer through the window and can just see the rear of the car disappearing around a corner and away.

'Simon? Someone's shooting at us! (Pause) I think they've gone. (Pause) Okay.'

I sit down heavily on a bed.

'He says to pack and be ready to leave in five minutes.'

In less than four we're both done. Simon knocks a moment later and when I open the door he's over to one side, examining the holes in the bricks.

'Got everything?' he says calmly, and grabs our big bags, and throws them into the tray of his dual-cab ute. We toss our backpacks after them. Jess slams the door of the unit shut and we pile into the front seat. Simon takes off smoothly.

I think it's been less than twenty seconds since he knocked.

Matthew and Aidan are at Simon's house. They've been packing too, and as soon as we stop they throw more bags into the back, plus eskies and boxes. I can see tools in one, and food —bread, fruit, spreads—in another. Matthew quickly locks the house then gets into the back seat beside Aidan.

Simon accelerates away. I ask, 'This may be the bleeding obvious, but where the hell are we going?'

He looks at me. I'm aware we're squashed in beside each other and he smells rather nice. He changes gear smoothly and I notice his hands are brown and lightly work-scarred. We turn onto the big road leading to the port and he says, 'The only place I can think of where we'll be safe. Out at sea.'

Jessie says firmly, 'Good idea.'

'But there's a *cyclone* out there, dear little Cyril, remember?'

'It's heading south-west,' says Aidan. 'We're going north.'

'What about my hire car?' I ask.

'How long have you booked it for?' asks Matthew.

'Two weeks.'

Simon smiles. 'We'll be back a lot sooner than that.'

I'm feeling confused. I like Matthew and Aidan and it certainly hasn't escaped my attention they're both lovely young men, either of whom might be right for Jessie. And despite not trusting Simon, it's difficult not to like him too, dammit.

But we seem to have been caught up in some insane alternative world where people actually fire guns, *guns*, at other people! In quiet little Australia too, not weapons-crazed

America. But then, deliberate drownings and gas blasts aren't very common here either. Or boats covered in glowing powder and rotting corpses.

I shake my head in despair. 'This is *awful*. How do you know we're not just putting ourselves into further danger?'

'Because we haven't got much alternative, Lena,' says Simon. 'Whoever these people are, they're stunningly reckless, and they've made it abundantly clear they're not giving up. At least if we can get away to sea we'll have time to try and figure out what the hell is going on.'

He turns hard right onto a road and after a couple of kilometres turns left onto another, with orange soil along the edges and low green scrub all around. A few more kilometres then we turn down a track to a broad white stretch of sand.

To the left are rust-red boulders and low cliffs, and to the right the beach stretches away into the distance to the Cable Beach resort.

'*Minyirr*,' says Aidan happily, waving towards the cliffs. 'Deadly place.'

Lined up on the sand are other utes, some with trailers. Out on the water, boats large and small are bobbing around. And on one mooring, half-hidden by a large catamaran, I can see lugger *Sparrow*. The sea is a bit rough but the air is warm and the sky hazy.

Simon pulls up near a tinny I vividly recognise from our previous outing on the lugger. We load half the gear into it, then Simon says, 'Okay, kids, you take that lot out and get it aboard. Jess, you stow it, Matty, you check the engines and be ready to go. Ade, you come back for us and the rest of the gear.'

'Aye, aye, cap'n,' says Aidan, grinning, and the three of them push the tinny out, climb aboard and start the motor.

Simon and I finish unloading the ute, then he drives it up

the beach to above the waterline and leaves it among the others parked there. He jogs back to me, and we watch Matthew and Aidan throwing bags onto the deck and Jess moving them out of the way.

'We sailed the lugger around from the port this morning,' says Simon. 'I'd already been thinking about getting away but it's hard to do anything unnoticed at the port. Here, you're just one among the other boats.'

He gazes at me. I'm standing there, arms clasped, anxiously watching the lugger. Beyond it, from side to side on the horizon, all I can see are long, ominous, gunmetal-grey clouds.

'Did you get your hair cut?' he says.

'This morning—before the world turned upside down. Again.'

'Looks good. But it looked good the other way too.'

'I know quite well you're just saying that to keep me calm.'

His eyes crease slightly. 'You reckon?'

The tinny roars back to the shallows and Aidan jumps out. We load it up with the remaining gear, push it further into the rough water and get in.

Soon I'm standing on *Sparrow*'s deck, Jess beside me. Simon revs the engine and we head straight out to sea. Astonished, I realise it's been barely three hours since Jess and I returned from our light-hearted shopping trip.

The white sands and Minyirr's rust-red cliffs recede in our wake until they're just a line on the horizon.

PART II. WALMADAN

9. Mutations

Aidan calls out from the galley, 'Tea's ready, shipmates!'

Simon, at the tiller says, 'Would you bring it up here please, Ade? We need to talk.'

We sit on the deckhouse while we wait for Simon to gather his thoughts. It's late afternoon and the dark clouds to the west seem larger.

'Okay, guys,' he says, after looking at the horizon for a time.

'Least we're not kids any more,' says Aidan.

'I'm including Lena, who's a bit more grown-up than you lot.'

'Hey, I like being a guy,' I say. 'Makes me feel tough.'

'You've been pretty indestructible so far, but best not to push your luck,' says Simon. 'First off I want to ask you and Jess what you actually saw when someone took a pot-shot at you.'

'A brownish car,' I say.

'A Jeep, four-door hard-top, reinforced military issue,' says Jess, who knows all sorts of odd things from years of playing bloodthirsty online games.

'And there was a young man with something that looked like a gun,' I say.

'Looked like a gun?' says Matthew. 'You're not certain?'

'Well, I've only ever seen guns on TV. But whatever it was, it was making explosions near my head.'

'What sort of a noise was it?' asks Simon.

'A kind of a pop, not a bang,' I say. 'What do you think, Jess?'

'I saw it briefly—a semi-automatic with a suppressor. Maybe the new Heckler & Koch.'

'What?' I say.

'A fairly lethal gun with a silencer,' says Simon. 'Okay, that's not good. What did the man look like?'

I think for a moment. 'A red face, like the guy who tried to drown me. No, more like sunburned. Muscular, tattooed arms. Really short blond hair. A silver chain round his neck and wearing a khaki-green T-shirt.'

Jess shrugs. 'Some bozo.'

'Put the two of you together,' muses Aidan, 'and you'd make one bloody brilliant eyewitness.'

Simon is silent, looking at the horizon. The only sound is the engine, the creak of the rigging, the waves slapping hard against the hull. I look around and shiver. It's getting cold out on the water.

'I think I'll go and put something warmer on,' I say.

'Good idea,' says Simon. 'Matty, would you please bring me my jacket and break out the anti-nausea meds? Let's talk more later. I need to think.'

We take anti-seasickness pills and Simon gets the boat to stay face-on into the wind—he calls it something salty like *hove to*— so it's stable and he can leave the tiller and come down to the galley in the evening with the rest of us.

Jess and Matthew have made sandwiches. We're all tired, drinking coffee in the glow of lamps, seated on the benches each side of the table.

The lugger does a bit of a belly-flop crossed with a

corkscrew. I grab my mug and say to Simon, 'Well, we're out at sea just as you wanted. But are we really safe? The weather's getting worse and it's pitch dark outside. How do you even know where we're going?'

'There, see?' says Simon, pointing. I hadn't noticed a dark area behind a partition with some serious-looking hardware. 'We've got radio, radar, Internet. Trust me, we know where we're going.'

'So where *are* we going? And what'll we do when we get there?'

'That's what I wanted to talk to you about.' He turns to me. 'Remember you said Glenn Garrod gave you invitations to the Worm Turning opening?'

I nod. 'They're in my suitcase.'

'I want you to take me.'

'What? To Worm Turning?'

'Yes. I really need to have a look,' he says. 'There's no way I'd get in otherwise.'

'But it's a big evening gala. You won't see much of the plant.'

'It's not the plant I want to see. It's the people, the politicians, the military, the event. Something's not right about it and I'd like to get closer and check it out.'

I suddenly realise I haven't told anyone about Max's warnings. The events of the blue boat had followed so quickly afterwards I'd quite forgotten.

I lean forward. 'Listen. A guy at the conference I was talking to was really worried about the gala. He thought it might be dangerous with protesters and, I quote, psycho Yanks together in one spot and feeling edgy. But he was probably exaggerating, he often does—'

'A guy?' asks Jess.

I look at her and say, 'A guy called Max.' I don't feel like explaining about my soon-to-be ex-husband right now.

Jessie understands and changes the subject. She asks Simon. 'So do you think Worm Turning and the contaminated boat are connected?' she says.

'Lena and I talked about that in the hospital. We wondered if the caesium was for some kind of attack on the plant pointing the finger at the Chinese. But then there was no follow-up at all. Doesn't make sense if you want to put the blame on someone.'

'I can't think of any connection between the plant and the boat either,' I say. 'From what Geo-Garrod says, their technique is only for fuel rods, not caesium assemblies.'

'Then what about the hafnium?' says Matthew, his bearded face troubled. 'Could caesium be used to do anything with the hafnium from the Wormhole?'

'I can't imagine what, Matthew. And remember, the hafnium has to first be extracted from the sands in some long industrial process overseas before it's even available.'

'But have you read those papers I sent you, Lena? Something is definitely wrong with the hafnium story.'

'Not exactly had a free moment the last few days,' I say wryly. 'But promise I'll have a good look tomorrow.'

Jessie gets up and brings slices of fruit cake back to the table. We eat quietly for a time, then Matthew says, mopping up crumbs from his plate, 'Isn't caesium the major contaminant in the dead zone around Chernobyl?'

'Hey, I'm just the ambo on this boat,' says Aidan. 'Wasn't Chernobyl some explosion, years ago?'

I nod. 'Nineteen-eighties. Worst nuclear accident in the world until Fukushima. But of course Hanford's taken pole position now.'

'So what happened at Chernobyl?' asks Aidan.

'They were testing the safety controls at an old power station in the Ukraine and screwed up. Contaminated most of Europe.'

'Jesus,' says Simon, clearing his throat. 'Um, Lena, there's no chance Worm Turning could blow up like that is there?'

I shake my head. 'No. Totally different.'

'What about the people?' says Aidan.

'Supposedly about sixty died at the time, mostly from fighting fires at the reactor, but thousands of kids went on to develop cancers of the thyroid.'

'Why thyroid?' asks Simon, puzzled.

'Growing bodies need iodine and thyroid glands just suck it up. The explosion released masses of radioactive iodine and the children took the brunt of it.' I hesitate. 'Brave kids, too. Their thyroids had to be removed but they—usually survived. Called their scars Chernobyl necklaces ...'

My breath catches and I can't speak.

Jessie says to the others, 'Lena worked with an aid group over there. She burnt out.'

I rub my face. 'It's okay, Jess.' I sigh. 'There was one little girl I was very fond of called Irina. She didn't survive.'

'But apart from the thyroid cancers,' says Matthew gently, 'I've read that the long-term death toll hasn't been as great as first feared.'

I lift my head. 'Look, there are highly respectable organisations claiming the death-rates are minimal—no problem here folks, move right along. But they carefully limit exactly where and what they measure. Those who examine the wider picture come up with rather more hair-raising numbers. Perhaps hundreds of thousands of additional deaths.'

'But why won't they acknowledge the larger exposure?' asks Matthew.

'Because it means world-wide liability for a massive, government-backed industry,' I say. 'And if they start investigating the true effects of the accidents, the bomb testing, the reactor pollution, the *criminally* sloppy storage— they're terrified at what might emerge. What they might have to pay in compensation, what they might have to do to clean up this fucking, *fucking* mess.'

I look around at the surprised faces. 'Yes, it's my life's work. And it breaks my heart.'

Matthew says, 'But surely the technology will improve ...'

'Oh, Matthew, it's never been that,' I sigh. 'It's some of the most amazing technology you could ever dream of. But then the owners are allowed to skimp on training or upkeep or storage because there's no profit in it.'

'Yeah,' says Jessie. '*Another flaw in the human character is that everybody wants to build and nobody wants to do maintenance. So says Kurt Vonnegut.*'

I laugh despairingly. 'So they hire a bunch of poor bastards to run things with a shelf of manuals, minimal pay and little support. She'll be right, mate. *People* are the weak link and that's not changing any time soon.'

A long silence. Finally Aidan stands and collects our plates and carries them to the small sink. He fills it with water, his back to us. I can feel he's upset.

'I'm sorry, Aidan,' I say. 'I hate it that Worm Turning was built on Indigenous land, but I'm still desperately hopeful it can do what they say it will.'

He turns and looks at me, his amber eyes sceptical. 'More people die of tobacco and fast cars than ever died of radiation, Lena,' he says.

'Of course—but that ends with them, right then and there. And yes, nature can be incredibly resilient, but not against radiation. And some nuclear material can kill invisibly for thousands of years.'

'Lena showed me some amazing pictures,' says Jess. 'By a woman called Hesse-Honegger who paints insects, mutated bugs, collected from around nuclear plants.'

She taps at her computer for a few moments and brings up some images, jewel-bright and exquisite. We cluster around and everyone becomes silent.

I remember when I first saw these paintings. First, I felt awe at the artist's craft and the perfection of the tiny creatures, each shimmering scale and faceted eye lovingly depicted hundreds of times larger than life.

Then growing disquiet as the artist compared the mutated insects to healthy ones, then sickening horror at the sight of the twisted wings and legs, the bulges, cysts and tumours, the genetic devastation on such an agonisingly minuscule scale.

After a time Matthew runs his fingers through his curls and says, 'Christ. Why isn't this work better-known?'

'She's ignored. Called eccentric, axe to grind, a liar,' says Jess. 'You know, the usual.'

Aidan stares at the images and puts a hand on my shoulder. 'Yeah. Sorry, cuz. Gotta get rid of anything that can do *that*,' he says, his voice husky.

He sits down again and sighs. 'All right, reprocessing's gotta happen—but, hey, put the plant somewhere else! If it's so bloody safe why is it at Walmadan and not the middle of Perth?'

'Well, we all know the answer to that, mate—screwing over Indigenous land rights is the national sport,' says Matthew.

'But why so set on Walmadan itself for the plant?' says

Simon. 'It's not as if we don't have plenty of other old nuclear sites like—where were those bomb tests in the fifties, Lena?'

'Maralinga, Emu Field.'

Aidan groans. 'This just goes from bad to worse.' He puts his head in his hands, the light glancing off his silver earring. 'You forgot one there. The Montes.'

'Oh, yes,' I say. 'Where they did the first tests.'

'Where?' says Jess, her slim fingers moving on the computer. 'Ah, I see. Montebello Islands.'

'Aren't the Montes part of your country, Ade?' asks Simon.

He nods slowly. 'My mum's from Broome, but my dad comes from the Pilbara and I grew up on Murujuga—they call it the Burrup Peninsula now.'

He shakes his head sadly. 'Gas refineries and the greatest collection of rock art in the world. The Monte islands are a hundred kays west—Dad and I used to go camping there when I was a kid.'

'Can you still see where they let off the bombs?' asks Jess, curious.

'There's a three hundred metre crater on the floor of one bay where they blew up a ship,' says Aidan. 'Even today nothing lives in it.'

'That was a plutonium bomb.' I say. 'Plutonium didn't even exist in nature till humans created it. And now just one particle in your lungs will slowly kill you.'

Simon rubs his stubbled jaw slowly. 'This is just too weird. I have no idea what's going on.' He looks up, his dark-fringed eyes intense. 'All right. Let's try to make some sense of it. What have we got?' He counts off. 'One, a boatload of caesium and a couple of corpses.'

'Two,' says Aidan. 'A plant fast-tracked on stolen Indigenous land.'

'Three,' says Matthew. 'A mine full of suspiciously high-yield hafnium.'

'Four,' says Jess. 'A bunch of bozos trying to murder Lena and Simon.'

They all gaze at me expectantly.

'I haven't got a five!' I say. 'I can barely get my head around bloody *one*.'

10. A Bewildering World

Aidan and I are finishing off the washing-up later when Jess says, 'Hey, here's something we haven't thought about.' She looks around at us. 'Where did that blue boat *come* from? And when?'

'How could we figure out something like that?' says Aidan.

'Satellite images, like the weather maps.'

'But they're low resolution,' says Simon. 'You can't see something as small as a boat.'

'The public ones are, but the originals are highly detailed.'

Matthew smiles slowly. 'Great idea. But gee, cyber-Jess, how could we possibly get to those originals?'

'Hey, Parrot-man,' she says, lifting an eyebrow. 'The people I work for store most of the world's data. What do you reckon?'

'Parrot-man?' I ask.

'Have you *seen* that abomination he calls a shirt? Makes my eyes bleed.'

'Oh, how unkind,' says Matthew, amused. 'I just like a bit of colour and movement.'

'As in a massacre at a tropical aviary?' says Jess.

'You think that one's bad? Doesn't even rate compared to what he usually wears,' says Aidan. 'Coolness quotient zero.'

Jessie half-smiles to herself. She turns to her computer and taps and thinks and flicks images and phrases here and there on the screen. After a little while she says, 'Yeah,' to herself, then 'Fuck,' and 'No way.' Time passes.

Simon asks, puzzled, 'Wait a minute, Jess, how have you got connectivity, anyway? The boat's Internet link isn't up.'

She says, 'Satellite. Amazing how much traffic flying around unsecured networks you can just blend with even out here.' She puts her head down again, concentrating. A few minutes later she says, 'Ah,' and smiles.

'All right. I'm into the archives. Let's start with the day we found the blue boat. Simon, how far from land were we and where?' She brings up an image of Western Australia and starts to zoom in on Broome.

'Okay, stop there, Jess,' says Simon. 'Come over a bit more—is that us? Go further in.'

She expands the image and we can see the lugger in startling detail, figures on the deck, shadows cast by the sails. And over to our west is another boat, a dark shape lying on its deck. I can even see light glancing off the metal drum near the tiller.

'I'll get a chart,' says Matthew. 'We can plot the positions.'

'Only if you put on something less psychedelic,' says Jess. 'I can't concentrate otherwise.'

Matthew glances at her hair. 'Seriously, you have a problem with *colour*?'

'Where clothes are concerned, yes.'

Matthew smiles and gets a grey T-shirt out of a cupboard and pulls it over his tropical bird shirt. He looks absurd.

Jess shakes her head in despair. They sit together at the table bickering amiably, and work backwards through the days plotting the blue boat's path.

Aidan and I sit at the other side of the table drinking tea. I glance at him—such a sweet-natured man. He plays the clown to Matthew's quiet thoughtfulness but he has a calm I find deeply reassuring, and I've got secret hopes he might suit Jessie.

'What was the place you come from again?' I ask.

'Murujuga.' He laughs. 'They call it the Burrup Peninsula nowadays, after a dead bank clerk.'

'That's in the Dampier Archipelago, isn't it?' I say. 'Seem to be lots of places named Dampier round here.'

'Too right. We're near the peninsula now, but the archipelago's eight hundred kays south-west of here. And Dampier town is on Murujuga itself.'

'A real lack of imagination in the cartography department,' I say. 'So you say there's a gas plant at Murujuga?'

'And fertiliser and explosives plants. I reckon we'll never be able to stop fighting to save what's there.'

'And what *is* there?'

'Oh, maybe a million rock carvings from the last sixty thousand years. Pictures of extinct beasts like the Tassie tiger. The oldest image of a human face in the world. Woops sorry, they crushed *that* one for road-fill, but the second-oldest one's out there, somewhere. Being eroded away by gas emissions.'

'Oh, Aidan, that's horrible. Can't the place be protected?'

'It is, sorta. Part of it's a national park—the type the pollies can dig a mine in if they really want.' He sighs heavily. 'Sorry, Lena. Drives me mental. It's where I grew up, brilliant place for kids. Camping, beaches, bush food, fishing—used to run wild.'

'Sounds idyllic.'

'It was. But then the funny thing was I got a job at the gas plant after leaving school and that was amazing too,' he says. 'Incredible feat of engineering, and I know half the blokes there, still good mates.'

'Wow! Can't imagine you in a hard hat.'

He smiles for a moment then says, 'But you know, when I'd

come off shift I'd stare at the hills around the plant, and I'd just feel dizzy, knocked out. The rocks—they're awesome, all piled up in heaps and tumbling down the slopes. And dark, sort of reddish-black, like they're glowing in a fire.'

'And you say there are maybe a *million* carvings among them?'

'Yeah. Some are well-known, but most are hidden.'

'Did you see them when you were a kid?'

Aidan nods slowly. 'Yeah. But a lot are in places you can't go till you're an adult and initiated.'

'How did you know which ones you couldn't go to? Did the elders tell you?'

He shakes his head. 'Not many elders around, Dampier was a company town. No, mostly you'd just know. You'd be scrambling up a hill and feel it. Not this way, that way. Stay out. Funny feeling, but you don't ignore it.'

'Why did you leave Murujuga, then?'

'Trying to cope with both sides of the place at once, old and new, started doing my head in. So I went to Broome to visit my mum's mob and stayed on. Guess I just couldn't bear being there any more.'

'But now you're fighting for Walmadan instead.'

'Yeah.' He smiles. 'Tangled up in this shitfight instead. Love Paddy and Maggie, gotta help them if I can.' He glances at me shyly. 'There's someone in Maggie's family, too ...'

Damn. Looks like he's taken, Jess.

Aidan goes for a nap because he's taking the next watch in a couple of hours. Simon restarted the engine earlier and is up on deck at the tiller. I take him a mug of coffee and say, 'We didn't finish talking about Worm Turning. How long would it take to get there?'

'Just a few hours directly, it's only about sixty kilometres north of Broome. The gala's in two nights from now so we've got plenty of time.'

'But where would we land?'

'There's a big wharf for loading mineral sands not far from the plant.'

'Surely they wouldn't let just anyone moor there?' I say. 'It'll be under heavy-duty security.'

He nods, checking the faintly-lit compass in front of him and moving the tiller arm slightly. 'Right. But not far from that is a jetty—I think your mate Glenn Garrod needed a berth for his glamorous yacht. Fishing and tourist boats can tie up there without any problem.'

'He's hardly my mate.'

'Favourite nuclear physicist wasn't it?'

I smile a little. 'So how far from the water is the plant?'

'About two kilometres or so inland.'

The wind is noisy and it's very dark. Before dinner we lowered the sails and I felt pleasingly nautical hauling on the ropes. Now, in the glimmers of light from the boat, we're motoring against what seem to be terrifyingly large seas.

We hit a big wave and I grab the handhold on the deckhouse and say, 'Simon, really, are we safe?'

He nods. 'Remember, luggers were built to work on this coast in all sorts of conditions.'

'That was a hell of a long time ago,' I say.

'I've done a lot of modifications and I'd say this boat's stronger and more seaworthy than most. So don't worry Lena, we're safe. And remember, *Sparrow* used to be your great-grandmother's—she survived didn't she?'

'Granddad said his mum would go out sailing sometimes, but

she didn't do the pearl-shelling—that was a business and she hired Asian men to do it. But he also said she simply loved the lugger for itself, all her life, so I'm glad *Sparrow*'s still around.'

'Me too, she's a bloody good boat.' After a time he says, 'So how did you end up in this radiation racket, anyway?'

'Oh, studied physics at uni, then my dad married Suyin and had Jessie. Suyin's a lovely woman, worked in nuclear medicine and inspired me a lot. And then a funny thing happened—'

'Funny amusing?'

'Funny odd. I only met my grandfather Mike for the first time when I was twenty, and didn't even know we were related then—nobody did. He'd had a secret fling with my Nana in the old days, and it turned out he'd actually fathered my dad.'

'But how did you know?' asks Simon. 'They didn't have DNA testing back then.'

'We'd all inherited the same small brown birthmark on our backs. You must have seen it when we were both scrubbing off caesium.'

'I wasn't looking at your back at the time.'

'I suppose we were too frantic to notice anything much.'

He smiles gently. 'Not precisely what I meant. So how did Mike lead you to a life of science?'

'He was a professor of engineering and gave me lots of encouragement to do research. To do anything, really. Such a funny, dear man. Tough as nails too when he had to be.'

'Sounds like a great bloke. Is he still around?'

I sigh, thinking of Mike's gentle gaze, his jokes, his tall spare frame, his lifelong passion for my darling Nana who went so quickly after him.

'Died a few years ago, just when I needed him most. Could have done with somebody sane around,' I say, my throat tightening painfully.

'Why was that?'

I'm stabbed by my old grief at the double bereavement, the incomprehensible absence. My burns hurt like hell and I'm exhausted from this long strange day, the attacks, the dash into such a bewildering new world.

Tears come to my eyes. I'm suddenly pissed off with everything and everyone, Simon especially. Attractive, deceitful Simon, who seems so nice but reminds me of painful things and tells me lies and *cannot* be trusted.

'Oh, rotten marriage. To a shit of an army man, a pathological bloody *liar*,' I say. I force myself to stop and take a breath. 'Okay. Maybe I'd better go and see how Jess and Matthew are doing.'

Leaving a slightly startled Simon behind I climb down to the galley, sit at the table and try to concentrate. 'So. What have you guys found?'

Matthew pushes the large chart towards me. 'Here's where we were when we ran into the blue boat. We think it'd been drifting for nearly a week.'

Jess says, 'About two weeks before that they were a long way out in the Indian Ocean and met a ship.' She turns her computer so I can see the images on the screen.

On a shimmering ocean etched with tiny waves, the small blue boat sits beside a large grey vessel with the oddest shape. It's long and broad at the rear, narrowing suddenly to a tapering bow—a bit like a wine bottle with a pointed cork.

'What on earth's *that*?'

Jess shrugs. She clicks, and the next image shows a crane on the ship and men around it. The sunlight is so bright it's just their shadows I see—one man with arms out directing, others standing casually nearby. A drum is dangling from the arm of the crane.

Click. The arm and its cargo are hovering over the boat, the shadows vividly outlined on the deckhouse. Then the drum is on the deck and the blue boat moving away, with one figure at the tiller, the other seemingly waving goodbye.

Shaken at the sight of the two men so blissfully unaware of their gruesome fates, I say, 'Okay, they got the drum from that big ship. But what *is* it?'

'Naval vessel of some kind. Need to do a bit more digging,' says Jess. 'Have to find a satellite in the area doing oblique scans so we can see it from the side.'

We sit chatting, gazing at the images. Aidan takes over on deck and Simon comes into the galley to say good-night. I'm a little embarrassed at my earlier outburst and avoid his eyes.

Matthew and Jess show him what they found. 'Really odd shape,' says Matthew. 'Look at the helicopter deck at the stern.'

'Who the hell has vessels like that?' says Jess.

Simon stares at the image. 'Not sure,' he says.

Jess gazes at him poker-faced and I realise she doesn't believe him. Neither do I.

'Look, I've got to go and get some sleep,' he says. 'It's all going round and round in my brain.'

After sitting there a while longer I start yawning. I expect Simon is asleep by now so I say good night, go to the forward hatch and climb quietly down the steep stairs. I wash in the bathroom, remembering showering there, terrified, just a few days ago.

Now all I want is a bed. Two single berths run along the hull opposite the bathroom and two are inside the triangular bow section. A double berth fits against the wall between the bathroom and the bow, and that's where Simon is asleep, breathing softly.

I move silently forward to the bow and curl up in a bunk, sighing with the relief of relaxing at last.

After a few moments Simon asks, 'Are you okay, Lena? It's been a bastard of a day.'

'For all of us,' I say, feeling a little ashamed. 'Sorry I got cranky earlier, Simon. Hit a sore point.'

'Well, we've all got those. See you tomorrow.'

11. The Eerie Warship

Next morning sunlight is reflecting around the walls from the hatchway. I lie there feeling the slow rocking of the lugger, enjoying the pleasing, unfamiliar sense of security.

Jessie is just waking up too. We wash and try to look vaguely civilised but it's a losing battle. Okay, that's me: Jess runs her fingers through her multi-coloured hair and looks fabulous.

When we climb to the deck I see Matthew at the tiller, curls ruffling in the wind. Jess says, 'Heya, Parrot-man.' He replies, 'Morning, cyber-Jess.'

The sky is partly cloudy, the seas rougher than yesterday. We find Simon and Aidan sitting at the table in the galley.

Aidan says, 'Good, you're up at last. Come on Jess, tell us what you found last night. Matthew won't, says you should.'

'Coffee first,' says Jess in a drone. 'Must have coffee.'

Finally we're at the table with some breakfast. Jess pulls out her pink-orange device and taps for a moment or two.

'All right, here's what we discovered at about two in the morning—the ship that loaded the caesium into the blue boat.'

She pushes the computer towards us. It shows a large grey vessel from the side, broad at the stern and tapering to a long sharp bow that's beaked like a bird of prey. It's eerie and brutal.

'Wow. What a weird beast,' I say. 'Do you have any idea ...?'

Jess touches the screen and zooms in on the large number 12

painted on the hull.

Simon murmurs, 'Hell.' I look at him with eyebrows raised. He clears his throat.

'Littoral combat ship, the latest. Trimaran hull, armed, fast, manoeuvrable. Built especially for shallow waters like the coast around here.'

'Can you trace that number?' I ask.

'We have. Matter of national pride and all that,' says Jess. 'It's USS *Jameson*. The American warship assigned to protect Worm Turning.'

Simon puts his head in his hands and groans softly.

'The *Americans* put the caesium on the blue boat?' I say. 'Why? And where on earth was it going?'

'Don't know why,' says Jess. 'But if those men hadn't died the boat's route would have landed them pretty damned close to Worm Turning.'

She turns to Simon. 'Okay. Time to stop messing around, dude. What do you really know about all this?'

He spreads his hands. 'I didn't know, Jess, I just suspected. The man who attacked Lena, the one who shot at you, the gun, the Jeep—it all suggested the US military. Plus Colonel Zukowski's weird story about destroying the boat when it was evidence in a crime.'

'Remember he said they recovered most of the caesium?' I say. 'Perhaps that's all they wanted anyway. But why would they move it from the ship to the fishing boat in the first place?'

'Deniability,' says Simon. '*Jameson* has to moor at the Worm Turning wharf and that's too public. But a fishing boat can come ashore unseen almost anywhere on the Dampier.'

'So they wanted to secretly land a nuclear contaminant near a plant for nuclear decontamination?' I say. 'That's ludicrous.'

'Could they be trying to undermine the plant—make it appear unsafe?' says Aidan. '*Bunch of losers—look, they've dropped caesium all over the place!*'

'But the Yanks have put billions into backing the plant,' I say. 'They desperately need it to handle their own mountains of nuclear waste. Why on earth would they want it to fail?'

'*Simon,*' says Jess. She's staring at him. 'Keep going.'

He takes a breath. 'All right.' He looks at me. 'I'm not precisely who I said I was or do precisely what I said I do.'

I feel a tightness in my chest. 'You lied to me in other words. Why am I not surprised?' I say coolly. 'Okay, Simon—who or what are you?'

'You remember I said I was working in the Environment department? And retired after they split it into Alise Berg's fiefdom and merged the rest of us with poor old Recreation?'

'Yup, I remember,' I say. 'Keep going.'

'I only sort-of retired. I still work in a government group.'

'What, Iceberg's your best buddy after all?'

'Never,' he says flatly. 'Look, governments come and go but public servants remain. And despite the stereotype, some are appalled at the devastation taking place. People with environmental backgrounds, even people from the intelligence services.'

'Aha,' says Jess. '*There* we are.'

Simon grins. 'There we are. Well, a few mandarins in the Commonwealth government set up a small monitoring group and I was recruited into that. It's hidden deep inside a committee with a name so dull it'd put anyone to sleep. But we observe and quietly try to head off the worst abuses before they go too far.'

'So that's why you *sort-of* retired to Broome?' I say.

'We already knew this region was threatened, but Worm

Turning was a massive shock. The fast-tracking caught us off guard, then the lies about mining profits and hafnium yields set off warning bells. And now *this*? The Americans smuggling in radioactive caesium? None of it makes the slightest sense, and we're desperate to know more.'

'What about your hard-faced mate, Jumbo?' I ask.

'Liaison. And he's nicer than he looks. Breeds endangered marsupials.'

'Yeah. Ex-army too, I suppose?'

He nods. 'Lena, look, I'm sorry for lying to you.'

I shrug. 'Par for the course.'

'But you see now why I must get into Worm Turning tomorrow night.'

'Yes.'

'And will you help?'

I gaze at Simon and his silver eyes meet mine. The cabin is silent. I glance again at the image of the eerie warship that handed over a drum of caesium to two men, and left them to die in agony on a small blue boat.

I slowly nod.

Later I make tea and take it up to the deck. I work my way forward to where Simon is sitting on the deckhouse watching the sky. I hand him a mug.

He says, 'Thanks. I was getting a bit dozy.' After a moment he says, 'Talk to me, Lena.'

I sit down at enough of a distance to show I'm still pissed off with him.

'I'm sorry, truly. I know you hate lies,' he says. 'But I had to be discreet—didn't want to say anything till I knew what was happening.'

'And do you?'

He laughs briefly and shakes his head. 'No, still don't, feel a complete fool. But I'm glad you know all my secrets now.'

All? There's a silence. I wait. Nothing.

The sea is rough, the ship rising and falling. Oddly, I find I'm getting used to the rocking and anticipating it with my body. It feels good.

I say, 'How's the weather going?'

'Cyclone Cyril's stalled about four hundred-odd kilometres off Broome. Nothing very dramatic, though.'

'Why would it stall?'

'Weird things, cyclones. Power up over warm water but over cold they lose their grunt. Perhaps it's run into a bit of cool sea but that won't last forever. It'll move south again.'

After a time I ask, 'And are we near Worm Turning yet?'

'Almost, but I've taken us a long way off-shore for now,' says Simon. 'We'll land tomorrow afternoon. We've just got to ride out tonight at sea—I hope it doesn't get any worse. But you and Jess seem to be handling it well.'

'I'd like to think our lugger-sailing great-grandmother gave us a genetic advantage.'

Simon grins. 'Landlubber's dream. Everyone gets sick as a dog in truly bad weather.'

I smile politely and move away.

Oh, Simon. All your secrets? What about that family you pretend not to have?

Sitting in the galley with Jessie later that morning, I get out my own laptop. A titanium, thin, powerful marvel, which now looks clunky beside her feather-light iridescent oval. Bloody technology, you can never catch up.

I finally start reading one of the papers Matthew emailed me, a report by Chinese scientists on their experiments with the isomer hafnium-178m2. By the time I've got to the end I'm feeling puzzled. They'd had some interesting results—not world-shattering but certainly enough to suggest a fruitful line of research, and not at all the tinfoil-hat stuff I'd expected.

I read another paper, this one by Russian researchers. Like the Chinese they were looking at the unexpectedly large amounts of energy released when they hit hafnium with high-powered beams. Different technique, but surprisingly similar results.

I'm stunned. If this work is correct it might one day be possible to create bombs from hafnium: a whole new era of radioactive weapons. I feel sick at the thought.

Matthew comes down to the galley and looks over my shoulder. 'Good, you've had a read. What do you think?'

'It's scary stuff. But I don't understand why is no one talking about it? It's remarkable work.'

He goes to the sink and starts washing up cups for coffee. 'But the gods of scientific credibility—and funding—have deemed this topic off-limits. Too embarrassing. No one can ever forget the cold fusion debacle.'

'That shouldn't be—'

He turns and looks at me, his eyes amused.

'Oh, all right,' I say. 'Yes, I know that's how it works all too damned often, but I can't imagine the vast and various defence departments around the world letting something like this pass by unnoticed.'

'I don't expect they have, either,' Matthew says, leaning back on the sink, drying the cups with a tea-towel. 'I suspect that's why no one's talking.'

'I hate conspiracy theories. Too easy.'

'Lena, if your funding was coming from those very defence establishments, why would you rock the boat?' he asks. 'And you'd probably be covered by stringent confidentiality agreements, anyway.'

Jess looks up from her computer and says, 'Makes sense. So you think it's the military buying the Worm Turning minerals?'

'Yes,' he says, pouring coffee into the mugs. 'Even if there's no bomb today, one day there might be and whoever's got a hafnium stockpile will be way ahead of the game.'

'Let's check it out,' she says.

'Find out who's buying the minerals, you mean?' says Matthew. 'I've tried, but keep on running into dead ends.' He hands me a coffee.

'I'll give it a go,' says Jess. 'For something like this you don't necessarily need the transaction details, just algorithms to recognise patterns and analyse differences.'

'And you've got algorithms to—?' I begin, then stop. 'Of course you have.'

She looks up, tucking a strand of orange hair behind her ear, and says seriously, 'It's not like in the movies, Lena. It might look as if I just magically go tap-tap—'

'That's exactly what it looks like,' says Matthew, with his quiet grin, sitting down beside her with two mugs. 'Shove over, I want to see all the magic.'

'Suppose something was encrypted, Jess, and you didn't have the key,' I say. 'You couldn't just find out what it is?'

'No way. I'd need a large chunk of the resources of my esteemed employers to decrypt even something small. They'd notice the power drain if nothing else.'

'Better get started then, cyber-Jess,' says Matthew, rubbing his bearded chin. 'Sounds like this might take forever.'

'Not necessarily, Parrot-man.' Her eyes are amused.

Oh good, I think, and close my laptop.

In the afternoon we put out a sea-anchor and set the sails so we're stable again. The air is warm and gusty, clouds are high in the sky. We take turns on watch at the bow to make sure we don't get run over by a bulk carrier, but the wide ocean around us remains empty.

Matthew and Jessie cook a delicious noodle dish in the evening then we sit on deck in the fading light and drink tea.

After a pleasingly quiet time, Jess muses, 'What does Worm Turning mean, anyway?'

'Remember the shock jock who made up the name?' says Aidan.

'That spiteful little horror in Sydney?' I ask.

'Yes. Thought it was a wonderful joke,' says Matthew. 'Calling the serpent—the aquifer—a worm.'

'And it's where the road turns inland,' says Aidan. 'Worm Turning. Hilarious.'

'But that's not the real meaning is it?'

Jess searches. 'Shakespeare. *The smallest worm will turn being trodden on, and doves will peck in safeguard of their brood.*'

Matthew, leaning lightly against her shoulder, quotes further, 'The worm turns: someone previously downtrodden gets his revenge; an unfavourable situation is reversed.'

'It's sheer arrogance to use a name like that,' says Simon.

'Nah,' says Aidan. 'Just straight-out contempt for country.'

'Ade, once we're closer to shore, will you call Paddy and Maggie?' asks Simon. 'If they're at the protest camp I want them to leave for the evening of the gala, take everyone with them. Go a long way away.'

'Why?' I ask.

He shakes his head. 'Just got a bad feeling. Like your mate Max said—there'll be too many thugs around in uniform that night, tense and trigger-happy. And we already know how dangerous they can be.'

'But will *Lena* be safe?' asks Jess sternly.

'She's the big boss's favourite nuclear physicist, so I reckon so.' He rubs his neck. 'I hope so.'

Jess and Matthew try to track the buyers of the hafnium-rich mineral sands but after several hours of subtle enquiry don't get anywhere.

So they change tack and go back to the satellite images and simply follow the path of a ship carrying Worm Turning mineral sands.

After a yell of triumph from Jess we gather to have a look. She shows us a sequence of pictures, starting with a ship crossing the Pacific and docking at Los Angeles. The cargo gets loaded onto a train, then the train travels to Las Vegas.

The cargo is emptied into trucks and carried north-west for a hundred kilometres or so, then dumped into cone-shaped hillocks. Around the same site there are hundreds of similar hillocks, in a vast tract on the map marked "Federal Land".

I sit down and run my fingers through my hair. 'But that's the Nevada *test* site—tourists used to come to Las Vegas especially to watch the mushroom clouds.'

'They call it the National Security Site nowadays,' says Matthew. 'Have to get that S-word in somehow. So now we know. Must be the American government buying the hafnium-rich minerals: no one else is allowed into that region.'

Jess is still flipping through other images, zooming over the ground. 'Wow, check this out, where they did the underground nuclear tests. Like the face of the moon! Each of those circular *things* is a crater.'

'But there must be hundreds of them, Jess,' I say, puzzled. 'I thought they only used this place in the 1950s.'

Tap-tap. 'Over one thousand tests, Lena. Continuing to the present day.'

'One *thousand*?' I say. 'They'd do that to their own country?'

Aidan says, 'Better their own country than somebody else's.'

'The Japanese might agree with you there,' says Matthew dryly. We're silent, shocked.

I take my turn on watch, then sit on the galley steps and listen to the news on the radio. Still no word about the contaminated boat, but there's a breathless piece on the new era heralded by the ingenuity of Worm Turning and the glittering grand opening tomorrow evening.

Then the weather report says Cyclone Cyril has become a category two, and is four hundred kilometres away and moving south-east towards Port Hedland.

'How bad is a category two cyclone?' I ask Simon, who's reading a book on the other side of the table from Matthew and Jess, who are lost in more detective work and occasionally murmuring to each other.

'Cat two?' says Simon. 'Um, minor damage to buildings. Winds up to, oh, 160, 170 kilometres an hour. You wouldn't want to be out at sea in one but you wouldn't be too worried on land in a strong building.'

'In case you hadn't noticed we're not on land. Or in a strong building.'

He smiles. 'No, but Cyril's a long way away.' He closes his book. 'I'm off to wash and sleep—on watch at four a.m.'

Jess looks up. 'Is it ten already? I'd better relieve Aidan.'

Matthew says, 'I'll come with you. Can keep trying some other leads.' Jess glances at him, pleased.

I sit alone in the galley for a time, pondering these last few strange days, then go up to the deck and along to the sleeping area. Simon, dressed in clean T-shirt and shorts, is sitting on the big berth with the first aid box.

'Can you help me?' he asks. 'I need to change the dressings on my legs and can't fit one on the back of my knee.'

I sit beside him, aware of his freshly-washed hair and strong brown legs.

'Okay,' I say coolly,' where do you need the dressing?'

'Here.'

'That's definitely healing now and the others are looking good too,' I say as I open the large patch and press it carefully over the red, half-scabbed area.

'Ow. Still annoying as hell. What about you?'

'Yes. The one on my ankle's driving me mad. I didn't change my dressings last night either, too tired. I'll have a wash and do them too.'

A little later Simon helps dress my ankle and the back of my calf. 'Healing up well, I reckon,' he says. He leans back and says quietly, 'Do you think we got away with it, Lena?'

'With being nuked, you mean?'

His quick grin. 'Yeah. With being nuked.'

'I hope so,' I say. 'I haven't felt severe exhaustion, have you?'

'No, just normal tiredness.'

I nod. 'Same for me. Finger crossed, yes, we may have been very lucky.'

'I just can't believe how *quickly* it happened—such a short exposure to the stuff and we end up with damage like this,' he says, shaking his head.

I gaze at him, part of my mind diverted by his long black

eyelashes, another part trying to remember something. 'Oh, that's what I wanted to figure out,' I say.

I go forward to the bow section and riffle around for a few minutes in the suitcase for my booklet and pen, then sit beside Simon again.

'These tables give you an idea of the strength of the radioactive source from the time of exposure and damage caused—approximate, but let's see.'

I lean against the head of the bed, looking up tables and jotting down figures.

'You don't use a computer for that?' he asks.

'Oh yes, but paper's fine too. And more portable in emergencies.' I finish and look at the result, puzzled. 'Give me a moment, I'll just check this again.'

Simon leans back beside me, watching my calculations. And my face too, I think.

I get the same result.

'What is it?' he says quietly.

'The caesium concentration is stupidly high,' I say, confused. 'It worked on us nearly twice as fast as you'd expect even for medical-grade isotope. It doesn't make any *sense*.'

'Why not?'

'What would you *do* with something like that? They stopped using caesium for radiotherapy ages ago. It has no other use!' I slam the booklet down beside me. 'This is insane—someone must have deliberately created this loathsome crap, stored it in the assemblies and put it on that boat.'

'Not someone. Our special friends.'

I put my hand over my mouth, tears starting in my eyes. 'What the hell is *happening*? Why would anyone do something as evil as this?'

'I don't know. It's all right, Lena.' He puts his arm around me.

It is astonishingly comforting and I long to rest my head on his shoulder. But after a few moments sanity returns.

This man feels wonderful, yes. He says nice things, yes. But he's still telling me lies. Yes.

I wipe my eyes and sit up. 'Well,' I say briskly, 'Better go and get some sleep.'

'All right. I was so comfortable, just about to drop off myself.' His eyes crease a little. 'Anyway, we both need lots of rest before our second date tomorrow night.'

I get up. 'Second date?'

'Surely you remember our first? The steamy atmosphere, both of us stark naked? I know I'll never forget it.'

'Simon, that wasn't—and it's not a *date*—'

He grins and I turn out the light. Despite myself I'm smiling as I get into my bunk.

12. The Sunset Gala

Next morning the weather is mild, but the sea's rough and the lugger is bobbing about. There's lots of high cloud and a strong wind from the south. After lunch Simon starts the engine and we begin to motor towards the coast. I sit beside Aidan on the deckhouse, feeling a little on edge and wondering what the evening will bring.

Gradually land comes into sight. At first just a smudge on the horizon but soon I see low cliffs topped with green, and dark red rocks along the aqua shore. The cliffs, in shades of rust and copper, are mesmerisingly beautiful and for some reason tears come to my eyes.

'It reminds me of one of my great-uncle's paintings,' I say, my throat tight. 'The shapes, the colours.'

'Liam Whalen and Paddy Bull were good mates,' says Aidan. 'He'd have spent a lot of time on this country. That gives you a connection too.'

'It's not my country.'

With a pang I think, I have no real home anywhere.

'Hey. If you love it, respect it, protect it, then it's part of you. It's your country, cuz.' Aidan puts an arm round my shoulder and gives me a quick, comforting hug.

Over to our left as we approach is a long industrial wharf. Beside it is a grey shape, which slowly becomes the massive warship USS *Jameson*, number 12 distinct on its beaked bow.

Two large guns sit in openings on either side of the stern, another on the bow. The superstructure rises sheer, almost windowless, and bristles with aerials and radar domes.

I shiver. That thing, that high-tech *monstrosity* loaded the caesium onto the blue boat?

The red cliffs here dip down to sea level. On the shore I can see a cluster of low buildings and rail lines and a massive conveyor belt, not moving, on tall stanchions. The belt extends from somewhere inland out to the end of the wharf.

'Why is the wharf so long?' I ask Aidan. 'Must be at least a kilometre or so.'

'The sea's really shallow here. Gotta be able to reach deep water when the tide's out.'

Perhaps five hundred metres from the industrial wharf is a narrow timber jetty. A large white yacht is tied up to it, and behind that a Sea Rovers boat.

'What did I tell you, Lena?' says Simon. 'Garrod's brought his toy. Play your cards right and you might get to see the famous gold-plated bathroom.'

He slows the engine almost to a standstill then turns the lugger in a wide curve so it glides back along the side of the jetty, its bow pointing out to sea. Jess and I lower rubber buffers to protect the hull, then Matthew leaps on to the jetty and Aidan throws him ropes to tie up.

I'm glad to see the bulk of Garrod's yacht on the other side obscures us from the warship, although I know perfectly well we've been monitored every moment of our approach.

'Ahoy, *Sparrow*,' someone calls out.

A fair-haired young man in a Geo-Garrod shirt walks towards Matthew and they shake hands. More of the yacht's crew, another man and two women, come onto the jetty and they seem an amiable bunch.

We also exchange greetings with the Sea Rovers crew, busy preparing to leave for Broome, but they've still got enough time to admire historic *Sparrow*. Lots of obscure nautical jargon gets thrown around, apparently to everyone's satisfaction.

The Sea Rovers finish their preparations. We wave goodbye to them as they leave, while the crew from Garrod's yacht return to their tasks.

I check the time and say to Simon, 'It's three-thirty and the gala's supposed to start at five. I'll go and get ready.'

Below, I find the tickets Glenn Garrod gave me a week ago and put them in my shoulder bag. I get the lovely long dress Jess bought for me out of my suitcase. It's low-cut, with silky layers in rose and copper and rust, rather like the cliffs of Walmadan themselves.

The dress flatters my fluffy red-gold hair and hides my burnt legs, while pretty sandals complete the outfit. I put on my make-up and feel like a brand new woman.

Jess, lounging on a bunk while I get ready, sits up. 'Lena, you look amazing.'

'Thanks to you of course.'

'Of course,' she says. 'Come on, let's go and knock Simon out.'

'This isn't for Simon's benefit,' I say. Jess laughs.

On deck the reaction is equally gratifying. Aidan calls me deadly and Matthew nods his head in admiration.

Simon looks me up and down and says, 'For last week's hospital patient you brush up pretty well.' Then he says ruefully, 'But we've got a problem, Lena.'

'Oh?'

'I'm going to have to ask you to take off that very nice dress and put on some jeans and sensible shoes.'

'Are you crazy?' says Aidan. 'She can't wear jeans to the big event.'

'Come on, Simon, why on earth?' says Jess.

I can't say anything I'm so surprised.

He says gently, 'I have no idea what may or may not happen tonight but so far someone's tried to kill both of us. I want you to be able to run if you have to, perhaps through the bush. We've got to be practical.'

'All right,' I nod slowly. 'That makes sense. But I'm going to wear a good top, okay?'

'Okay. But bring a dark coat. And I promise, one day I'll take you out in that dress for a fantastic dinner.' He grins. 'It can be our third date.'

Matthew says, puzzled, 'Third—?' but Jess elbows him.

I go below again feeling gloomy. Boring jeans, boring shoes. For the biggest event I'll ever get invited to, by a billionaire who calls me his favourite nuclear physicist. I'd rather hoped to show him—and everyone else—I wasn't just a drab scientist. No bloody chance of that now.

I go to get my old jeans out, then suddenly remember Jess bought me some new ones. I put them on and they're tight and blue and fit me rather nicely.

I add some pretty flat shoes and aquamarine earrings and a turquoise silk top that matches my eyes. Okay, not bad. I grab my shoulder bag and a black linen coat and I'm ready to go.

Simon says, 'Excellent,' when I come back on deck.

I give him a scathing look. 'I'll *never* get to see the gold-plated bathroom at this rate.'

He grins. 'Chances are still pretty good, I reckon.'

He goes to get changed too, and is soon back on deck dressed in dark casual clothes, his hair tidy. He gives me a torch to carry in my bag and puts his camera and another torch into a small backpack.

'Aidan spoke to Paddy Bull earlier,' he says. 'He's been

picking up some goods from the camp and he'll drive us to the gates. He says there's plenty of transport laid on for the guests so we should be able to get a lift back here once it's over.'

'All right.' I take a breath. 'Guess we'd better get going then.'

Jess hugs me and whispers, 'Don't forget to use your comcuff if you can.' Of course—it feels so familiar on my wrist now I'd almost forgotten how useful it might be.

Simon jumps onto the jetty and gives me a hand up. One of the women from Garrod's yacht calls out, 'See you guys at the gala!' and we wave to her.

Then we stand there, looking at each other.

'Okay?' Simon asks. I nod.

We walk silently along the jetty to the shore. It takes ten minutes to get to the road, then a battered people-carrier arrives and turns around and pulls up.

Paddy grins at us from the front seat. 'Jump in, you blokes. Got to get you to a party.'

We sit in the front seat beside him as the vehicle starts off again. He chuckles. 'You look really nice, cuz. Better than last time I saw you, anyway.'

'Not at my best in an isolation suit, Paddy, I'd have to say.'

'Jeez,' he says, shaking his head. 'That was a bad night. Glad you're okay now.'

As we climb a rise I can see part of the coast, the blue ocean washing against rusty rocks and pink sand. On the landward side, layers of low green scrub are rooted in red soil, and slender trees with creamy trunks beyond.

The earlier cloud cover has partly broken up in the wind and the late afternoon sunshine is turning the dusty road to brilliant copper.

'You've got everyone away from the protest camp now, Paddy?' asks Simon. His leg is warm against mine. I try to move away but there's not much room.

'Yeah. They weren't happy to go, looking forward to a few cross words with Garrod tonight, but they saw the sense in backing off after the attacks on you two.'

'Where've they gone?'

'Most are at Maggie's daughter's place, just out of Broome. But you don't really think there'll be trouble tonight, do you?'

'Don't know,' says Simon. 'But if there is, at least no one from the camp'll be in the firing line.'

We arrive at the T-junction and turn inland onto the sealed road. After two kilometres or so we slow down. A line of cars is waiting to pass through the security gates up ahead.

'Okay, Paddy. Let us out here, please?' says Simon. 'You get back to the others now—say hullo to Maggie for us. And thanks again for the lift.'

'Take care tonight, you two. Hope you can dig up some dirt on these buggers.'

'We'll do our best,' I say.

Simon and I walk the few hundred metres to the gates. To one side I see the protest camp, or what's left of it: it's in the process of being flattened. Two men in uniform are feeding bits of chairs and tents to the flames of the camp fire.

Simon mutters, 'Bastards.'

We stop at the pedestrian entrance to the gates. I show a soldier my invitations and he runs them through a small machine which imprints them with a little silvery seal, then hands them back to me. Amused, I think, that's a bit more high-tech than a pass-out stamp on the wrist.

Another soldier is standing to the side with a gun. The first man waves a sort of paddle near my body, front, back, sides. He sees something on the display and says, 'Alert.'

The other soldier's gun makes a lethal-sounding kerchunk and he points it at me. 'Give it here,' says the first soldier abruptly, and looks through my shoulder bag.

He takes out my lipstick and opens it, then the torch. He unscrews that and examines the batteries, then reassembles it and hands it back. He then waves the paddle over Simon.

'Metal in the backpack. Out. Slowly.'

Simon says calmly, 'Just another torch. And my camera.' He takes them out and the guard inspects them to his satisfaction.

The first soldier makes notes on his machine then hands Simon's things back. 'Have a pleasant evening. Sir. Ma'am.'

We pass through the gates, putting our things away, and I say, 'Wow. They weren't mucking around.'

'Yes. But at least we're in.' He looks at me. 'Would you care to take my arm? We're on our second date at an elegant affair, don't forget.'

'First. And it's not a date.'

I put my arm through his and we stroll along the road. I notice he's wearing a light, rather pleasant cologne.

Clusters of people are walking and chatting in front of us, a limousine driving slowly between them, so the view ahead is obscured. Then it isn't, and even though I was here the other day I'm amazed at the sight.

The sun is low in the west behind us and the whole area has become a glamorous amphitheatre. Ahead, the double-height glass foyer is filled with tables and flowers and twinkling candles, and a red ribbon is stretched across the foyer doors.

In front of that is a deck with a podium, while elegant chairs for the audience are laid out in semi-circles facing the deck. To our right there are linen-covered serving tables and waiters pouring drinks, and behind them an open parking lot full of shiny cars.

At the base of a low hill to our left are discreetly screened portable bathrooms. Large glimmering lights on stands are dotted at intervals around the whole area, while a big audio-visual installation with banks of electronics and cables runs along the rear.

An Aboriginal teenager in a Geo-Garrod uniform comes past and offers us a tray of drinks. There are three kinds of champagne she tells us, reeling off the brands, and they're all the ludicrously expensive kind.

We take the crystal glasses and sip. 'Yum,' I murmur.

In the evening light the processing plant looks dramatic, the sculpted swirls of metallic crimson and green along the side of the building suggesting the brilliant landscape around us.

Simon nudges me and says, 'Won awards, you know. Aesthetic *and* technical excellence.'

'Deservedly, too. Have you had a chance to see the mine, the Wormhole? Jess and I did the tour the other day. It's enormous, unbelievable.'

'When Matty sneaked in last year to get samples for testing I came too. We camped over behind that hill and I had a good look around. They'd excavated much of the Wormhole by then but the plant itself wasn't finished. Got to admit it's bloody impressive now.'

People are laughing and chattering loudly. Through a gap in the crowd I see Glenn Garrod, handsome in an evening suit, beside Minister Alise Berg. And—oh *no*—Max is there too, a martial peacock in his uniform. My mood sinks for a moment then rises again when Glenn sees me and smiles and beckons me over.

Simon and I approach. Alise, in an exquisite silver evening gown, glances at my jeans and flat shoes. She gives me a politician's smile, but I feel her contempt and wish bitterly I was wearing my glamorous dress.

Still, Glenn doesn't seem put off. I see his eyes lingering on my low neckline, then he holds my hands and kisses and hugs me rather more warmly than socially required.

'So glad you got here, Lena! You look wonderful. Are you completely well again?'

'Yes, perfectly, Glenn. And thank you *so* much for your flowers, they were simply beautiful. May I introduce my companion?'

Simon leans forward and shakes Glenn's hand earnestly. 'Dr Simon Rossi, ex-Department of Environment. Great occasion, Mr Garrod.'

I introduce Simon to Iceberg. Her eyes linger on him speculatively and she says, 'What a pity you didn't end up in *my* department.'

'A pity indeed,' says Simon with apparent sincerity. He may not be wearing an evening suit but he looks rather good all the same, and I give Alise a dazzling smile.

'And Simon,' I say, 'this is Minister Berg's chief of staff, Brigadier Leopard.' They shake hands and nod.

'Oh, Lena, what a formal introduction for your own *husband*,' says Alise sweetly. 'Call him Max at least.'

Simon smiles blandly. 'Great to meet you, Max.' Max stares at him without expression, then says to me, 'So. You came after all, Lena.' His disapproval could have glaciated the tropics.

A plump man with cynical eyes joins us and Glenn introduces him as Mr Edward Crichton, ambassador for the United States.

'Call me Ed,' the man says, and looks around, spreading his

arms. 'Say, isn't this just something! What a show of cooperation between our two great nations, don't you think— uh—Lena?' There's something more than usually false in his enthusiasm.

I nod. 'Certainly is, Mr ... Ed.'

Colonel Zukowski comes up behind Alise and murmurs, 'We're ready.'

She nods and he moves to leave, then sees me. His boyish face is surprised. 'Well, good evening, ma'am. You're looking remarkably fine.' Then he glances around and says with a smile, 'I *do* hope you enjoy this unforgettable occasion.'

I have the oddest sense his words have more than one meaning. He ignores Simon, turns away and walks to the podium. I gaze after him, puzzled.

He taps the microphone and says in his deep voice, 'Everyone, please be seated now.'

'That's our cue,' says Glenn. 'Lena, there'll be an orchestra and dancing later. I hope you'll keep a dance or two for me.'

'Of course I will, Glenn. See you then.'

Max nods at me severely, the line between his eyebrows etched deep.

Simon and I turn to find seats. He goes towards the chairs near the portable bathrooms.

'We won't see very well from over here,' I say.

'We won't be seen very well, either.'

The sun is setting and the banks of lights around the amphitheatre are slowly becoming brighter, casting long shadows.

I take another sip of the delicious champagne.

'So, um ... Max?' says Simon. 'The man who warned you off this event?'

'Uh-huh.'

'Husband?'

'Separated.'

'Ah.'

After a moment I say, 'Did you notice anything strange about Zukowski?'

'Now you mention it, a bit slimier than usual.'

'Simon, something in his voice worried me. Do you think he might know about the caesium having come from *Jameson*? That would explain his rush to sink the blue boat.'

'Which could also suggest he's behind the attacks on us, too.'

'Oh, *God*.' I take a gulp of champagne.

Now most of the crowd is seated, I realise the whole area is ringed by soldiers in black, with large guns and an array of lethal-looking objects dangling from their bodies.

I'm suddenly shocked at the sight of one not far from us. Luckily he's not looking my way.

'Simon, that man over there,' I whisper, 'with the tattoo on his neck. I think he's the guy who tried to drown me.'

'Don't worry, he won't recognise you. You're hair's different, you're all glammed up.' He looks around casually for a time. Then he leans forward and says calmly, 'Hell.'

He takes a deep breath and murmurs near my ear, 'Okay, Lena. In a little while I want you to go over to the bathrooms, slip away and hide in the shadows behind them. I'll follow soon after. Enough people are still moving around, we shouldn't be too obvious.'

'Hide? Really?' I stare at him in surprise.

He says, 'Yes, please,' and after a moment I whisper, 'Okay.'

Just then Glenn starts speaking. He gives his familiar, amusing spiel on the reprocessing project, enlivened with some new patter on how the plant has been built to withstand cyclones.

He even lifts a chair and throws it at the glass foyer behind him, making everyone gasp and squeal as it simply bounces off.

'*Toughened?*' he asks. 'You haven't seen toughened like this place! It can handle anything and starting tomorrow, it *will!*'

Everyone applauds.

He ends his talk. 'And now I'd like to ask the United States ambassador, Mr Edward Crichton, for some words on the American perspective.'

The ambassador speaks for only five minutes or so—short by the measure of events like this—his tone flat, almost bored. But he's smirking, his eyes restless as if he's watching for something.

Simon whispers, 'Does he look edgy to you?' and I nod.

After applause for the ambassador, Glenn says, 'Let me introduce the Honourable Alise Berg to offer the Australian view of this historic project.'

She smiles triumphantly as everyone applauds, then she makes her way in her silver gown to the podium. A few people get up for fresh drinks, a few others weave through the crowd to the bathrooms, but most of the audience's attention is focused upon Alise.

'Okay,' whispers Simon. 'Off you go.'

I regretfully leave my glass of delicious champagne beside the chair and cover the short distance to the bathrooms. Out of the corner of my eye I can see even the soldiers are mesmerised by Alise.

I go to the loo—never know when I'll have the chance again—then move quietly out and into the shadows behind the building, my heart thumping, and put on my dark coat.

In a few minutes I hear a soft noise and Simon appears beside me. Alise's voice, spouting cliché after cliché, bounces off the rise behind us.

'See there?' murmurs Simon, close to my ear. He's pointing at a gully in front of us leading up the low hill. 'Go, now. Quietly.'

I move ahead and can hear him following me. I try not to make any noise. After a short scramble the slope levels off and we reach the top, bending low. Simon leads me to one side then whispers, 'Down,' pointing in front of us.

The twilight shows a flat wide boulder on the top of the hill and I lie on my stomach, Simon beside me. We wriggle forward and peer carefully over the edge.

13. The Ambassador Weeps

The lights are dazzling, shimmering on Alise as she speaks. The boulder feels warm, like an animal, and lying there I'm intensely aware of Simon's long body stretched out beside me.

He lifts his camera and takes photos of the scene, then he passes it to me and shows me the camera's miniature telephoto. Looking through it is like using binoculars and I can see exquisite detail.

I train it on Glenn's happy face. He seems a nice enough man and this can't have been an easy project. I like his vision of this new method of reprocessing and hope it succeeds. Yet I hate the idea of his plant being foisted on this beautiful country, causing such grief to Aidan and my new friends.

I can see the ambassador in his chair on the stage, clearly checking his watch, his foot tapping slightly. Beside him Colonel Zukowski is expressionless but his posture is tense. Max is in the shadows to one side, scanning the audience. I hope he's not trying to check up on me.

The Iceberg is in her element, the focus of all eyes, but dear God her speech is dull. I take some images discreetly with the comcuff.

'He doesn't remember me because I was a subordinate,' says Simon quietly, 'but I knew Max in the old days, in the army. He was a bully even then, too fond of bending the truth.'

'Didn't change over the years.'

'I can see now why you might not trust military men.'

I glance at him, remembering his own lies. If he really works for who he says he does then I can understand professional reticence: but the invisible family?

Alise drones on and on. All right, I think.

'Um, Simon,' I murmur. 'On the subject of trust, I'd like to ask you something.'

'Mmm?' He's peering through his camera and puts it down.

'When we were in hospital you told me you had no family, just Matthew. But at your house I saw a photo of you with your wife and son. I don't understand why you lied to my face.'

He's silent for a time, then sighs. 'Yes. I did have a family once. But a drunk drove onto the footpath one night and now I don't. I was telling the truth. Matthew's my only relative.'

'Oh *God*, Simon, I never imagined—I'm so sorry!'

'No. It's something ...' He shakes his head. 'It was many years ago but it's still hard to—' He clears his throat and rolls onto his side and gazes at me. 'I'll tell you all about it one day but this might not be quite the right time.'

'Probably not.' I feel a sweet sense of relief. 'Forgive me.'

'Nothing to forgive. I understand you don't trust anyone much, Lena, but I promise you can trust me.'

He leans forward and kisses me lightly on the forehead, then leans back and grins.

'And while we're speaking of trust—you and Jess and your sparkly high-tech bracelets. What the hell's *that* all about?'

'Ah.' I'm flustered. 'They're not bracelets, they're cuffs, communication cuffs. Some secret technology Jessie's been working on.'

'Do they take photos?'

'Yes.'

'Then take them for Christ's sake, don't pretend to be

scratching your ear. I'm more afraid than ever we're going to need evidence of whatever happens tonight.'

'Why? What's made you afraid?'

His brow creased, he says, 'Those soldiers down there. They're not regular military, they're not even Delta Force or SAS. They're a top-secret group who do the filthiest of black ops. You wouldn't use them to guard a social event even if the President was there.'

'Then what on earth—?'

'They're for killing. Killing whoever they're told to kill. Without accountability, without a qualm.'

A chill of sweat runs down my back.

I can hear Alise saying something surreal about *key performance indicators*. She winds up at last and the audience claps as she sits, pleased with herself. A few people move around and get their glasses refilled.

Glenn says, 'Some words now from our allies, whose support made this whole project viable. Colonel?'

Colonel Zukowski walks confidently to the podium. He says in his deep voice, 'As the representative of the United States military here tonight, I'd just like to add some observations on this joint venture between our great countries.'

Lights glitter off his insignia as he looks around the audience. 'I have to say I'm proud of our agreement, I'm proud to offer the protection of our superb forces, and I'm particularly proud of the custodial obligation the United States bears for any contingency.'

'*Custodial* obligation?' Simon says slowly. 'I wonder what's really in that agreement. They never released all the details, usual crap about security. And the Commonwealth's *seriously* pissed off at the state for signing the agreement—negotiating with a foreign power is a Federal role. They're still arguing over it in the High Court.'

Glenn stands. 'I'd now like to call upon Minister Berg to cut the ribbon.' He hands Alise a large pair of gold scissors.

She turns to the foyer doors saying, 'I'm *delighted* to declare the Worm Turning Nuclear Reprocessing Facility—'

Suddenly a large truck screeches to a halt behind the audience. A soldier jumps out and runs to Colonel Zukowski. They speak quickly then the man dashes back to the truck.

Zukowski comes to the microphone. 'Ladies and gentlemen, we have a report of some possible terrorist activity in the area. For your own safety I'd appreciate it if you'd take your places in the totally secure foyer. Just enjoy this great event prepared for you while we deal with any issues. *Minister?*'

Alise says '– *open*,' and cuts the ribbon.

Glenn and the colonel pull the big doors apart. 'No panic, please,' Zukowski calls out, shepherding people inside.

'If you say *no panic* it's guaranteed to make people rush,' whispers Simon.

He's right. The guests, the media, the photographers, even the waiters are pushing to get inside. It doesn't take long. Then Glenn enters laughing, his arms out welcoming his guests and ushering them to seats.

He takes a glass of wine and moves confidently through the large room. People start to relax, the waiters bring more trays of drinks and nibbles and the party resumes inside.

Finally only the ambassador, Alise, Max and the colonel are left standing on the deck, amid a cluster of soldiers in black. But something very odd is happening.

The ambassador is shaking his head furiously and waving his arms, yelling, 'What the *fuck*? No way!'

Two of the soldiers grab him and shove him into the foyer. They slam the doors shut and take a bar or piece of timber—I can't quite see—and slot it into the large handles.

'No escape,' says Simon slowly.

I can see the ambassador inside banging on the windows. He grabs a chair and slams it without effect into the glass. The unbreakable glass.

People come up to him and try to calm him down and he punches and flails at them. They move away shrugging, back to the candle-lit tables.

The ambassador slumps to the ground, his face hidden by his hands. Simon is looking through the telephoto, snapping image after image.

'He's crying,' he says flatly. 'The American ambassador is sitting on the floor crying. You getting all this?'

'Yes,' I say, taking video with the comcuff, breathless with shock. 'What does he know that the rest of us don't?'

A limousine glides out of the car park. Colonel Zukowski ushers Minister Berg towards it, his hand lingering on her silvery hip. Max is staring around, and Zukowski leans forward aggressively and says something to him. Max slowly takes a seat beside the driver.

Zukowski opens the rear door for Alise and slides in beside her. Max's white face gazes back at the lights of the foyer as the limousine purrs away.

A soldier goes to the audio-visual desk and the screens go black one by one, as the event's media transmission is halted. Two of the soldiers take up guard, guns at the ready. The others, including those surrounding the area earlier, gather at the rear of the truck.

With effort they extract a large metallic rack, perhaps two metres tall, put it onto some sort of trolley and push it towards the building, parking it out of sight of the people inside.

One man leans over the rack touching things and tiny green lights glimmer. The two guards at the door remain behind, while the other soldiers climb back into the truck and leave with a rumble of engines.

A hum of party noise comes from the foyer and I hear music begin to play. People gather at the tables and waiters bring them dishes. Everyone seems to be content to ignore the bizarre behaviour of the ambassador sitting slumped against a window, silent now, his head on his arms.

Simon and I look at each other in astonishment.

'What the hell just happened?' I ask.

He focuses his telephoto camera on the rack with its small winking lights and draws a quick breath. After few moments he passes me the camera.

I focus in and see that the rack holds a big, squat metallic cylinder with an instrument panel and, lying sideways above it, a horribly familiar container.

'But that's the *drum* from the blue boat!' I say.

'I'd imagine the caesium assemblies are back inside it too.' Simon's voice is hard.

'What's that thing it's lying on?'

'Pretty sure it's a bomb.'

'A *bomb*?' I say, horrified. 'But, Simon, why on earth would the guards just stand there?'

'Probably don't know what it is.'

'Their commanders would just *leave* them to be blown up?'

'I doubt their commanders are too much concerned about the fate of anyone within the vicinity, Lena.'

I gasp. 'The people in the foyer? But that unbreakable glass might protect—'

'Not unbreakable where a bomb's concerned.'

'But dear God, what can we *do*?'

Simon looks down for a few moments.

'Nothing,' he says quietly. 'Nothing at all.' He lifts his head and gazes at me. 'We'd be shot in an instant if we went near it. And I promise you, disarming something like that is not how it looks on TV. It's basically impossible.'

He puts his hand briefly on mine. 'Lena, we're going to have to do something incredibly brave.'

'What?' I stare at him.

'Leave. We have to leave. We can't stop what's happening below. Perhaps it's not a bomb, I hope not. But we've got the evidence of what's happened and we must get it out safely. That's all we can do.'

'*Leave*?' Tears of horror come to my eyes. 'Leave those poor bastards to whatever that thing is going to do—and loaded with *caesium*? If it's a bomb it'll go everywhere, this place'll be contaminated for *generations*!'

'We must, Lena, think. We must. It's all we can do. If we don't get away soon ...'

We look at each other in despair and after a few moments I slowly nod.

Simon wriggles backwards and I follow him, and when we're out of sight we get up. I find the torch in my bag and Simon takes his out of his pack.

'I know the way,' he says. 'We just have to get out through the fence and follow the conveyor belt back to the water.'

We move quickly along a path in the bush lit by our torches. I can hear the orchestra behind us growing fainter and fainter, and I think of the band playing on the Titanic as it sank beneath the waves.

Our feet crunch along the ground and I hear rustling in the bush around us. Away from the lights of the plant I can see a half-moon floating serenely in the sky. This can't really be happening I think, appalled. All those *people* back there—

'Only a few hundred metres to go. Matty and I found this path when we got in last year,' says Simon. 'It leads to the electrified fence.'

'Of course,' I say. 'There'd *have* to be a fucking electrified fence, wouldn't there?'

Simon grunts, 'Okay, down here.'

He slips and slides down a slope below the path. I follow him, thankful for my flat shoes.

'Good. Still there.'

'What is?'

'A hollow beneath the fence.'

There's a rounded dip in the dust. Above it is a metal barricade almost twice my height.

'I'll go first,' he says, turning to me, taking off his backpack. 'Whatever you do, don't touch the fence. It's not only electrified but it'll trigger sensors. Those guys in black will be here in minutes—'

'Yes, yes, I understand.' I'm trembling.

He gets down on his belly and caterpillars slowly under the wire. I gasp when he seems to touch it but it's just a trick of the light. My heart pounds, my throat is dry.

After an endless time Simon makes it through to the other side. He sits for a few moments, arms on his knees, breathing deeply.

He looks up and says, 'Okay, ready? Pass me your bag and my backpack first.'

I push the bags carefully underneath so he can get them. I look up at the soaring fence and the moon beyond. I lie down and slowly, carefully, wriggle myself through. Simon gently pulls my shoulders to help.

At last I'm free of the menacing wire and sit, gasping for breath. Simon stands and helps me up too.

'You all right?' he says.

I hold onto his arms, shaking. 'Yes,' I whisper. 'I think so.'

He hugs me suddenly and I cling to his warmth and solidity.

'Next bit should be easier,' he says, his hand stroking my hair. 'Oh—'

'So long as that bomb doesn't—'

'Hush,' he says, his face warm against mine. 'Lena, if—'

'Hush,' I say. 'Simon, *oh* ...' I kiss him fiercely.

He groans and pulls my hips towards him and holds me tightly, and I feel a pang of lightning lust flare from my thighs to my throat.

After a time we slowly separate. I whisper, 'Just fear, that's all, the great aphrodisiac.'

'You reckon?' Simon laughs softly. 'Hey, why don't we test that theory later? Let's go.'

We start off. It's not too difficult because there's a narrow sealed road beside the conveyor belt, and we run, our torch beams jumping around in front of us.

I feel a thud of terror at a flare of eyes reflecting back from the bush, but we're past before I can even wonder what it was. (Please let it not be a crocodile.)

I'm used to jogging, as I go out for a run every few days, but terror shortens my breath. After ten or fifteen long minutes the brush around us starts to thin out and I see lights ahead.

We slow, breathing heavily, and cautiously step onto the side of a road near the shoreline. Lights dazzle the length of the big wharf. It's empty.

'The *Jameson's* gone!'

'They knew they had to get away,' says Simon. 'Probably took Iceberg and her mates—yes, look, their limousine's parked at the far end.'

We gaze around, up and down the road. No one's about.

'All right,' he says. 'There's the jetty, the lugger. We're okay. Come on.'

He takes my hand and we run along the road, then onto the jetty to the boat. Aidan and Matthew and Jess wave from a distance. After what seems like forever we finally reach them.

Simon gasps, 'Start the engines, Matty,' and without a pause he does so.

'Glenn's boat!' I pant. 'Some of the crew may still be there, we've got to tell them to go too! Hullo? *Hullo?*' I yell.

The yacht rolls slowly in the swell. No one responds.

'They're all at the gala,' says Simon. 'Lena, we *must* go.'

He helps me jump aboard. Within moments the ropes are released and the engine is roaring.

As we draw away I look behind, at the lights from the gala glowing on the horizon, and the beautiful white yacht whose owner and crew are now locked up in a glittering glass foyer, eating and drinking and dancing to an orchestra.

I wonder if Glenn tried to find me for that dance I promised him. Oh, I'm *sorry*, Glenn, I'm so sorry.

Then I think—but maybe nothing will happen, maybe we've just spooked ourselves! Perhaps that thing we thought was a bomb was really some kind of monitor to protect people, not *kill* them, for heaven's sake.

And then I remember the drum full of caesium.

14. A Dome of Golden Light

The lugger is perhaps ten kilometres away from the coast now and we're gathered at the stern, Matthew at the tiller. Simon and I have told everyone what we saw, still hardly able to believe it ourselves. None of us can take our eyes from the horizon and the glow from Worm Turning.

The sea is rough, the sky cloudy. Aidan says the last weather bulletin had cyclone Cyril two hundred and fifty kilometres away and moving east towards the coast, but landfall was not expected for a day or more.

'Surprising change of direction,' says Simon. 'Could even head for Broome now. But don't worry, we'll get there long before it.' His face is drawn as he sits close beside me on the deckhouse, his shoulder warm against mine. We stare at the distant glow.

Matthew and Jess bring us tea and sandwiches. The tea is good but I'm not hungry, and the light on the horizon seems to dance before my eyes. I'm tired but can't go below.

Simon murmurs to me, 'You should get some rest—'

Suddenly a dome of golden light blossoms silently and expands in the sky, brighter and brighter. I stare, astonished. It's so *beautiful* ...

'Get down, all of you!' roars Simon. 'Down!' He grabs me and pulls me to the deck, hugging me tightly, protecting me.

Matthew and Jess and Aidan lie beside us, hands over their

heads. In the astonishing light I can see the texture of Simon's skin, a curl of silver hair against his ear, a small scar along his chin. I press my face into his neck.

I hear a distant noise, a whispering growing louder, and suddenly a wave of pressure crashes over us, pounding, roaring, shaking the boat like a toy. Just as I think we don't have a chance, it starts to fade. The roar recedes and my ears ring in the silence.

'Are you all right?' Simon whispers to me. I nod against his shoulder. I don't want him to let go, the world is suddenly too bizarre to cope with.

Finally we roll over and sit up. No one is hurt, but our voices are subdued. After a time we stand. The golden dome in the sky has faded away, but on the horizon a line of red flames is flickering against roiling clouds of black smoke.

I sit down on the deckhouse.

'Oh, thank God. It wasn't a nuclear bomb.' I feel light-headed with relief.

'And you'd be certain of that precisely because—?' Aidan's voice is wobbly.

'If it was, the clouds would be a totally different shape.'

'But what about the caesium?' asks Matthew.

'Caesium doesn't explode in itself, it just turns a normal bomb into a dirty bomb,' I say. 'The bomb blows things apart and the caesium leaves the area radioactive.'

'For how long?' asks Simon, turning to me. 'How long will the radioactivity last?'

'The good thing—' I laugh in dazed horror, 'well, it's hardly good but at least it wasn't fucking plutonium. That's got a half-life of twenty-four thousand years.'

'Half-life?' asks Aidan.

'The time it takes for the level of radioactivity to fall by fifty percent.'

'And here's me thinking that was just a video game,' says Aidan glumly. 'So what's caesium's half-life?'

'Thirty years.'

'Not too bad,' says Matthew. 'Not like centuries.'

'But if exposure for, say, two hours kills you now, then in thirty years it's four hours. Sixty years it's eight, ninety years it's sixteen. So even after a century it's still lethal, just takes a bit longer—'

'This place'll be radioactive for *hundreds* of years?' says Aidan in shock.

Suddenly I'm trembling. 'Oh, those poor, poor people—'

Simon puts his arm around me.

'What on earth do we do now?' asks Jess forlornly.

'Get somewhere out of this area as soon as possible,' says Simon. 'We don't know where *Jameson* is but we certainly don't want them to know we survived. We've got to show the world what those bastards did.'

'Did you take lots of images?' Matthew asks him.

'As many as possible.'

Jessie nods. 'Lena, sync with me.' She taps dots and holds her wrist beside mine for a few moments, then says, 'Right.'

'Jess—I told Simon about the cuffs—'

'It's okay. I told these guys as well. It was way too cool to keep secret anyway.' After a moment Jessie looks at her cuff and says, 'All right—it's totally misted now.'

'Misted?' I say.

'You've heard of the cloud? World's greatest cliché?'

'I haven't,' says Aidan. 'Remember—ship's ambo?'

'Virtualised, decentralised data, server and application infrastructure,' says Jess.

'Extraordinary,' says Matthew thoughtfully. 'For a moment

there I almost understood what you were saying.'

'Well, even better than that, all my information is stored in a mist,' says Jess. 'Encrypted, highly dispersed, untouchable.'

'But I thought the security services could decrypt just about anything,' I say.

Jessie scoffs. 'They like to believe they can. Not this though.'

'So it's safe, yes?' I say.

'Oh, yes.'

'Can you take copies from my camera too?' asks Simon.

'Hand it over.'

Simon gives it to her then says, 'Lena and I are half dead. We've got to get some sleep before we hit Broome. Can you guys cope with things here now?'

'No probs,' says Aidan. 'we're going straight there, only take a few hours.'

'I just remembered something,' I say, chilled. 'Zukowski said he hoped I'd enjoy this unforgettable occasion. And he *smiled* as he said it.'

Going down the steps to the sleeping area I stumble on the last one, but Simon catches me and we hold each other. I relax into his arms, smelling his delicious hair and skin.

He kisses me for a moment then steps back and eases my coat away from my tired shoulders, then nuzzles my neck.

I pull off his coat and whisper, 'Weren't we going to test that theory? Fear as an aphrodisiac—'

He kisses me slowly and caresses my breasts. The nipples tighten exquisitely.

'Hypothesis disproved,' he says. 'Certainly not fear.'

I laugh and cling to him. He strokes my hair and we lean against the wall together, braced against the rolling of the lugger in the heavy seas. We hear Matthew and Aidan talking and moving about on deck above us.

'Guess the definitive experiment has to wait until we're alone,' I whisper.

He laughs quietly. 'Yeah. Let's rest. We've only got a few hours before Broome and that marathon back to the lugger just about killed me. Try to forget what happened for a while.'

We climb into the big bed and he holds me from behind. I sigh at the peace and warmth.

'Anyway,' Simon murmurs in my ear, 'Aren't you still married to laugh-a-minute Max?'

'Separated for a year. Untouched for a long time before that. I think I actually qualify as a virgin by now.'

'Untouched?'

I roll over to face him. 'Soon after we married Max decided he found me ... undesirable. Wish he'd figured it out before then.'

'How could he not find you *desirable*? Man's a moron.'

'He's got a thing for Asian women. Believes they'll be more submissive than me.'

'In his dreams.' Simon kisses me. 'Well, isn't it lucky I've got a thing for bossy, cuddly nuclear physicists?'

'Have you met many?'

'Not till now, but I've lived in hope.'

I laugh and snuggle into his shoulder. The boat rolls and my eyes close. Such contentment.

I suddenly come awake, my heart thumping from a terrible dream. I lie still for a moment gradually realising it's not a dream at all.

Simon is standing next to the bed pulling on a clean T-shirt.

'Hey,' he says softly. 'It's about six a.m. and we're nearly there. Better get up soon.'

He leans on the bed and kisses me briefly, then climbs the stairs. I soon follow and when I get on deck the seas are high and the wind is strong. I'm stupidly surprised it's still dark. The evening of the gala seems a lifetime away, yet I know it's only been a few hours.

We gather in the galley, the boat hove-to. Matthew and Aidan serve us all bacon and eggs, which taste wonderful. I ask what's happened while we were asleep.

Jessie says, 'There was a news flash earlier saying there'd been a bombing at the plant, assumed to be terrorists, but no other details.'

'How long before we reach Broome?'

'About an hour,' says Simon. 'We can't wait around now, we're low on fuel. I can see plenty of other boats on the radar trying to get into port ahead of the cyclone, so we won't be too conspicuous.'

'Cyclone? Is Cyril coming this way now?' I ask.

'Yeah. Turned towards Broome while you were sleeping. But it's at least a day or so away,' says Aidan. 'And it might shift, anyway. The Law men'll be at Minyirr doing their best.'

I don't have time to ask what he means because Jessie says, 'Holy fuck!' She looks up at us in shock. 'The Yanks have just taken over the Dampier Peninsula!'

We read the screen over her shoulder.

> *Broome, 20 April: Colonel W. Zukowski, Head of US Forces, Worm Turning, announced today that the terrorist bombing of the plant had set in motion the security provisions of the Dampier Peninsula Pollution and Protection Agreement, and the region is now under the full custodial supervision of the United States. Satellites have confirmed the presence of radioactive substances in the bombed area but emergency services cannot attend*

> *because of the contamination. To safeguard citizens and*
> *property, security checkpoints have been established at all road,*
> *sea and airport facilities, and travel is restricted.*

'They're saying the agreement gives the US complete control of this region if a terrorist attack occurs,' says Jess, quickly scanning another document. 'To, you know, *protect* us.'

'Jesus,' says Simon, stunned. 'Has someone just annexed a chunk of Australia?'

'Looks like it,' says Jess. 'And there's nothing about them ever having to hand it back, either. Funny that.'

> *Col. Zukowski was appointed Administrator of the region early*
> *this morning. The Minister for the Industrial Environment, the*
> *Honourable Alise Berg, announced that the Western Australian*
> *government is appreciative of the swift US response to the*
> *terrorist bombing.*

> *Minister Berg is to be appointed as liaison with the US*
> *administration. Fortunately, Col. Zukowski, Minister Berg and*
> *staff had left the plant and were returning to Broome in the USS*
> *Jameson before the tragic explosion occurred.*

'Wow. Way fortunate. Must be psychic,' says Aidan.

'I thought the Americans were supposed to be our *allies!*' I say. 'We've always supported them.'

'Like the school yard bully,' says Matthew quietly. 'While you go along with them you're safe, until the day you say no. Then you're the enemy.'

> *Over three hundred people, including billionaire Glenn Garrod,*
> *owner of Geo-Garrod Ltd, the US ambassador Mr Edward*
> *Crichton, and numerous local political figures were attending the*
> *gala. Due to the intensity of the explosion no survivors are*
> *anticipated.*

'Poor Glenn, poor *people*,' I say.

'But it all starts to makes sense now,' says Simon. 'Bombing the plant. The perfect "terrorist" excuse.'

'And no one can check it out,' says Aidan. 'Because the region's contaminated.'

'And that prevents anyone else mining the Wormhole,' finishes Matthew. 'So the Americans now have the only stockpile of hafnium-rich sand in the world.'

'Wow. What a nice train of logic,' says Jess admiringly.

'But they've *destroyed* the reprocessing plant,' I say. 'Don't they care about getting rid of nuclear waste?'

Jess says, 'Oh, Lena. Little-dick men in power love waving lots of scary nuclear stuff around, makes them feel bigger. Why would they give a fuck about cleaning it up?'

'Hey, listen to this bit,' says Matthew, reading aloud:

> Unconfirmed reports suggest the bombing may be the work of
> Sea Rovers, the extremists supporting the protests at Worm
> Turning, and an associated sea-going group.

'Extremists?' says Aidan. 'The only thing extreme about the Sea Rovers is how many trees they want to plant. And they're going to get the blame?'

'I wonder,' says Simon slowly. 'What about that associated *sea-going group*? That could mean us. We'd better keep a very low profile.'

15. Sanctuary

It's morning when we reach the Port of Broome and I shiver to see grey, ominous USS *Jameson* tied up at the wharf. Around it is a frenzy of activity.

Larger boats are being moored to cyclone buoys, while on the sand four-wheel-drives are lined up, winching small boats out of the water onto trailers.

Leaning on the rigging beside me, Matthew says, 'Looks like everyone's been taken by surprise at how quickly the cyclone's turned this way.'

'But what will you do with *Sparrow*?' I ask. 'She's too big to put on a trailer.'

'There's a slip further round in the bay. We'll fasten her to a cradle and a tractor will pull her out onto the hard.'

The skies are full of dark clouds and to the west I can see flashes of lightning, but they're so far away I can't hear the thunder. It's windy and gloomy and raining.

'We've cut it bloody close,' says Simon. 'Only half an hour of fuel left. We'll have to fill up later after the storm.'

As we slowly approach the slipway I notice a Sea Rovers boat not far away. It's the one we met at the Worm Turning jetty and we exchange yelled greetings with the crew.

As we're throwing necessities into bags and securing *Sparrow*, a large inflatable motors towards the Sea Rovers boat, carrying American soldiers with raised guns. They loudly order the crew to tie the boat to a nearby buoy.

Then, to our astonishment, they force them roughly into the inflatable and take them away to the shore. It happens in just a few moments and we can't do anything.

We look at each other, shocked, and keep going. We've just finished preparing *Sparrow* for the slipway—a yacht is being pulled out ahead of us—when we see another inflatable with soldiers heading towards us. It comes alongside and a man yells, '*Stop.*'

We stop.

'Tie up to that buoy,' he says, pointing to one nearby.

Simon says calmly, 'That's not a cyclone buoy. It won't hold in a major storm.'

'Tough shit,' says the soldier. 'How many? Where from? IDs?'

'Five of us,' says Simon smoothly. 'Tour from Port Hedland. Had no idea the storm was—'

'IDs? Licences, passports?'

We produce driving licences and the soldier notes our names and addresses on a small machine he's holding, then presses a button. Five plastic rectangles appear one by one, the size of credit-cards. He hands them over to us.

'Keep these with you at all times or you'll be detained,' he says. 'You're now under the protection of an Official Overseas Special Region. Get outta here.'

I drag Jessie back before she can ask what's so bloody special about it.

'But—' says Matthew, and two soldiers lift their guns at him.

'Fine,' says Simon, quickly adding more ropes to the buoy. 'Be with you in a moment.'

'*Now.*'

We grab our bags and pile into *Sparrow*'s tinny and motor away to the shore. We see the soldiers move to another boat and start harassing its crew. We land on a strip of sand and pull the tinny up and secure it.

Aidan says, 'I rang Maggie a while ago—yes, there she is!'

The people-carrier comes along the nearby road and Maggie Everett waves to us from the driver's seat. We throw our bags into the back and clamber in.

'Bloody glad to see you, Maggie,' says Simon, as she releases the handbrake and accelerates away.

She shakes her head in disbelief. 'I was worried, I can tell you. I saw them arresting some Sea Rovers, roughing them up too.' She looks across Simon and smiles wryly at me. 'Strange times, eh, Lena?'

'Thanks heaps for coming, Aunty,' says Aidan. 'Didn't know if you could—'

'Had to bring Paddy over to Minyirr. Easy enough to get here from there.'

'Paddy's at Minyirr?' asks Matthew. 'Excellent.'

We're driving along the highway between the port and Broome. Rushes of rain are striking the van, the windscreen wipers are swishing back and forth. I can't believe how much traffic there is—every second vehicle is a military truck.

'Minyirr?' I ask. 'Isn't that the cliff where we launched the lugger?'

'Yeah,' says Aidan from the back seat.

'What on earth is Paddy doing *there* when a cyclone's about to hit?'

'Trying to get the storm to move sideways.'

I don't know what to say.

'Paddy's with the other senior Law men,' says Aidan. 'When a cyclone threatens the town they sing to it. Tell it who they are. Ask it to shift a bit. I think they become part of it and talk to themselves, but I'm not allowed to know much more than that.'

'Oh,' I say. 'Does it work?'

'Sometimes.'

I decide not to bring up the thorny issue of random events and confirmation bias, then I'm astonished to hear Jessie say, 'Saw a couple of great papers on that. Small variations in consciousness under ritual conditions can cascade through to a physical change event.'

'Jess?'

'Oh, *Lena*,' she says, shaking her head. 'Honestly. Haven't you been keeping up with quantum holographic duality at *all*?'

I sigh. Clearly not. I ask, 'So where are we going?'

'Too risky to go back to Simon's,' says Aidan. 'So we're going to Maggie's daughter's place.'

'Yeah, the youngsters can't wait to see you,' says Maggie, grinning. 'Hear you're pretty keen to catch up too, mate.'

'*Maggie*,' says Aidan, embarrassed, and I remember, oh yes, he likes someone in her family.

Simon says, 'If Zukowski and Berg think we died at the gala they might not be watching my place any more, but better to be cautious and stay away.'

'They'll know you're alive pretty soon,' says Jess. 'I expect that goon in the inflatable has already uploaded your details.'

'But if they think Lena and Simon are dead will they still be looking for them?' asks Matthew.

'Dunno,' says Jess. 'Let's hope the agonising strain of governing an *Official Overseas Special Region* keeps them too fucking busy to check.'

We're through the town now and heading out on the highway. The brilliant red earth and green trees around us seem to glow with light against the charcoal sky. We turn onto a narrow dirt road, then after a kilometre or so we pass through gates. Maggie pulls up outside a house with a wide veranda, framed by swaying trees.

Maggie says, 'Here we are. Get inside and out of the wet.'

We do so as several Indigenous people come to meet us on the veranda. A pretty young woman squeals and kisses a shy Aidan, while a handsome man with curly hair hugs him.

Everyone is laughing and talking and we're ushered into a comfortable lounge-room and given mugs of tea: I don't think I've ever tasted anything so good.

I lean against Simon with a sigh and he puts his arm around me and kisses the top of my head. The pretty young woman sits down on my other side.

'Heya, Lena, I'm Cath, Maggie's daughter. I knew your great-uncle Liam when I was a kid, his wife was one of my aunties. And this is my brother Russell—he's the chief herder.' She waves her hand at the man with curly hair.

'Oh? You keep sheep here?' I say dopily.

'No,' he grins. 'Tourists. Little eco-village going next door.'

I laugh and look up at Simon. He smiles gently and murmurs, 'Assumptions, Lena,' then closes his eyes and rests his head against mine.

Maggie looks us over critically. 'You guys are totally buggered, aren't you?'

'Been up most of the night, Aunty,' says Aidan.

'Yeah, looks like it. All right, got a couple of rooms here and one of the units is free. When you've finished your tea you all go and have a rest. Russell, you take Simon and Lena over to the unit. Rest of you, the rooms are down the hall there.'

Russell gives us umbrellas on the veranda, and in the pelting rain we follow him along a paved walkway to huts clustered around a pool and rockery. He steps onto the wet timber deck of one hut, unlocks the door and ushers us in.

'Fruit, tea, coffee and basics are in the cupboard. Milk and drinks in the fridge. Come over to the house when you've had a rest and we'll get the barbecue going. See you later.'

I sit down on the couch and look around. It's a lovely little place, with a big bed and sitting area, a small kitchen and bathroom. It's airy and light, all lattice and timber and soft fabrics. In contrast to the pristine room I feel sweaty and dusty, and say, 'I'm going have a quick shower.'

Simon takes off a few layers of clothes and says, 'Uh-huh.' He falls down on the bed and is asleep in seconds. I have a shower in the neat bathroom and pull on one of the cotton kimonos hanging there. I lie down beside Simon and am asleep in moments too.

I come suddenly awake to a loud crash. The wind is whistling around the hut, the rain hammering on the roof.

'Just a tree-branch,' says Simon sleepily. He leans up on one arm and strokes my face. 'How are you feeling now?'

'Much, much better. What time is it?'

'Mmm, nearly four.' He puts his arm around my hips and draws me close. 'We should probably go and see how the other are. In a minute.'

He kisses me and I can't believe how good he feels, the solid warm length of his body against mine. Delicious time passes and we're just getting serious when suddenly there's a thumping on the door.

'Go *away*,' I mutter furiously.

We separate. I sit up and pull my kimono together and call out, 'Come in.'

The door opens to show a small boy, a large red dog beside

him, wagging its tail. The boy looks at us wide-eyed and squeaks, 'Barbecue,' then turns and dashes off.

Simon groans quietly. 'Better be sociable. Barbecue it is.'

We dress and run back through the rain. When we get to the covered courtyard at the rear of Cath's house the smell of cooking makes me realise how hungry I am. Rain sweeps through the yard while we sit on the veranda, eating contentedly.

'What's the latest on the cyclone?' I ask.

'About 140 kilometres away, moving in this direction,' says Jess. 'They think landfall will be tomorrow at noon. It's a category three now.'

'Doesn't sound good.'

'Gusts to 220 kays an hour,' says Aidan. 'Want another sausage?'

'Yes please,' says Matthew. 'More onions too.'

'Where will we go if the cyclone hits here?' I ask.

'Some of my family died in Tracy in Darwin,' says Maggie, passing around a plate of baked potatoes. 'When Cath built this house I made sure it had a reinforced cellar. You're welcome to stay with us.'

'Will there be room enough with all your other guests?'

'Most have already gone to the Cable Beach shelter. They'll feel more secure there, but we reckon it'll be fine here, too.'

'Thanks a lot, Maggie,' I say. 'A reinforced cellar sounds pretty good to me.'

Later we move inside to the lounge and sit quietly over beers. Everyone else has gone. It's just the five of us plus Maggie, Cath and Russell, and they've already been told about the horrors of the gala bombing while Simon and I were asleep.

'Now we've had a rest we've got to have a good think,' says

Simon. 'For starters, if Zukowski and mates find out we're still alive they'll probably try again.'

'At least the bastards don't know where we are,' says Aidan, stroking the red dog beside him. She rolls onto her back, ecstatically grinning.

'While you two were ashore at Worm Turning, Parrot-man and I wrote up a report on the blue boat, complete with images,' says Jess. 'And then over the last couple of hours we did the same with the stuff from the gala. So we've got the whole package ready for release. Just say when.'

Aidan says, 'But what if they grab us before you release it?'

'Dead man's switch,' says Jessie. 'Or dead geek's.'

'What?' I ask.

'A fail-safe. If I don't send a signal every two hours then the information goes live automatically. Worldwide news within moments.'

The red dog thumps her tail in approval.

'Brilliant, Jessie,' says Simon, beside me on the couch. 'We'll release it as soon as possible. But I'd like to contact Jumbo first and find out what the government—other than the charming Alise Berg—thinks about handing over a chunk of Australia to another nation. May be able to coordinate something.'

'Evil bitch Alise, you mean,' I say. 'How could she? And *Max*? I knew he was a bastard but helping murder all those people?'

Simon says thoughtfully, 'I don't know. He looked pretty startled at the gala, when Berg and Zukowski weren't at all surprised. Maybe he wasn't in on the plot.'

'He's still a bastard, no matter what,' says Jessie.

Simon grins. 'Okay. Unanimous family opinion. But I'll find out what Jumbo's heard anyway.' He goes out to the kitchen and murmurs on his phone for a time. When he comes back his brow is drawn.

'Not encouraging news,' he says, sitting down beside me again and folding his fingers through mine. 'Jumbo says the state government isn't objecting to the situation. Quite the opposite. Apparently a large financial inducement arrives with the honour of becoming an Official Overseas Special Region.'

Matthew says, 'But surely money—?'

'An *unbelievably* large amount. An offer not to be refused, especially now the Dampier Peninsula has become a glowing waste-pile. If the Yanks want it they can bloody well have it, reckon our patriotic pollies.'

'But this is our *home*,' says Maggie. 'This town, this country, it's ours. We've got to live with those bullies, carry their stupid identity cards? They've already set up a camp outside Broome, for insurgents, they say. *Insurgents*? They took away my friend's eighteen-year old for painting an Australian flag in the window.'

We're silent, stunned.

Simon leans forward. 'Maggie, Cath, Russell—you've been bloody good to us, but as soon as we can get away safely we will. And we won't release the package till we're gone. Don't want you guys getting into trouble.'

'The day a meal and a bed for the night is a crime,' says Cath angrily, 'That's the day I'm—I'm—going to—' She puts her hand over her mouth. 'I don't know what I'm going to do. What can any of us do?'

The red dog looks at Cath and whimpers.

A sad evening passes. We sit in the lounge room checking up on what's happening in the outside world but it's not encouraging. Other countries have made barely a peep of protest about the annexation.

The state government is grovelling with joy to see the Yanks riding to the rescue, and the Commonwealth government just says blandly it's monitoring the situation.

Locally, the only ads on TV are about how fabulous the future will be and how seriously "anti-social behaviour" will be punished. And, oh yes, they've renamed the Dampier Peninsula to Liberty Province.

Aidan and Russell go to the kitchen to do the washing-up. Jessie yawns and Matthew dozes beside her. A lull in the storm arrives and Simon and I decide to return to the unit. Before we leave we all hug each other solemnly, shocked at the seriousness of what's happening.

Simon and I dash to the unit through the rain and close the door with a sigh of gratitude. We're safe and, thank God, we're finally alone.

I light candles and snuggle in bed while Simon has a shower. Then, smelling deliciously male, he gets in beside me.

At last, at last. We curl up together, and as the night goes on the rain gushes down, the thunder roars and the lightning explodes (while the storm's none too quiet either).

You want more? Recall the sweetest lovemaking you ever knew. It was something like that, only better.

16. Cyclone Cyril

I thought yesterday's weather was fierce: I had no idea. Today the sky is almost black and I don't understand how any of the trees are still upright.

Simon and I pack our few things with much affectionate foolishness, then we shut the door of the little hut where we've been so briefly happy and race through the storm to Cath's house.

We have a delicious breakfast, courtesy of Aidan and Russell, and Jessie tells us cyclone Cyril is now just seventy kilometres away. Landfall is expected in a few hours.

'You mean this still isn't as bad as it gets?' I ask.

'Cat four now,' says Aidan. 'Winds up to 280 kays an hour.'

'Two hundred and *eighty*?' I'm aghast.

Everyone else is packed too and soon we'll go down to the cellar. I'm feeling tense, my heart thumping. Simon and I catch each others' eye every now and then and smile. Oh, yes. Maybe that's why my heartbeat's so fast.

'Is your hand still on the dead geek's switch?' I ask Jessie.

'Yeah, did a ping about an hour ago. All good.'

Just when I think the noise of the storm can't get any louder it rises in a roar.

Maggie says, 'Okay, I reckon—' and suddenly there's a shuddering crash as the front door smashes open.

A large, wet, terrifying figure in black fills the doorway and moves into the room like some high-tech gorilla. It raises two massive arms and lifts off a dripping head cover.

I feel a chill sweat of shock. Colonel Zukowski.

Following him are three other figures, all as ominous, and two of them are pointing guns at us. Don't these creeps *ever* get tired of threatening people?

With despair I see the third man taking off his headgear is Max. Of course it is, the utter shit.

Then I realise how surprised he is to see me, how his face changes for a moment. Good heavens, Max is actually touched to find out I'm not dead.

'Okay,' says Zukowski. 'You five get your gear. Truck. Now.'

'You can't just *barge* in here—' says Maggie.

Zukowski looks at her, puzzled. He gestures at the dog, wagging her tail at all the interesting new people. There's a terrible noise and she dies, exploded into a redness that's grotesque against her soft russet fur.

The soldier lowers his gun. Cath sobs agonisingly, her hands over her mouth.

'Course I can,' says Zukowski. 'I can do whatever I like. You five get in the truck and the rest of you don't speak, don't move, and you might stay out of the insurgent camp.'

'What the *fuck*, Zukowski?' says Max. 'This isn't—'

A soldier hits him across the head with the butt of his gun and a line of blood starts dripping down Max's face. He falls against a wall in shock.

'Wimp,' says Zukowski. He turns back to us. 'Do I have to say it again?'

I wonder how I ever saw him as youthfully attractive: now all I can think of is a boy pulling wings off a fly.

We grab our bags and go to the door. An armoured carrier with rows of seating is pulled up next to the veranda. We clamber in and the soldiers with guns sit beside us.

With a shock I see a blond man looking embarrassed in the front seat.

Simon says calmly, 'Hello, Jumbo. Along for the ride?'

Jumbo spreads his hands. 'Mate, there was nothing I could do, had to inform them you were back.'

'But how did they know we were *here*? I didn't give you the address.'

Zukowski, in the front, sneers. 'You think those ID cards are just for fun, fucker? Once we knew we needed to round you up it was easy enough to find you.'

'Location trackers,' says Jess bitterly.

'Shut up, cunt,' says Zukowski conversationally. 'Go,' he tells the driver.

Max is seated in the front too, silently pressing one of Cath's tea-towels against his head to stop the bleeding. We're all quiet as the truck sways in gusts of wind, ploughing through walls of rain. There's almost no other traffic on the roads now.

We stop briefly in the town to let Jumbo out and he scurries away, his shoulders hunched. After about fifteen minutes we reach the gloomy port and drive out along the wharf, passing through several security gates.

To one side I can see *Sparrow* plunging up and down against the ropes holding her to the buoy. She looks so small.

We park beside USS *Jameson*. Zukowski turns to Max. 'Fuck off aboard, cretin.'

Max looks at me expressionless, then leaves and climbs the gangway to the ship.

'Out,' says Zukowski. We get out and stand in the rain shivering, the soldiers beside us.

A voice calls 'He-*llo!*' It's Alise Berg, coming from the gangway towards us. She's wearing a silk pants suit and a young sailor is desperately trying to keep an umbrella over her head.

'My *goodness*, Lena,' she says. 'You *are* indestructible. And we all thought you'd died so tragically at the plant. How did you escape?'

'We left early,' I say. 'I was—feeling sick. We walked back to the boat.'

'Oh? I didn't see you on the road.'

'Was that you?' asks Simon. 'Limo doing a hundred and twenty? No, you wouldn't have. I was helping Lena, she was being sick in the bushes. Must have been too much champagne.'

'She always was a two-pot screamer,' says Alise, pleased.

Zukowski clears his throat. 'I find it highly suspicious that this group has now been in the vicinity of two terrorist events. As regional Administrator I'm serving you with an exclusion order. You are to board your boat now and sail south out of US territory.'

'But a cyclone's coming,' I say.

'The *Jameson* will escort you part of the way. You'll be perfectly safe.'

'Alise, don't let him do this!'

'Lena,' she says sweetly. 'As government liaison to the Dampier Pen—to Liberty Province—I must concur with Colonel Zukowski. I'm afraid your behaviour lately has raised rather a few eyebrows, and the police will probably be interviewing you when you're back in Australia.'

'We're in Australia *here*,' says Aidan angrily.

'Shut your mouth, piece-of-shit,' says Zukowski, and a man jams the butt of his gun into Aidan's ribs. Aidan groans and doubles over, and Matthew grabs him and holds him up.

'Lena, it's best for everyone if you simply do what you're told,' says Alise kindly. 'I'm so sorry it's come to this. *Do* take care.' She turns and walks back to the ship with her sailor attendant trying to keep up.

From the front seat of the truck Zukowski looks down at us.'Okay, I'm only going to say this once. Get in your stupid little boat and cast off. *Jameson*'s heading out to sea now. You follow us at a hundred yards distance—got that? Don't fall back. Don't go ahead. Or we'll shell you, and we won't miss.'

'We've only got half an hour of fuel,' says Simon carefully.

'Yeah.'

'But we haven't got the speed to keep up with you,' says Matthew.

'Keep up. Or you'll be dead.'

Zukowski gets out of the truck and heads towards the ship. Above the roar of the storm he calls, 'One hundred yards, fuckers,' and climbs the gangway.

Sodden and subdued we climb back into the truck and the soldiers drive us to our tinny on the shore. We pull it into the water and get in.

'Straight out to your boat,' says a smirking goon pointing his gun at us and I realise it's the man with the flag tattoo on his neck, the one who'd tried to drown me. 'Don't change course or we'll kill you.' *With pleasure* is implied.

We motor out and fasten the tinny to *Sparrow*. We throw our bags onto the deck and climb wearily aboard. We untie ropes in the rain then Simon starts the engine, and I hear a rumbling noise coming from *Jameson*.

A spotlight shines dazzlingly from its stern onto *Sparrow*, onto us. The warship moves slowly away and we follow, soaked and freezing.

Through the wind Simon yells, 'Everyone put on dry clothes and get into wet-weather gear and life jackets. And take anti-nausea meds.'

We do so, and Matthew takes the helm while Simon gets changed too. I put long strips of sticking plaster on Aidan's bruised side, hoping nothing is broken: luckily he still seems to be able to move.

Waves crash against our bow as we chug along, lit up like the shooting target we are, behind the great stern of the ship ahead. I'm shivering and holding on as the lugger sways sickeningly.

The wind seems to take the breath from my lungs. The waves are breathtakingly high and the rain is almost horizontal, foam flying through the air.

Matthew shouts, 'What do they think they're doing, going to sea in a cyclone?'

'They're 'Muricans,' laughs Aidan. 'They create their own reality, doncha know?'

Jess, down in the galley, comes half-way up the stairs and calls, 'Bad news. They've been aboard, smashed the modem, destroyed the radio. But they've left the radar and a radio phone—probably to keep telling us *one hundred yards, fuckers*. Who uses yards in this day and age anyway?'

'USA, Liberia, Myanmar—beacons of sanity and progress,' yells Matthew.

Jessie laughs and climbs down to the galley again. Miraculously she manages to boil water in these conditions and brings us flasks of coffee.

I can see *Jameson* ahead is turning and we follow like a lamb. I tell myself, don't think *to the slaughter*, but it's too bloody late. We're leaving Roebuck Bay behind, Minyirr over to starboard.

I wonder if Paddy and the other senior Law men are still

there, singing to the cyclone. Becoming the cyclone. Ahead of us lies the wide Indian Ocean, now a maelstrom churned up by the wrath of cyclone Cyril.

How could I ever have thought that a silly name? I'm sorry I laughed at you, Cyril, please don't drown us, I silently pray.

I make my way hand-over-hand to where Simon is grimly holding the tiller against the kick of the waves. I take some of the weight of it and he says, 'Thanks, love,' and kisses me briefly.

I stand beside him. There doesn't seem to be anything to say.

The stern of *Jameson* is like some nightmare cliff face that's perpetually receding. The spotlight glistens on us and the wet lugger and the gigantic waves. The guns in the bays on either side of the stern are manned, and pointing directly at us.

Why on earth are they forcing us to follow them? They *know* we don't have enough fuel to go anywhere safely!

And suddenly I realise what a fool I am. They're not taking us anywhere but out to sea. To where Cyril will deal with us. To our deaths.

Deniability, I think bitterly, of course. 'Tragic loss of historic lugger', I expect the headlines will read.

I look at Simon in anguish. It's not fair, we've had so little time together. He gazes back at me reassuringly. 'Don't worry, love. We'll get out of this, I swear.'

Oh, my darling man. How can you keep a promise like that?

It must be close to midday but it's as dark as evening, the spotlight blinding, glinting on the foam and the rain flying past. In the distance I can see Cyril's charcoal cloud-banks lit up by flickers of lightning.

The eye of the cyclone must not be far away now.

We're out in the ocean now and well past Minyirr, but instead of turning south-west for Port Hedland—with a hope of avoiding the storm—*Jameson* turns north, into Cyril's path.

The boat is lifting to the peaks of the waves then plummeting into the troughs. I feel sick, but that's probably because whenever we rise up I see the pale glimmering line of Cable Beach. It's coming closer and there are reefs not far off those pretty sands. Oh, God.

It must be nearly half an hour since we left port.

Jess comes up on deck with the radio phone for Simon. 'Ronald McDonald wants a word,' she says.

I can hear Zukowski's deep voice. 'How's the fuel situation going?'

'Just a few minutes left,' says Simon. 'Give us some more or we can't keep up with you.'

Zukowski snickers. 'You don't have to keep up any more, fuckers. Enjoy.'

The dazzling light clicks off and for a moment I can't see in the dark. Then, faster than I could have imagined, the shadow of the looming stern of *Jameson* moves away and is gone.

We're alone on that nightmare sea.

And a few moments later *Sparrow*'s engine sputters. And coughs. And stops.

All around us is darkness and freezing rain and screaming winds and violent buffeting waves reaching taller than the boat itself. And Simon says, bizarrely, 'Okay. Need to wait a bit, make sure they're gone.'

Wait? Is he mad? Minutes pass. My heart is hammering. The silvery strand of the beach is growing brighter, wider, *closer*.

Just when I think I'll faint with the suspense, Simon says calmly, 'Matty? Engine room, please.'

Matthew launches himself flying down the galley stairs and

into the engine room beyond.

'Mind moving sideways a bit, love?' says Simon.

I do so and he leans down and pulls some panelling off the side of the boat. What's he *doing*? I can see dials and switches and buttons, and his hands are touching and turning.

The line of the beach is now a bright strip, the wind shoving us relentlessly towards disaster.

Matthew bellows from below, '*Ready!*'

Simon hits a button and the engine leaps into life again. He swings the tiller wide and roars, 'Hang on, everyone!'

The lugger accelerates in a long, leaning curve away from the beach, and slowly that terrifying line starts to recede behind us.

I sob with excitement and Aidan yells, 'Holy fuck!' Jessie screams with joy and Matthew leaps up the stairs again and hugs her, laughing.

Simon looks at me, eyes delighted, and says, 'Didn't I say we'd get out of this?'

'You did! Oh, darling man. You *did*.'

'Remember those expensive modifications I mentioned? Secondary fuel tanks, a superb engine that looks pretty ordinary. Discreet. Useful.' He laughs, throwing his head back. 'I had no idea how unbelievably useful till today.'

After a time we calm down. We might have escaped one disaster but we're still at the mercy of the looming storm.

'So where do we go now?' says Jess. 'North of here's been nuked and Cyril's closing in. Broome?'

'No way,' says Aidan. 'Zukowski'd just line us up and shoot us himself.'

'We'll go south and use Cyril to help us,' says Simon. 'Matty, will you and Aidan take the tiller? I need to have a look at the radar.'

In the galley the roar of the wind is less, though the leaping and corkscrewing of the boat is the same.

Simon checks the radar. 'Look. There's *Jameson*, heading back to Broome. At least they're out of the way and won't care about us. They'll think we're matchwood by now.'

'And that great mass there,' I ask, pointing at the radar. 'Is that Cyril?'

'Yes. We're ahead of it right now, that's why the winds are pushing us towards the shore. But if we can get round to the east of the eye, the winds'll start coming from behind and we won't have to fight so hard to go south-west, away from the coast.'

'Is that as easy as it sounds?' says Jessie.

Simon laughs wryly. 'No. If we get caught up in the wind it'll drive us into the eye wall. We'll have to to keep turning away at an angle and that'll be hard. But we don't have any other option.'

'But I thought the eye of the cyclone was supposed to be calm,' I say. 'Couldn't we go there?'

'We'd have to get through the eye wall itself, love, where the winds are twice as powerful,' he says. 'We wouldn't stand a chance.'

'Oh, Simon. Can't we send out some sort of distress signal?'

'No, Zukowski's already demolished anything that could do that. Except—Jess, what about your Internet connectivity? You said you didn't need the boat's link, you use other people's or something weird like that.'

'Hey, I would if I could, but the power's out everywhere, courtesy of Cyril. No power, no links—not even for me.' She sounds surprised.

A thought strikes me. 'Jess—did you update your dead geek's switch?'

She shakes her head. 'No, a ping was due when *Jameson* left us to die but I was sorta preoccupied. So the package has gone live automatically: all the evidence is out now, worldwide. Wonder what'll happen?'

'We can worry about that later,' says Simon. 'For now we're going on deck and taking a detour around Cyril. Are your life jackets on properly?' He slightly readjusts mine and kisses me.

We take cushions and bedding up to soften the hard edges of a small area in the lee of the deckhouse, then Simon seals every hatch. The tiller is lashed to keep us roughly on course but it still needs two people to handle it.

We all take turns, then try to recover a little strength, braced in the half-sheltered space beside the deckhouse, held onto the boat by safety harnesses. Without them we'd simply be flung overboard.

The next five hours are hallucinatory.

We're submerged in a world, far beyond anything I could ever have imagined, of the possible extremes of noise and movement. It's rather like being inside jet engines: jet engines rotating in every conceivable dimension.

We're pummelled against surfaces barely softened by our sodden padding. The air is basically freezing water and simply taking a breath is hard work.

There's not even room in my mind to think about my far-away family, except to wish with every fibre of my being we were there with them and not here on a boat.

And despite the anti-nausea meds we're seasick, more than I ever imagined was humanly possible. Oh dear Lord, we are so sick. At least we don't have to clean up after ourselves—waves gush over us continually and we only have to open our mouths to get a drink of fresh rainwater.

But eventually I lose all hope and can no longer even

imagine surviving. I simply want the sickness to stop. I want to die. Where's a lethal US warship when you really need one?

After a long, long time I notice the feeble light is beginning to fade and assume something worse is descending upon us. Then, in my agony, I slowly realise it's just the approach of night.

And surprisingly the wind's howl is lessening a little, the buffeting isn't quite so painful, the rain is now a solid sheet rather than a brick wall.

Have we managed to get through the worst of the storm? My retching eases and I start to think I may not die after all, although it still remains an attractive option.

An hour or so later it becomes possible to move around safely. Simon, red-eyed, re-opens the hatches. Matthew and Jess remain grimly at the tiller, the rest of us collapse below.

After a few hours of blessed unconsciousness we force ourselves awake to give the others a chance to sleep. By then it's night-time and the cyclone has become no more than a vicious storm.

We heave-to and heat some soup in the galley. I'm surprised to be able to eat, but the food is good.

Despite the blow to Aidan's ribs from the soldier's gun he's held up amazingly well, but now he's pale and in pain and I dress all our various cuts and abrasions.

Simon starts the radar again. We can see the ragged mass of Cyril a distance to the north-east, passed over the coastline. Without the sea as its power-source it's already diminishing.

'Looks like it missed Broome, thank God,' says Simon. 'Paddy and the Law men seem to have had a win.' He looks at me, one eyebrow raised. 'It's actually made landfall at Worm Turning.'

'Will that help get rid of the caesium?' asks Aidan.

'Well, it won't change the levels of radioactivity but there'll be less dust, always a good thing,' I say. 'Thank you Cyril, for that at least.'

We sit in silence for a time, too tired to talk. Eventually Aidan says, 'I'll take the helm now. You get some sleep. We can work out what to do in the morning.'

'Keep on motoring down the coast towards Port Hedland, Ade,' says Simon. 'I want to make sure we're well out of Zukowski's clutches.'

When Simon and I go forward I'm amused to see Jess and Matthew, still in their wet-weather gear, fast asleep in each other's arms on the double bed.

'Damn,' whispers Simon. 'Only the single berths left.'

I kiss him, sit down and collapse.

PART III. MURUJUGA

17. Operation Sparrow

Next morning we're all sore and sorry for ourselves, painfully stiff with bruises on top of bruises, but we're alive. Above us is broken cloud and glimpses of sunlight and blue sky, and slowly our spirits rise. A week ago I would have called the water rough but now it looks like a millpond.

We're only about seventy kilometres from Port Hedland so we're hoping to put in there and find out what's happened while we were battling the cyclone.

Jess still can't get an Internet connection, so it must be taking some time to repair the power ashore. She gets a small tool kit from her bag and starts trying to fix the boat's smashed communications gear.

The rest of us go up on deck and start tidying the mess from yesterday. But mostly we sit on the deckhouse and enjoy the glorious day: we made it through that terrible storm and we escaped the monstrous Colonel Zukowski. I sigh with relief.

The empty coastline passes by in the distance, red-brown shores smudged with green. When I'm at the tiller after lunch I notice an enormous ship on the horizon, then another and another, and a line of low buildings in the distance.

We motor into Port Hedland in the afternoon, the dusty town along one side and a row of bulk carriers loading at the wharves on the other. We tie up at a small marina and Simon goes to the office and arranges our mooring for a few days.

After we secure the lugger we go for a walk to get groceries and stretch our legs. I'm stunned at the bizarre feeling of the ground swaying beneath my feet. I'd noticed it before when we returned from Worm Turning, but after the storm it's intense.

Simon laughs. 'It'll wear off in a few days.'

'Inner ear motion compensation,' says Jess. 'Wow, that's *totally*—' She grabs Matthew's arm to stay upright.

There seems to be a layer of red dust over everything. Tree branches and rubbish are scattered around and some sheds are without roofing iron.

'The man in the office said Cyril didn't do too much damage here,' says Simon, 'but it came on top of a direct hit a few weeks ago from cyclone Brenda. So the place is still something of a shambles—communications are flaky too.'

'Good,' I say. 'Less chance of Zukowski talking to anyone.'

We walk along a road with warehouses and maritime businesses, and ask a man for directions. He points us towards a shop a few blocks away where we load up with groceries.

As we're leaving Jessie runs back and buys a couple of prepaid mobiles.

'We need to be careful about using our own phones,' she says. 'The comcuffs are fine but the mobiles are probably being monitored. In fact we should take out the batteries and just not use them.'

'Even now?' I ask. 'After Berg and her mates think they've drowned us on Cable Beach?'

Jessie nods. 'Probably automatic monitoring. People don't remember to turn those sorts of things off and if they notice our phones are still working we could be in trouble.'

'But, hey, we're back in *Australia*,' says Aidan dryly. 'Gotta be safe here.'

We carry our purchases back to the lugger, passing a hotel on the way, then refuel and clean up and take on fresh water.

In the evening the sky is startlingly red, as we wander in the warmth to the hotel for a meal. A TV in one corner of the room is showing horse races but the reception is bad and the barman has turned down the sound.

A few beers and steaks later we're all feeling rather pleased with ourselves. We're groaning at one of Aidan's jokes when I remember something I'd meant to ask Simon earlier.

'What did you tell the man at the marina?' I say. 'Did you say we'd come from Broome?'

He shakes his head. 'I said we'd been fishing around Depuch Island—about a hundred kilometres south of here. I'd still like to keep a low profile.'

'But won't the lugger be noticeable?' asks Jess. 'I thought there weren't many left.'

'There are a few modern replicas around nowadays, people love the style, so we won't be too obvious.'

'When do you reckon your information package'll be hitting the airwaves, Jess?' asks Aidan.

'It's out there already, but I've no idea who's paying attention,' she says. 'Depends on the news cycle. A celebrity scandal could bury it.'

Just then the TV reception comes good. The races are over and it's a news conference. We stare silently—Zukowski behind a microphone, Minister Berg in a grey suit beside him.

Zukowski is reading something from a paper but we can't hear what. The ticker at the bottom of the screen says TWIST IN WORM TURNING TRAGEDY, then reception breaks up again.

We're suddenly very sober.

Aidan stands. 'Going to see some rellies of mine a few blocks from here. They'll know all the goss from Broome.'

'Make sure you're back by morning, Ade,' says Simon. 'Just in case we have to make a quick getaway.'

Jess says to me, 'Parrot-man and I'll watch the boat. You and Simon get a room here and have a good rest.'

'But we don't—'

'Here's the necessities.' She hands me a small backpack.

'Really? You guys'll be all right by yourselves?'

She smiles.

We pay for the accommodation up front, telling the clerk we might be leaving early on a fishing trip. The room looks comfortable and in the bathroom there's a big shiny spa.

'Let's give it a go,' says Simon.

Some enjoyable time later, the bathroom a haze of steam and bubbles, we lie contentedly side by side in the warm water.

'So good of Jess and Matthew to suggest this,' I murmur.

'Good? They wanted to be by themselves too.'

'Is that okay with you, the two of them? I know she's eccentric, but—'

'Eccentric? Woman's a genius, she's perfect for Matty.' He kisses me. 'Remember his broken engagement? The ex wanted him to forget science and get a job with a mining company. I was glad when it ended. But Jess lets him be himself. They'll be good together.'

'How did you go from being such a bastard of an army man to someone so nice, Simon?'

He strokes my wet hair back from my forehead. 'Ah, you're just impressed by my extra fuel supply.'

'Got us out of a nasty situation, that's for sure.'

'You calling a spa a nasty situation?'

I tickle him. After we stop splashing around we lie quietly in the warmth.

After a time Simon says quietly, 'You could actually thank my wife. I was miserable in the army. She encouraged me to leave and do ecology, she knew I'd love it. And I did.' He's silent for a moment. 'She supported me through the degree but she didn't live to see it awarded.'

I hug him. 'I'm so sorry. That must have been dreadful.'

He nods slowly. 'And losing my son was ... inconceivable. The only comfort was knowing nothing could ever hurt me again after that. Not much of a comfort, though.'

'You don't have to talk about it.'

'First time in ages I've been able to.' He sighs. 'Perhaps the first time it seems I might even get beyond it, one day.'

I stroke his face. 'How old was Matthew when he came to live with you?'

'Just six. I'd been in mourning for two years by then with no end in sight. But he was all alone. His mother—my sister—died in an accident, and his father had abandoned them long before that. So Matty saved *me*, became a reason to go on. He doesn't realise, even now, what he did for me.'

I kiss him and hold him for a time, then say, 'Sweet man. We need to get out of this bath before we turn into prunes.'

'Yes. I was just thinking, you're rather slippery and elusive in these bubbles. I'd quite like to be able to pin you down—'

'And then what?'

'Something like this?'

'Oh, *yes*.'

I'm sleeping the best sleep of my life when the prepaid mobile beside us rings. I come awake cursing and grab it. The curtains are open and I can see it's barely dawn.

Aidan says, 'Lena, I've just heard, Zukowski's saying crazy, awful stuff! We've got to get out of here right now—'

'Okay. We'll meet you at the lugger as soon as we can.'

'*Hurry,*' he says, and hangs up.

Simon is already awake. 'Trouble?'

'I haven't heard Aidan sound so scared before. I think we need to go. Sorry, love.'

'Me too.'

We dress quickly and get back to the boat in ten minutes. Jess and Matthew, wrapped in a blanket with their heads together, are sitting on the deckhouse watching the sun rise.

They look around in sleepy surprise when we run towards them. I'm charmed to see Jess is in one of Matthew's lurid shirts, while he's wearing something black.

Aidan is just behind us. 'Jessie!' he calls out. 'Got your link going again?'

She smiles contentedly. 'Yeah, last night, but then I had better things to do.' She realises he's serious and becomes alert. 'Ade, what's up?'

Breathing heavily he says, 'Check out the news!'

We rush down to the galley and Jessie starts tapping. 'What am I looking for?'

'Try Zukowski—propaganda—terrorists,' says Aidan bitterly. 'That should bloody well do it.'

We gather around and read.

PACKAGE IS "TERRORIST PROPAGANDA"

Broome, 23 April: Colonel W. Zukowski, Administrator, Liberty Province Official Overseas Special Region, has announced that the information package released yesterday world-wide is no more than terrorist propaganda. Col. Zukowski stated:

"US security agencies have now examined this material. It is an

amateurish attempt to divert the blame for the attack at Worm Turning from the terrorists themselves onto US Forces. A number of brave young American soldiers died at the scene, so we can only dismiss this as a cruel deception aimed at grieving widows and children."

'Brave young American soldiers *you* killed,' I mutter.

"The ludicrous story about a boat with corpses and radioactive material is obviously a fabrication based upon the recent salvage of a drifting vessel. The images purporting to have been shot aboard are fake—the glowing powder special effects are obviously computer-generated."

'Special effects? Kidding me, dickwit?' says Jessie scathingly.

"We are still scrutinising the Sea Rover extremists, and are confident we know who and where their terrorist associates are. They will not escape. Port Hedland authorities will be cooperating with us in a capture-or-kill mission, Operation Sparrow. We hope to have further news for you soon."

Col. Zukowski and newly-appointed Minister of Special Regions Alise Berg are aboard USS Jameson and the warship will depart Bush Maritime Facility (previously Port of Broome) at dawn.

'Operation bloody *Sparrow*?' says Matthew despairingly. 'The bastards. It's going to be us taking the blame.'

Aidan sits down, stunned. 'Capture-or-kill?'

'Port Hedland authorities will be cooperating,' I say. 'We've got to get away!'

Jess is silent.

'*Jameson*'s top speed is about forty-four knots. It could be here in six or seven hours,' says Simon slowly.

'But why is Zukowski so certain we're alive?' I say. 'As far as he's concerned we ended up in pieces on Cable Beach—and we disabled all our phones.'

Jess comes out of her daze. 'He knows we're alive, the creep.

Something else gave us away. Those *cards*, those fucking location trackers! We were too busy surviving Cyril to even think about them. Where are they?'

We check our bags for the innocent-looking pieces of plastic, and soon have all five of them in a pile on the table.

'Burn them!' says Jess.

'No, no,' I say. 'Do we have anything that might float?'

Simon smiles at me. 'Yeah. Good idea.'

He goes to the galley bin and finds a plastic juice bottle and we stuff the cards into it. Then we seal it, take it on deck and throw it over the side. The tide begins washing it up-river.

'That'll buy us some time if nothing else,' says Simon. 'Okay, let's go.'

He starts the engine, Matthew and Aidan release the moorings, and in moments we're heading out of the harbour. The sun is just rising over Port Hedland as we leave.

'But what do we do *now*?' I say, sitting down on a deckhouse. 'They've smeared our information as propaganda and us as terrorists. Australian authorities are cooperating to track us down and *kill* us, for God's sake. Where on earth can we go?'

'We have to get to Perth,' says Simon. 'I've got a high-level contact there, someone with a bit more backbone than bloody Jumbo. But we don't have enough fuel for the whole trip—it's about eighteen hundred kilometres.'

Aidan is gazing out to sea, a far-away expression on his face. He turns and says, 'I know somewhere we can go. Somewhere I've got friends, somewhere we'll be safe.'

We all stare at him.

He's suddenly beaming. 'Murujuga, my country. *Murujuga*. Less than two hundred kays from here. We can be there by this evening. And my cousin's in Dampier, the main port—he can get us fuel or even smuggle us out by road.'

We look at each other silently then Simon suddenly laughs. 'Okay, Murujuga, here we come.'

It's a beautiful clear morning. After the exertions of the last few days it's a relief to simply do nothing as the lugger motors along.

I'm sitting peacefully against a cushion enjoying the sound of waves on the hull and the endless blueness all around. Interesting, I think, the water's just ordinary old water here. It's lovely but not the luminous turquoise of Broome.

Matthew is at the tiller and Simon and Aidan are dozing on sleeping bags. Leaning against the deckhouse, her computer on her lap, Jess says, 'Well, I've got the crowdsourcers onto it.'

'Onto what?' says Simon sleepily.

'Onto proving that our evidence from the blue boat and the gala isn't fake. Got to be the first step in saving our skins.'

'Crowd—?' murmurs Aidan.

'People working together online to solve a complex problem. Like supercomputing with humans.'

'But even the best evidence can be smeared, Jesso,' says Matthew. 'Yes, we need it authenticated but we still need to stay alive to back it up. And if Zukowski gets to us first ...'

'Simon,' I say, 'your mate in Perth, can we contact him from here?'

'We're too far out from the coast now for phones,' he says, leaning up on an elbow. 'And email's too easily traced. Could be dangerous.'

'Anonymisers,' says Jess.

'Translation, please,' says Aidan sleepily.

'We send email through networks that remove any evidence of their source. Simon, want to try to get through to your contact?'

'Okay.' Simon gets up and sits on the deckhouse beside Jessie. He tells her an email address then looks out to sea. After a time he shakes his head slowly. 'But I don't know what to say. The whole thing is just insane.'

'Dear friend,' says Matthew, deadpan. 'The might of two governments is chasing me in a warship. I have proof of a conspiracy to steal your country and if you pay my expenses I will send you five million dollars from my bank in Nigeria.'

Simon laughs and says, 'Come *on*, guys. We've got to figure out something sensible.'

After half an hour of effort we cobble together a message that outlines the essentials of the blue boat, the caesium, the explosion at the gala. We don't point the finger at Iceberg or Zukowski, just say we're being blamed for events at which we were simply witnesses.

Jess sends off the message, but I think we all feel it's going to be hard to convince anyone of the truth now.

After lunch I'm at the tiller. Matthew is sitting nearby, jotting down something in a notebook. We can hear Simon and Aidan and Jessie in the galley laughing as they clean up. Matthew and I catch each other's eye and smile.

He shakes his curly head in wonder. 'I never imagined meeting someone like Jess in a situation like this.'

'I don't expect any of us ever thought we'd be in a situation like this. Surreal.'

He nods. 'It's early days yet but I'm hoping—well. Is it all right with you?'

'Couldn't be happier. Simon mentioned you'd had a rough break-up a while ago, so it must be nice to meet someone new.'

'Beyond nice,' says Matthew softly. 'She's amazing.' He looks up. 'And I'm glad about you and Simon. He's been alone for a long time.'

'I have too. Relationships aren't easy.'

'Absolutely. So let me get this right—that yes-man hanging around with Zukowski is really your husband?'

'To my shame, yes, but he'll soon be an ex. Can't be soon enough.'

'He did *try* to tell Zukowski to back off at Cath's place.'

'Didn't try very hard,' I say.

The others come up on deck and settle down. Aidan says, 'I wonder where bloody *Jameson* is. Radar still broken, Jess?'

'Yeah, I managed to patch the cables, but we're too far away from Port Hedland now to see the destroyer,' she says. 'But have no fear, the Internet, as always, has an alternative.'

'To radar?' I say.

'Not precisely. But some people just want to know where ships are. They're not in peril on the sea, but they're simply obsessives who wanna *know*. And there we are.'

'But I thought naval vessels weren't included on those sites for security reasons,' says Simon, looking over her shoulder.

'Ah, but this is the geek version,' says Jess.

She runs the pointer over a cluster of icons near a tracery of the coastline near Port Hedland. Names, countries, speeds, directions flicker for a moment.

She zeros in on a grey arrow inside the harbour and information appears: *Jameson* (US) 2 knots 185°.

As we watch, the arrow changes to a large dot and the speed to zero knots. 'Okay,' says Simon. 'Looks like it's just mooring at the port now. Guess they'll soon see we're not there.'

'Does *Sparrow* show up on that?' asks Aidan in alarm.

'No, she wouldn't,' says Simon. 'Large ships carry data

transponders, but it's optional for small vessels, and we don't.'

'Zoom out a bit, Jess,' I say, feeling anxious. 'Just check.'

The coastline image widens. It shows a multitude of icons, swarms of coloured dots for moored ships, and arrows for moving ones. Purple for tankers, blue for cargo, orange for tugs, and grey for unspecified, according to the key.

Jameson is a big grey dot moored at Port Hedland. Down, to the left, is the Murujuga peninsula.

And out at sea, a little more than halfway between them, is a small grey arrow. Jess focuses on it. *Sparrow* (AU) 7 knots 255° appears. I feel weak.

'But we don't *have* a transponder on board,' says Matthew. 'How can they possibly be getting that data?'

'Could something else be giving our position away?' I ask.

'But what?' says Simon. 'Jess, when you were fixing the electronics was there anything Zukowski might have left behind?'

'I'm pretty sure not.'

'But why didn't *Jameson* come straight to us then?' Matthew asks. 'Why did they bother going into Port Hedland at all?'

'Maybe they were blindly following the tracking cards,' I say.

In silence we watch the grey dot. I imagine inflatables with fast engines zooming up and down the harbour searching for *Sparrow*, and finding a juice bottle instead.

'What'll we do?' says Aidan. 'That transponder's got to be *somewhere* on board.'

'We'll have to search everything,' says Simon grimly. 'Lena, would you please take the tiller? The rest of us'll turn over everything below.'

After about half an hour they come back on deck, dispirited. They've looked through bags, cupboards, hidden spaces and everywhere possible, and found nothing. On the screen

Jameson is still a dot moored in the port.

The wind comes up and we hoist the sails so our passage through the water becomes a little faster. We make some afternoon tea and cluster around the small screen again.

'Perhaps they won't even think to look for our transponder data,' I say.

'They'll use everything they—' says Simon. 'Oh, hell.'

Jameson's icon has suddenly changed from a dot to an arrow.

'They're on the move. Guess they found the bottle, then,' says Aidan.

Wonder what direction they'll take,' says Matthew slowly.

We watch in suspense. After the grey icon has moved away from the coast, Jess focuses on it.

Jameson (US) 35 knots 255°, appears.

Simon groans. 'Our direction.'

'Could they be heading for Perth?' I say. 'They'd have to follow roughly the same path as us.'

'We'll know for sure when we're in range,' says Aidan. 'If they don't shoot—hey, they're going to Perth.'

'How long till we get to Murujuga, Parrot-man?' says Jess.

'About two hours, Jesso,' says Matthew. 'But at the speed *Jameson* can go, they'll get there just after us.'

18. Red-Black Rocks

In the galley Simon spreads the chart for Murujuga. The peninsula itself is perhaps five kilometres wide and twenty long, divided from Dolphin Island by Searipple Passage. Clusters of small and large islands lie towards the west and north.

'Bit like a dick pic,' says Jess.

'I see what you mean,' I muse. 'The way it thrusts itself so boldly from the mainland.'

Aidan grins. 'The old men told the missionaries that Murujuga means hipbone sticking out. They knew how easily shocked the priests were.'

'Well,' says Simon, 'whatever it is, we can use Searipple Passage to get to the far side and luckily that's too shallow for *Jameson*. They'll have to use the shipping lane around the top of Legendre Island, so we might gain some time then.'

'And Dampier's only about ten kays from Searipple,' says Aidan. 'I can call my cousin.'

'But we might get your cousin into strife too,' I say. 'We've got to find that transponder first. What would it look like, anyway? Big or small?'

'For commercial shipping, about the size of a book,' says Simon. 'But those for recreational boats can be pretty compact. And the latest ones are tiny.'

'Perhaps Zukowski hid one in the bilges,' I say. 'Not that I know what bilges are but they sound like the sort of place you could hide anything.'

'I've got an idea,' says Jess absently. 'I may be able to hack our comcuffs to detect it.'

'Oh,' I say sadly. 'I'd hate to lose my beautiful cuff.'

'Not physically, Lena. In software.'

'Really?'

Jess shrugs. 'The electronics are flexible. Perhaps.' She sits for a moment staring at her computer. 'Not easy. Okay dudes, go away. I've got to check code.'

Simon, Aidan and I return to the deck and sit near Matthew at the tiller. The sun is low and on the horizon ahead is land. Murujuga. I look at the lovely dappled sky, something niggling my mind. A tiny metallic object that's been put on the boat—or perhaps brought along by one of us?

Of course we've got devices galore—not just the cuffs, but phones, laptops, cameras, torches ... Torches? Why did that pop into my mind? I suddenly think of the night of the gala, madly dashing back to the boat with our torches flashing around and lighting the way.

I remember the guards at the Worm Turning gates opening our bags and checking the torches. Could they have slipped something inside them? I don't want to raise anyone's hopes so I just get up quietly and go down to the sleeping area.

Simon's backpack is stuffed in the corner. I find his torch and open it but there's nothing inside apart from ordinary old batteries. Nice idea, I think gloomily, but no.

I close the backpack. I almost give up but I have a habit of completeness (some describe it a little more unkindly than that) and go to my suitcase.

The shoulder bag is lying at the bottom and I pull it out. I open my own torch and check it over but find nothing unusual.

I look deeper into the bag—just a lipstick and eyeliner and the tickets Glenn Garrod gave me.

I put the torch back and move to close the bag, and something catches my eye: a metallic glint. I reach in again and pull out the tickets.

The tickets the soldier's machine impressed with a sort of seal: a flat, silvery seal I'd simply assumed was the rich man's equivalent of a pass-out stamp.

Bloody *assumptions*, I think with a sigh.

I take the tickets to Jess in the galley. 'Bring up the ship-tracking page again,' I say.

She knows I'd only interrupt if it was important, so she does. On the screen I see the large arrow of *Jameson*, perhaps one hundred kilometres behind the small one of *Sparrow*.

I get a pair of wire cutters from Jessie's kit. I cut through one of the flat metallic seals and it gives way, exposing flexible golden circuits. But our small grey icon sails serenely on.

I cut viciously through the seal on the second ticket.

Sparrow disappears, and *Jameson* is alone on the digital sea.

I rush up to the deck to tell everyone the good news.

'But how did those things on your gala tickets even know what boat this is?' says Aidan.

'Probably interrogated *Sparrow*'s electronics somehow,' says Matthew. 'Amazing what information's stored in every bloody device nowadays.'

'And even if *Jameson* can't see the transponder any more we'll soon be in range of their radar,' says Simon, at the tiller.

'But did you notice how many vessels, big and small, are moving around Dampier?' says Matthew. 'If we can get in and refuel and get out quickly we might become lost in the crowd.'

Simon nods. 'Hope so.'

After a time Jessie comes up on deck, her computer under her arm, and sits on the deck. 'Okay,' she says. 'We've had a reply from your mate in Perth, Simon.'

'Read it out please,' he says. Jess says:

> Jesus, Rosso, I heard they were chasing some silly bugger in a boat, should've realised it was you. Yeah, I'm pretty sure you're being fitted up too—my guys checked out those Internet pics and they don't look fake at all.
>
> Trouble is, this latest bout of federal vs state arm-wrestling has gone stupid, so we've got to move carefully. But I'll send a small team with transport to Exmouth, so if you can reach there they'll get you back. That's the best I can do for now. Hope it works out.

'Exmouth?' How far's that?' I ask.

'Oh ... three hundred kays from here,' says Aidan. 'We are *really* going to need that fuel.'

I look ahead. In the golden light of the setting sun we're just inside the entrance to Searipple Passage.

Matthew goes down to the galley to check the depth of the water on the radar. He calls out to Simon, 'Five metres ... six metres ... four metres ...'

'The tides are massive here,' Aidan says, leaning on a stay beside me. 'It's a bit of a race to get out the other side of the passage before it's too shallow.'

'How low will it go?'

'This'll all be one big sandbank soon,' he says. 'But I reckon we'll make it.'

Searipple Passage is perhaps four hundred metres wide, with hilltops on either side covered in long spills of red-black rocks, rough-edged and cubic, with occasional tall, narrow stones standing among them.

'Look at it, Lena,' Aidan says wistfully. 'Murujuga. Older than the Pyramids. Older than Stonehenge. The most ancient archive of human culture in the world. Here.'

There's no gentleness to the rocks: they're fierce against the green hills, and seem to radiate heat and power like banked fires, like embers beneath charcoal. They shouldn't be beautiful, but they are. My hands tingle with the urge to touch.

Aidan says, 'Wish we could take a walk up there.' He points to a broad valley with rocks tumbled like dice down the slopes. 'Brilliant carvings, you'd love them.'

'One day, cuz. One day we'll come back, I promise.'

In something over an hour it's almost dark, and it's a relief when the water becomes deeper and the passage opens up as we emerge on the far side of Searipple.

'Where's *Jameson* now?' I ask Jessie.

She switches to a screen with the busy ship icons. 'There, approaching Legendre Island.'

'We've still got a chance of getting into Dampier before them,' I say.

'It's the getting out I'm more worried about, love,' says Simon wryly.

After a few moment of silence Jess says, 'Okay, everyone, good news. I've hacked my comcuff to pretend it's a transponder.'

'Um ... why?' says Aidan.

'Rather than being anonymous, it might be safer to blend in with the other boats. But we don't have to tell the world we're *Sparrow*, my cuff can transmit any name we like. So who will we become? Think of something stupidly nautical.'

'Lots of boats round here do boozy fishing charters to the Montebellos,' says Aidan. 'What about—I don't know—*Montes*

Mermaid? That's lame enough.'

'Right,' says Jess. She taps at her cuff then refreshes the shipping page. A small green arrow appears near the end of Searipple Passage.

Montes Mermaid (AU) 7 knots 210°.

'We're green now because we're a recreational vessel,' she says. 'Dozens of them round here.'

'That's brilliant, Jess!' says Simon, and Matthew gives her a quick hug.

A little later Simon checks his watch and says, 'Okay guys, we've got about eight kilometres to go, then we've got to make a decision. Do we try to get to Exmouth by sea or, with Aidan's cousin's help, try driving there?'

'Let's ask him,' says Aidan. 'He'll know what's happening—and don't forget, they blocked the roads round Broome. If they've done that here we won't have a choice.'

'Ring him, please Ade. But keep it as short and information-free as possible.'

Something's been puzzling me and I say, 'Those transponders I destroyed. They weren't put on board by Zukowski, they were sealed on the tickets of everyone who went to the gala. Don't you think that's odd?'

'The seals came from the Ministry of Monitoring Partygoers,' says Jessie. 'And the tracker cards were from the Ministry of Randomly Waving Guns. Bloody snoopers just can't stop themselves. But lucky for us they're bozos and not very good at pulling the threads together.'

'Let's hope they stay bozos forever then,' says Aidan, tapping numbers into a phone. 'Hey, Dreads, bro! How're you going? It's me. Yeah. Smoko Jetty, six-thirty? See ya.'

In the evening light the scene ahead of us is illuminated like a stage. Slowly we pass an enormous maze of buildings and pipes outlined with light, fires roaring and writhing from the tops of three tall chimneys. Two massive domed vessels are moored along a brilliantly-lit wharf.

'There it is, shipmates,' says Aidan. 'Natural gas plant.'

'In the Environment department,' says Simon, checking the compass, 'we did a safety study for that place, they wanted to expand it. Found it was a model of good practice, fire-fighting facilities, training, the lot. Full marks. But one of my colleagues decided to work out what would happen if it blew up, by accident or deliberate attack.'

'I expect it wasn't good news for the peninsula,' says Jessie, sitting on the deck, leaning against Matthew, her computer open on her lap.

'Peninsula? Try state. Or Indian Ocean,' says Simon. 'Plenty of variables of course, but even with the lesser amounts of inflammables back then it'd also set off the fertilizer and explosives plants.'

Fertilizer and *explosives* plants?' says Jessie.

'Lots of big bangs per buck around here,' says Matthew.

'Well, the outcome was Hiroshima-scale explosions, as well as serious pollution,' says Simon. 'But that wasn't the worst of it. Depending on things like soil instability, direction, intensity of blast, it could potentially generate a tsunami.'

'But wouldn't shock waves just disappear into the ocean?' asks Aidan.

'No, they can travel great distances in water,' says Matthew. 'Remember the 2004 tsunami? Crossed the Bay of Bengal in barely a ripple, then when it hit land—waves of twenty-five, thirty metres.'

'So what sort of waves could an explosion from here

generate?' says Jess.

'Potentially massive,' says Simon.

'What happened when your mate reported that?' asks Aidan.

'What do you think happened? Lost his job in a hurry and the plant got permission to expand,' says Simon.

The sun sets and the evening passes quickly into night. Lights glitter from small boats and great ships, from metal and moorings and shorelines, while red and green beacons blink on and off along the shipping channels.

We pass tanks and jetties and cranes, and approach a large wharf where two bulk carriers are being loaded with iron ore from rumbling conveyor belts.

'So if a tsunami did start off here,' says Aidan, 'where would it hit?'

Jess brings up a map on her computer. 'Um, Indonesia first, then Sri Lanka and southern India,' she says. 'And the Maldives, Diego Garcia—'

'Those islands are barely metres above sea level,' says Matthew. 'They were lucky in 2004 but they'd have trouble coping with anything worse.'

'Diego Garcia?' asks Aidan. 'Isn't that where there's a big American base?'

'Yes. The one they used for bombing Iraq and Afghanistan,' says Matthew, his face troubled. 'And torturing the people they kidnapped.'

'What?' I say, horrified.

'You've heard of *rendition*, love?' asks Simon gently. 'That's what it really means. A lot of seemingly normal folk out there think Orwell's *1984* is an instruction manual.'

'Used to be you could tell who were the baddies 'cause they were the torturers,' says Aidan gloomily.

'Your info's a bit out of date, dudes,' Jessie says. 'The Yanks have recently withdrawn from Diego Garcia. They've been renting it from the Brits since the sixties, but now they've closed it down.'

'Why did they leave?' I ask.

She taps, then is silent for a moment, reading. 'They've been stalling for ages, but the place was about to be investigated for human rights abuses—torture, disappearances, murder. So they did a runner.'

'But who'd give them a base now?' asks Matthew. 'They've alienated most of Asia and the Mideast.'

'Everything's been shifted temporarily to the Philippines but that's costing big money,' says Jess. 'No one knows where they'll go.'

Aidan laughs and says cynically. 'I do.'

We look at him in surprise.

He holds out his hands and shrugs. 'Where else, shipmates? The country they've just stolen. The Dampier Peninsula.'

We're stunned into a long silence.

'Of *course*,' I say slowly. 'It was probably never about the hafnium, that was just insurance for the future. The bombing of the plant was the main game, a ploy to take over the region for a new base.'

'But surely they'd be in danger from the caesium contamination?' asks Simon.

'Perhaps not.' I shrug. 'Thinking about it, the peninsula's pretty big—possible to fence the worst-hit areas off. And the threat of radiation itself means no one else will go near the place. They'll be left alone to do whatever they like with it.'

The infrastructure around us is lit up with raw orange light. We pass the conveyor-belt wharf and turn into a bay where a scattering of work boats and tugs are moored. Aidan stands at the bow and directs Simon at the helm. We sail between the wharf and the dark bulk of what the chart calls Tidepole Island, and slowly approach the shore.

Further down the bay I can see the modest streetlights of Dampier. It's a small, no-frills town, Aidan tells me, built in the sixties for iron ore exports from the open-cut mines. This is where he grew up, his dad a wharfie at the port.

We approach a small jetty where Aidan jumps out and fastens a line from the boat. A tall man in overalls with a magnificent head of dreadlocks comes to meet him, and they hug and talk for a time then climb aboard. Aidan introduces us all then says to Dreads, 'Tell them what you told me.'

'Was just saying the cops've put roadblocks everywhere, no one knows why,' Dreads says shyly. 'Just checking IDs. The truckies are pissed-off big time, hate hold-ups. Anyway. All roads out to the highway are blocked.'

We look at each other without speaking. So we can't get away from here by car: *Sparrow* is still our only means of escape. In a way I'm relieved—for all the frightening times we've faced, the lugger is the centre of our small happy world and I'd hate to leave her behind.

Dreads is an operator for a harbour refuelling barge, so he returns to shore and a little while later his barge motors alongside us. We don't want to use our traceable credit cards to pay for fuel but Jess does some anonymous transaction straight into his bank account and all is well.

I keep checking the computer for *Jameson*'s location, then staring out to sea. The grey icon of the warship is only a few kilometres away on the screen but it's impossible to work out which of the moving lights on the harbour it might be.

'It's close to the port wharf now—could be going to tie up

there,' says Aidan. We watch in silence as the icon doesn't stop.

'It seems to be coming straight towards us,' I say, a knot of terror in my gut.

'Cyclone buoys're just over there.' Dreads points back along the way we came. 'Naval vessels use them sometimes.'

Filling the tanks seems to be taking forever. On the computer the grey icon moves closer. I stare back along the approaches. Why can't I see it? Surely it'd be obvious, it's less than a kilometre away! Then I realise I'm looking for the wrong thing.

Jameson isn't lit up like the other vessels: it's an absence, a great gliding darkness, blotting out the distant lights and their lovely reflections, as if deliberately turning them off one by one. I see a vast shadow coming closer and closer, and I'm surprised at how quiet it is.

With a whirl of backwash it slowly turns and halts, the bow pointing towards the wharf. Light suddenly floods the deck and figures move about, tying up to a large buoy.

Fuel is still quietly pumping from the barge. Simon puts his arm around me and I stare at the warship in horror, looming like a predator just a few hundred metres away in the glittering sea.

We're trapped beside the small jetty.

Agonising time passes. I'm waiting for the armed, shouting men, the inflatables to roar towards us, but nothing happens. Dark figures keep moving about quietly on *Jameson*.

The brilliance from the ship glows deep in the water, extending perhaps fifty metres on each side, and Simon murmurs, 'I'm not sure they can see very well outside the range of their lights. How much longer, Dreads?'

'Ten minutes'll do it, mate,' he replies. Dreads and Simon stay on deck but the rest of us go below and wait as time ticks slowly by. Finally we hear the sounds of the pump stopping, the clunk of the nozzle being removed, the equipment being closed up and locked.

The barge quietly motors away, then about ten minutes later Dreads returns on foot with a shopping bag full of fresh bread, milk and fruit for us. We gratefully thank him, then he wishes us well and leaves. We make a pot of tea and some sandwiches and sit silently in the galley.

'We'll have to try to slip away while it's dark,' says Simon. 'But if we pass between *Jameson* and the loading wharf we'll be lit up by the port lights. In any case, the wharf's surrounded by an exclusion zone and we don't want to set off a security alert.'

'So we'll have to navigate between the ship and Tidepole island,' says Matthew, pointing at the chart. 'A lot darker there and it looks like a fairly broad passage.'

'No,' says Aidan. 'There's a reef running out from Tidepole.'

'So how close to *Jameson*'s stern will we need to sail?' asks Jessie.

Simon checks the chart. 'Within, oh, thirty or forty metres I reckon. Too bloody close.' He rubs his chin. 'High water's at three a.m. so that'll give us the best odds. And with luck no one on the ship will be too alert at that time of night.'

We sit aimlessly in the galley, then Jessie brings up a news broadcast on her computer showing an interview with an apparently furious state premier.

'Would you call that foaming at the mouth?' Aidan asks.

'Cranky, for sure,' says Simon. 'What's it about?'

Jess turns up the volume.

'This state has had *enough*,' the premier roars. 'Where was the Commonwealth when terrorists were nuking our technology of tomorrow? We've known for a long time Canberra's no friend to this state! Tree-hugging, loser-loving Canberra!'

'Just in case the subtlety's zipped right over your heads, fellas,' says Aidan, 'loser means Aboriginal.'

'Look at his complexion,' says Jess. 'Heart attack city. He really needs to relax.'

'I tell you this,' says the premier ominously. '*One* more insult to our territorial integrity and Western Australia will go it *alone*. And, I promise you, we'll be be a lot better off without being sucked dry by those vampires on the east coast!'

'What?' I can't believe what I'm hearing.

'Secessionists, Lena, remember?' says Matthew. 'I imagine if they called a vote in Parliament today they'd declare independence.'

'You know who one of the prime movers is?' Simon asks me. I shake my head.

'The mining magnate, Alf Berg. Iceberg's father and her biggest backer.'

'Nasty piece of work, too,' says Matthew. 'Rich beyond fantasy, but if they gave him the cash he'd sell his own mother for medical experiments.' He stands up. 'Coming on watch, Jesso? The rest of you get some sleep while you can.'

19. A Green Gully

I toss and turn until it's two-thirty and time to get up. The air is cool and I pull on a beanie to keep my ears warm. We quietly prepare the lugger to leave. We can see one or two men on *Jameson*'s deck but they don't appear to be watching us.

Simon starts the engine on low revs. We manoeuvre away from the jetty and head towards the gap between the warship's stern and the dark island. Aidan and I are standing at the bow watching for obstacles.

As we come closer and closer to the ship we simply can't avoid the edge of the circle of floodlights. I see silvery fish glinting and swirling deep in the water below.

I've never felt so naked.

As we get closer I see the mounted guns in the pods on either side of the stern. With a shiver I remember the night of the cyclone when they were pointing directly at us.

I can't stop myself looking irresistibly upwards as we pass. My heart thuds in terror as I see the pale face of a man standing beside one of the guns smoking a cigarette. He looks down.

We stare at each other.

It's Max.

He slowly raises one hand to me and in some strange reflex I wave in return. In a few moments the lugger has passed beyond and out of the light into the dimness ahead.

Oh, no! I'm shaking with horror.

My shoulders clench as I wait for the yells of recognition, and I stumble to the tiller to tell Simon. He comforts me and I become calmer.

Slowly I realise all I can hear is our engine puttering quietly, the soft rumble of the conveyor belt, the gulls mewling along the waterfront. Everything behind us is peaceful.

We keep gliding into the night, away from Dampier. Away from *Jameson.*

'Maxie didn't rat on us?' asks Jessie, surprised. 'Not like him to be helpful.'

I shrug, puzzled. 'Perhaps he didn't see me as clearly as I saw him. I had a beanie on so perhaps he didn't recognise me— thought I was just some random sailor.'

'He would've seen the big white *Sparrow* written on our bow,' says Simon wryly. 'Hard to miss that.'

'Yes he could,' says Matthew. 'While you were all asleep earlier we painted out the name.'

'On both sides too. At great risk to life and limb,' says Jess.

Simon shakes his head in admiration. 'Bloody good idea, you guys. Looks like we got away with it too.'

He takes out one of the charts and sets it on the table. 'Okay. I think we'll go north for a bit now, around Malus and Rosemary Islands, then head south-west for Exmouth. Matthew and Jess, you go and get some rest.' He looks at me and says, 'You too, love. Aidan and I'll keep us going.'

I fall asleep almost immediately but wake up a couple of hours later. I can see it's daytime outside now—light is beaming through the hatch. I roll over, ready to drift away again, then realise something is different. The familiar steady throb of the engine is absent and the lugger is swaying gently.

Matthew and Jess are still fast asleep. I get up, wash quickly and climb to the deck to find a brilliant blue-gold day all around us. To port I see a low island and a beach with a rocky platform at one end. Simon and Aidan have raised the sails and we're heading towards the sand.

'What's happened?' I ask.

'Looks like some floating rope got tangled in the propeller and burnt out part of the gearbox,' says Simon. 'Aidan snorkelled down but couldn't get it untangled. We'll have to beach to fix it properly.'

'But if you beach us won't we tip over?'

'No, these old luggers have shallow draughts, they can go aground safely.'

The tide is high and we float ashore as far as possible until the boat reaches the sand. Matthew and Jessie are awake now too so we set anchors and improvised sandbags to keep *Sparrow* balanced upright as the tide recedes.

We have breakfast, then Simon says, 'Can't do anything till the tide's out and we can reach the propeller. Why don't you all go for a walk up the beach? I've heard the fish here practically jump into your hands if you ask them nicely.'

'Too right,' says Aidan. 'Those rocks are deadly fishing. We can get lunch.'

I stay seated while the others gather hats and fishing gear.

Matthew says, 'Aren't you coming, Lena?'

'No. I don't like to see my food while it's still alive. You go, I'll stay here and chat to Simon.'

When they're a distance away, Simon and I look at each other grinning. We race along the deck and down to the sleeping area and start throwing off our clothes. We fall onto the big bed, laughing, and I breathe his lovely leathery scent.

How good it is to think of nothing but the delights of touch, of smoothness and roughness and shifting muscle, the warmth and weight and yearning of it.

I am open, I am known. Pleasure billows through me then softens to sweet animal shivers.

As we curl together, Simon says sleepily, 'Remember the night of the blue boat, when you told me to strip off and not mess around? I should have realised right then you were the woman for me.'

We doze for an hour or so then wake and nuzzle gently. Simon murmurs, 'I'm so sorry you've been caught up in all this, love. These are nasty bastards chasing us and I'm afraid we're way out of our depth.'

I nod slowly against his neck. 'I'd rather we weren't caught up in it too, but if I had to be anywhere I'm glad it's with you.' After a moment I say, puzzled, 'But you know, I don't understand why they're still after us. We're *irrelevant*—we put our evidence out for the world to see and Zukowski brushed it away like a mosquito.'

Simon shifts onto his side to look at me. 'Surprises me too. And when *Jameson* came into Dampier the crew didn't seem in much of a hurry. And they haven't done any more aggressive press releases about Operation Sparrow either. Maybe they're not after us now for some reason.'

'Bigger fish to fry?'

'I wonder. Remember Aidan joking they could simply be sailing in the same direction as us? Perhaps they are.'

'Oh, I hope so, sweet man.'

'Speaking of fish, I think the kids have come back.'

We hear the clanging of pots and pans in the galley. We dress and join the others.

'Good chat, then?' asks Aidan, grinning.

'Excellent,' says Simon. 'Good fishing, then?'

'The best,' says Matthew, deftly slicing silvery shapes apart. 'Jessie's a natural. Caught the biggest one.'

'I didn't think I'd like it, Lena,' says Jess, heating the frypan. 'But it is rather fun. And we saw sharks too, and so many sting-rays. Not the sort of place I'd want to go swimming.'

Aidan nods. 'Yeah, these waters are swarming with life. And most of it has razor-sharp teeth and really bad manners.'

Matthew drops fillets into the frypan and as they cook they smell wonderful. We chop up some salad then sit on deck and have a feast.

By early afternoon the tide is out and Simon and Matthew get busy with knives freeing the entangled propeller. It takes time but they finally succeed, then come aboard again.

'Matty and I'll strip down the gearbox now and check out the damage,' says Simon.

'I'll help too,' says Jess. 'I like gears, such nice logic.'

'While you're all having fun being grease-monkeys, the ambo and the academic'll go for a wander,' says Aidan. 'Got some rocks to look at.'

That sounds good to me, so we put on sunscreen and grab our hats and water bottles and a couple of apples, and leave the others chatting contentedly over some unbeautiful piece of machinery.

Before we left Aidan advised me to put on jeans and shoes and I'm glad I did—the innocent-looking grass is painfully spiky. We climb a low hill then clamber down into a valley littered with tumbled swathes of dark red rock. Aidan shows me some carvings there, the stone pecked away to paler layers with raised dark outlines.

Kangaroos and emus are easy to recognise but others are puzzling, as if they show something that hovers on the edge of recognition but can't quite be named. There are eerie staring faces too, and long dancing bodies and patterns of lines and dots, complex and mesmerising.

'They're just *beautiful*,' I say.

Aidan smiles. 'Picasso said Aboriginal art was what he'd been trying to do all his life, so it must be pretty cool.'

Ahead of us is another long hill which looks like the highest point on the island. We come to a point where the way separates into two gullies lined with rocks.

We sit down under a small shady tree to have a drink of water. Aidan looks around, the light glinting on his earring, and says, 'I used to come here as a kid, it's a powerful place. I was lucky—my dad knew an old man who taught me a little.'

'Are there many Indigenous people from round here?' I ask.

'No. Dad's own country was coastal, further south. From Murujuga itself? No one's left. They were all murdered.'

'*Murdered*? When?'

'Eighteen-sixties, Flying Foam Massacre. An expedition to 'punish' any black man, woman or child they could find, for a crime someone else had actually committed. The only thing those poor bastards were guilty of was being alive and in the way of the pastoralists.'

'And they were *all* killed?' I ask in disbelief.

'Yeah. The only mobs left round here are from the mainland. Doing their best to look after Murujuga, but since they're not direct descendants they can't legally get native title.'

I sit silently for a time, shocked.

Aidan sighs. 'Hey, Lena. All in the past in our modern

multicultural paradise.'

I want to weep. 'How do you bear it, Aidan?'

'I think the worst bit is that it just never bloody ends,' he says quietly. 'Stealing country. Destroying culture. Hating people who've lost everything.' He laughs shortly. 'Fuck. Hating people *because* they've lost everything.'

'A shrink once told me that when someone's done a wrong to somebody else, they often keep doing it over and over, simply to justify themselves. Or else they'd have to admit to the initial wrong.'

'Yeah. Sounds like White and Aboriginal relations in a nutshell.' He smiles wryly at me and gets to his feet. 'Come on. I've got a game for you.'

'A game?' I stand.

'Yeah. Go over there and choose which gully we should climb to get to the top of this hill.'

I wander over to where the path separates. Both gullies look the same, the stepped rocks similar sizes, both easy enough climbs.

'I don't know. Maybe this one.' I point to the left.

'Give it a go,' Aidan says.

'Why?'

'Go on.'

It looks straightforward enough. I take a few steps up, a few steps more, then stop, confused. The rocks now look treacherous, unstable, sharp-edged. The path seems steep and unfriendly too, almost dangerous. I clamber back down, then gaze at the rocks, puzzled: they look benign once more.

I set off again. After several steps upwards the same thing happens—the way ahead looks too threatening to proceed. I try a third time, a slightly different path, and it's almost terrifying. Confused, I make my way back to Aidan.

'Okay,' he says. 'Try the other one now.'

I shrug and start up the second gully. It's surprisingly easy and I smile at myself for imagining the two paths were even remotely the same. These rocks are nicely stepped, almost welcoming, and I reach the top in just a few minutes.

I look back and see Aidan is climbing the other path as easily as I climbed this one. I walk over to meet him. 'What on earth was that all about?'

'The gully you climbed is a women's place,' he says. 'I would have felt terrible if I'd used it. The way I came is for men. That's why you felt so unwelcome when you tried it.'

'That's—oh, *come* on, Aidan. I don't believe—' I stop.

'Doesn't matter if you believe or not. What did you feel?'

After a moment I say quietly, 'Something.'

'Remember when I said you don't have to come from country to belong to it? You've just got to love and respect it?'

I nod.

He slowly smiles. 'Welcome to country, cuz.'

We wander along the hill and Aidan shows me some more hidden carvings, eerie and beautiful.

'Should you be letting me see these—uninitiated woman and all?' I tease.

'You reckon these are the powerful ones? Dream on. They'd be too much for you to handle.'

'A bunch of rocks? Really?'

'Yeah. This isn't a joke, Lena.'

I feel abashed. 'I'm sorry, stupid thing to say, Aidan. I'd never want to hurt your feelings.'

'Hey, I know that. Family, after all.'

We sit down in the shade of a small tree and eat our apples.

'Are your parents still in Dampier?' I ask.

'Dad died,' he says quietly. 'On the wharves all his life, but it was a stupid heart attack got him in the end. Mum was pretty shattered, but a few years later married a nice fella from Derby and lives up there now. She's okay. What about you?'

'Parents divorced a long time ago. Mum's with a lovely man and they're Sea Rovers over in Queensland. Dad had a pretty rough time after Vietnam but he's mellowed now, and happy with Jessie's mum. It all worked out in the end.'

Aidan nods. 'Yeah, funny, how it seems to.' He stands up. 'Okay, time's getting on. Let's go back the other way, one last place I want to show you. I reckon you'll like it.'

We walk along the hill towards the sun, now lower in the sky. Aidan leads me down one side of the ridge until we're just above a shady green gully. I can see light sparkling here and there from rainwater collected in stone hollows.

'Go down and find a place to sit and be patient,' Aidan says. 'There's some carvings you'll like but you'll have to listen.'

'Listen?' I say doubtfully.

He grins. 'Well, pay attention. No *assumptions*, Lena. And keep an eye out for animals.'

'Small, friendly, non-venomous animals, I hope.'

Pushing my way down between the bushes I emerge into a space that surrounds me. I lean over a stone hollow and wash my dusty face and arms with cool water, and it feels oddly as if I'm preparing for a ceremony.

Looking around I wonder where I should sit, then see a shady flat boulder, a heap of carved rocks lying before it. It's comfortable, and despite the solitude I feel surprisingly safe.

After a time I stop thinking about anything much. I realise I'm profoundly relaxed, sinking, the way I felt on the jetty in Broome. I gaze peacefully at the rock carvings in front of me—

two sinuous dancing women, one on each side of an enigmatic, curved, diamond shape.

I can't stop my eyes following its lines over and over, up a curled fin-like arm, down a pointed sort-of leg. The dancing women have tassels swinging from their waists and they're nursing babies at their breasts.

My own breasts tingle in sympathy, and I wonder what it would have been like to have known such a thing in my life, to have nursed a child. The breakup with Max ended so many hopes. I sigh and feel an old familiar pain in my chest.

Yet still I feel a strange sense-memory of mothering, of holding a child—what *is* that? Of course I'd cuddled Jessie as a baby but this is quite different.

Then I remember Irina.

I wasn't part of the medical staff on the aid project to the Chernobyl children, I was collecting data on their thyroid cancers. But somehow I ended up helping on the wards too as there weren't enough hands to go around.

Seven-year-old Irina had steady brown eyes and a shy smile. Her father had been one of the many brave men who'd battled the burning Chernobyl reactor and died in agony soon afterwards. Irina's mother worked in a factory so she couldn't be there during the day, but she slept on the floor beside her bed at night.

Irina was a brave, bright child, easily my favourite. She taught me to count to ten in Ukrainian and would giggle in delight at my dreadful accent.

When she had her operation she seemed to recover well, but the following morning her temperature spiked and within hours she was gravely ill. The doctors gave her antibiotics but her immune system slowly failed.

No-one could find her mother. I held her small body against

me for hours as she drifted in and out of consciousness, desperately wishing I could share my own life-force with her. Her mother arrived, thank God, just before she died.

My arms, my breasts, my core, tingled with the sense of the child's reality for days. I couldn't believe she was gone.

But here, now, I feel Irina again.

Tears roll down my cheeks.

Time passes. Slowly I become aware there is something like a presence behind me, a vast, gentle, inhuman presence that is *breathing* in the still air. It has the shape of the carving before me. It's not Irina, it's not anything I can possibly conceive of, but I feel no fear at all.

Then a small brown animal wriggles from between the rocks and stops, gazing at me with large, intelligent eyes. It has white patches, a scruffy tail and a pointed nose, something like a mouse crossed with a spotted cat. It would fit neatly into the palms of my two hands.

The mouse-cat lifts a long paw and strokes an ear and I see a pouch: it's a female, a wary mother creature. She looks at me with liquid eyes for a long moment then turns and dashes away into the rocks.

Slowly understanding comes to me. I *had* nursed a child. I'd nurtured Irina when she needed it most, when her own mother could not. I'd known what it was to be a mother. I wipe my face and whisper *yes*. The ache in my chest eases, gently and unexpectedly.

I realise the great gentle presence behind me is changing now, it's somehow less vast, less inhuman. Absurdly (given the circumstances) it seems almost ordinary, kind, even familiar. Like the carvings I saw earlier it hovers on the edge of recognition, but in the end I have no name for it.

Curious, I turn around to see what is breathing behind me.

I'm only faintly surprised to find there is nothing and no one there.

Now all I can hear are soft bird-calls and leaves rustling in the tree-tops. With gratitude, I lean forward and lightly trace my fingers along the carved lines, the enigmatic presence.

It feels like the right time to go. I murmur goodbye, as if farewelling friends, and leave the way I came. I am almost dizzy with peace.

Aidan is waiting for me further along the ridge. When I get to him I say, 'I saw a spotted mouse-cat.'

'Sounds like a quoll, a northern quoll.' He gazes at me. 'Yeah, suits you. Did you know the females always raise their young alone?'

'It was a place of mothers I think. It helped me—come to terms with something.' I put my hand on his arm. 'Aidan, I heard something *breathing*.'

'Yeah?'

'Behind me. A ... presence, like one of the carvings. And then the quoll came out to watch me.'

'Perhaps the quoll is your dreaming.'

I shake my head, confused. 'But what does that even *mean*?'

He looks away, searching for words, then turns back. 'It's like the energies of the earth, the powers of every rock and plant and animal—they're really *strong*, Lena, sometimes too much to bear alone. Everyone needs a guide to trust, to protect them, to be the thing that *they* protect.' He shrugs helplessly. 'A still point, a focus, a connection ...'

'A dreaming. Oh, cuz. What a day.'

We wander peacefully along the ridge of the hill towards the setting sun. Gradually a wide white beach between rocky platforms comes into view.

'Great camping spot down there,' says Aidan. 'But where *Sparrow*'s stranded we're not supposed to stay overnight, it's a protected area. I wonder how that engine's going?'

'Guess we'd better get back,' I say. 'Feels like we've been away for days.'

Below us there are a few tents pitched on the beach and a scattering of vessels in the bay. One, a distance from the shore, catches my eye and I point.

'Isn't that the Sea Rovers boat from Broome? Remember the soldiers taking the crew away?'

Aidan gazes, frowning against the sunlight. 'No,' he says slowly. 'That one was smaller. But—I can't see properly—it looks sort of familiar ...'

The boat is painted blue with a Sea Rovers sun logo on its high pointed bow. It has a single mast and a long cabin towards the stern.

Recognition hits me like a blow and I sink to my knees, my serenity shattered. I grab Aidan's arm and pull him with me, saying hoarsely, 'Get *down*.'

We stare at the bay, making ourselves as small as possible.

'It can't be,' says Aidan, shaking his head. 'Oh fuck, it *is*.'

'We've got to tell the others,' I whisper, as if afraid of being overheard.

'I know a fast way back, come on!'

We keep low until we're out of sight, then turn and run.

20. Return of the Blue Boat

As we race down the hill towards the lugger, leaping over rocks and small bushes, I can see the others still working on the dismembered gearbox.

Aidan and I clamber up the short ladder to the deck.

'Hey ... fellas ...' he says, trying to catch his breath.

'What's happened?' Simon asks me as I'm bent over, gasping, hands on my knees.

'In the next bay ... the boat!' I manage.

'Boat?' asks Matthew.

'The blue boat. The *contaminated* boat!' I gasp. 'Moored in the bay over there and they've painted the Sea Rovers logo on it!'

'Who has?' says Jessie.

'Who knows? But it's *there*, it wasn't blown up like Zukowski said and now it's pretending to be a *Rovers* vessel!'

'Are you all right?' asks Simon, holding my shoulders.

I nod and straighten up, breathing heavily, in shock.

'Come on, sit down,' he says. 'Have some water. Tell us exactly what you saw.'

I rest on the deckhouse and gulp a few mouthful, then pass the bottle to Aidan, who takes it gratefully as he sits beside me.

'Nothing else to tell. But that dreadful boat is *here*,' I say, bewildered. 'How?'

Aidan says, 'It's anchored a fair way out. I didn't see anyone on board—did you?'

I shake my head. 'The gearbox—is it all right now?'

'Almost there, but we won't catch the high tide this evening,' says Simon. 'The next high is around midnight.'

'Oh, *no*. I want us to get away as soon as we can.'

'Yesterday we sailed right past that bay,' says Aidan, 'but we were wrestling with the propeller and getting the sails up. I don't remember even looking.'

'No, nor me,' says Simon. 'So we can't be sure if it was there then, or if it's just arrived. But look, we'd better check it out before dark. If lights come on then at least we'll know if someone's on board.'

'Or if there's just more dead people,' says Jess darkly. 'You go, I'm busy. I'm sick of being chased around by these gun-toting zombies. I want to find out what they're saying to each other.'

'You're going to break into a military network, Jess?' I ask.

'I can't. But I know someone who can—a genius called Roxy. She's amazing, but just too feral even for my esteemed employers. She's the only geek I know who could break in without screwing up. Guys as talented as that usually want to piss on something to prove they were there.'

Matthew nods. 'Sounds about right.'

'Okay,' says Simon. 'I'll get some torches. Do you want to stay here?' he asks me.

'No, I'll come with you and have another look. Maybe we got it wrong. I hope we did.'

The sun is setting now. The four of us go, leaving Jess still working away on the lugger. I feel a little anxious about leaving her by herself but she seems happy enough. We quickly get back to a good vantage point above the bay and watch the boat, keeping well down.

'The evening you and Simon were on the blue boat I had plenty of time to check it out,' says Aidan. 'I reckon it's the same one.'

'I agree,' says Matthew. 'Remember it well.'

'Really?' I ask.

'Every vessel's as different as a human face, love,' says Simon. 'That's it, for sure.'

'Then how come it's a Sea Rovers boat now?'

'It was already painted blue,' says Matthew. 'All someone had to do was put the sun logo on it and tidy the deck, and it's no longer an Asian fishing vessel, it's an ordinary old Rovers boat. Pretty clever.'

'But why tell us they blew it up when they obviously didn't?' asks Simon slowly.

'And why the hell is it *here*?' I say.

Lights suddenly appear on the blue boat. A figure comes on deck and moves around then returns to the cabin. We watch for a time and nothing more happens. It's almost dark now and mosquitoes are humming all around us.

'Let's get back to the lugger,' says Simon, and we retrace our steps carefully in the torchlight.

Jess is still seated at the galley table, working. Aidan and I make a light meal and we all eat quickly, not saying much. Simon fills the coffee pot. 'Going to be a long night,' he says.

Jess stops typing and looks up. 'Okay, Roxy'll have a look at *Jameson*'s network for us. She's bored with cracking the NSA, she says there's never anything cool. It's all selfies, even when they're spying on heads of state. In fact especially then.'

'Sounds perfect for the job,' says Simon. 'Meanwhile can we use the table for putting the gearbox back together? That's got the best light.'

Jess finds a corner of the floor and keeps working. Aidan

goes on deck and I sit on the stairs with a cup of tea warming my hands. Absently I watch Matthew and Simon's heads bent over the machinery.

As they adjust bits and pieces and fit them back together I smile at their family resemblance, Simon's wavy grey hair and Matthew's brown curls, their strong shoulders and long hands, their quick grins as they murmur to each other.

Then I mull over this very strange day, especially what happened in the small green valley. Perhaps it was sun-stroke? Yet I had a hat on and was in the shade. But that strange half-familiar presence—what on earth could it have been? I heard it *breathing*, clearly, unmistakably, breathing.

None of it made any sense.

I sigh. But of course it did: in the light of my past and my regrets and experiences, it made perfect sense. I recall the liquid eyes of the quoll, and suddenly the idea of that small spotted creature pleases me absurdly.

I scold myself, don't be silly, you're a scientist.

Then I think contentedly, yes, but perhaps that was my very own dreaming. I argue back and forth for a few more cycles, and just become more and more confused.

Then Simon looks up with satisfaction and says, 'Right, that ought to do it. We'll just put the gearbox back on the engine and test it and then we can sit down and think about everything else.'

After ten minutes of grunting and cursing and testing noises from the engine room, Simon and Matthew emerge triumphant. We gather in the galley again.

'Where's *Jameson*, Jess?' asks Simon. 'Still at Dampier I hope.'

'It was a while ago,' Jessie says. 'I'll check.'

She brings up the page with all the ship icons.

'There we are,' Matthew says. 'Good old *Montes Mermaid*.'

'Hey, I reckon we should disappear for a while,' says Aidan. 'We're not supposed to be on this part of the island at night and we don't want a Fisheries inspector coming by.'

'Good call, Ade,' says Simon. 'Can you turn your fake transponder off, Jessie?'

She taps at her wrist. 'Done.' Our little icon disappears.

Matthew points at the map of the nearby bay, where there's a small unknown-vessel icon, and says, 'Must be the blue boat.'

'But *Jameson*—?' says Aidan.

Jessie zooms in on Dampier and searches around for the ship's large icon, without success.

'Come out a bit, Jess,' says Simon.

She does so, then says, 'Oh, fuck.'

Aidan puts his face in his hands.

I stare at the screen. The warship isn't at Dampier. It's about twelve kilometres away, on the far side of the island, and it's heading in our direction.

A faint hope hits me. 'But what if it's not coming after us? What if it's going to the blue boat instead?'

'By the time we know *that* it'll be too bloody late,' says Aidan.

'And the tide's on the way out,' says Matthew quietly. 'We can't launch the lugger for hours yet.'

Simon rubs his eyes with the heels of his hands and sighs.

We silently watch the digital *Jameson* coming closer.

'No.' Simon suddenly stands. 'I'm not going to sit here waiting. Let's get in the tinny and go round to the bay. We can hide and watch *Jameson* arrive. It'll either stop at the blue boat, or come here, or just keep going. One way or the other we'll know. And if it's us they're after, then at least we won't be trapped.'

The blue boat scares me: I'll never forget what happened last time I went near it. 'I'll take my dosimeter,' I say, and get the tiny device out of my bag and put it in my pocket.

'Is that like a Geiger counter?' asks Aidan.

'Sort of.'

'Good.'

Simon hands out torches and Jessie puts her pink-orange device in a waterproof pack, then we climb into the tinny. It takes about ten minutes to motor from our part of the island around to a large rocky platform lying at one end of the beach.

Ashore, lights are glowing from the tents and a barbecue is lit up, while three yachts are anchored in the bay. The blue boat is a long way further out, perhaps five hundred metres away from us.

Simon guides the tinny so we're sheltered from view behind the rocks and puts out a small grapple. The water is almost still. We wait.

A soft light glows from Jessie's computer as she checks on *Jameson*'s progress. 'About nine kilometres now,' she says. 'Maybe fifteen minutes away.'

I lean into the comfort of Simon's arms and we watch the blue boat. Apart from red and green side-lights there's no indication anyone is on board. I can hear the soft lapping of wavelets and bursts of laughter from the people on the beach at the barbecue.

The air is warm and silky on my skin, the moon almost full, outlining everything in silver. 'Beautiful night,' I murmur. 'If we weren't being pursued by psychopaths it'd be perfect.'

Simon laughs then says, 'I keep wondering about that bloody boat. Why is it *here*?'

'They used it to orchestrate a disaster once before,' says Matthew. 'Perhaps that's the plan again.'

'Something to pin on the Sea Rovers?' says Aidan.

Jess lifts her head. 'Those creeps really like blowing things up. What were we saying earlier would make a great big bang?'

Aidan gasps. '*Jeez*, Jess. Don't even suggest it.'

'The gas and explosives plants?' I ask. 'They couldn't. Even they wouldn't.'

'And *why*, Jesso?' asks Matthew. 'What sense could there possibly be in that?'

She sighs. 'When the bozos wanted land for a new base they just stole it, with a bang so shocking they simply got away with it. Maybe they're after something else here, too.'

'Well, Iceberg and her father want the state to secede,' I say. 'What did the premier say? *Just one more insult to our territorial integrity* and—what?'

'They'll go it alone,' says Simon. 'But since their idea of going it alone is not to pay taxes I can't see it holding together for very long.'

'So Iceberg might want something shocking to happen as an excuse to secede,' I say. 'But what on earth could interest Zukowski here?'

'A tsunami?' says Jess.

Aidan shakes his head. 'Oh, Jess, come on, *no*.'

'I was looking at the places that'd be affected,' she says quietly. 'They're all on the shit list. Indonesia? Refused the US land for a base. India? Bought reactors from China. The Maldives? Keeps taking the US to court about rising sea levels.'

'And then there's Marao too,' says Simon slowly.

'Marao?' I ask.

'An island in the Maldives. Leased to the Chinese—massive installation, gives them access to the whole Indian Ocean, Africa, Mideast, Asia. Anything that could potentially damage Marao would make the Yanks pretty happy.'

'Those poor men on the blue boat looked Chinese,' I say. 'Perhaps Marao itself was going to be framed for the Worm Turning bombing. And all that fell in a heap when the men died and we discovered the boat.'

Jess sighs. 'Nice train of logic, but I don't much like where it's heading.'

'Well, here's another carriage for your train,' says Aidan, and sighs. 'Dreads told me on the quiet they've recently uncovered something pretty fatal at the gas plant: massive amounts of asbestos built into the infrastructure.'

'Isn't that illegal?' I ask.

'Wasn't in the old days, but it sure is now. It's a disaster,' says Aidan. 'Removing it would close the place down for years and cost the earth. Not removing it would close it down *forever*. But hey, if "terrorists" blew it up? Instant fix. It'd be insured, so the money'd still keep rolling in.'

'But—an explosion, a *tsunami*? That'd kill thousands, maybe millions of people,' says Matthew, horrified. 'No one in their right minds could justify that.'

'Didn't stop them justifying Worm Turning,' says Simon. '*Or* invading the Mideast, triggering the Endless War, and spreading carnage from Africa to Centrasia. People are just collateral damage, after all.'

'If governments were humans,' says Jess, 'they'd be locked away in high-security psych wards, never to be released.'

I sigh. 'So hypothetically some crazies might think an explosion around here would suit them. But we can't *assume—*'

Something flickers in my line of sight and I sit forward.

Out to sea a large shadow glides.

'Okay,' says Simon grimly. 'What now?'

Jameson comes closer, then slows and stops on the far side of the blue boat. Lights appear and we can see a man in silhouette on the boat, waving. An inflatable is lowered from a bay on the warship and speeds towards him.

The man climbs down into the inflatable, then it zooms back to *Jameson*. The lights disappear and we hear the purr of motors starting up.

In a primitive reflex we all shrink low, and Aidan says, 'Nobody here but us red rocks, you bastards.'

As *Jameson*'s shadow moves smoothly across our line of sight it's almost eerie how quiet the engines are. It doesn't turn towards us and it doesn't turn into the bay where *Sparrow* is grounded: it just keeps going.

'On the way to Perth it seems,' says Jess, consulting her computer. 'And good riddance.'

Simon turns and stares at the blue boat.

After a few moments he says, 'Lets swing past. I want to have a closer look.'

'Not too close,' I say. 'Who knows how well it's been decontaminated?' I get out my dosimeter, which fits neatly in the palm of my hand. 'I'll check as we approach.'

We motor slowly towards the blue boat, keeping an eye out for *Jameson* in case it returns.

'The hull's a bit low in the water,' says Simon.

'Something fairly heavy on board?' asks Matthew.

The bow points towards the departed warship, a ladder dangling down, just as on that dreadful evening ten days ago.

Only ten days since I so innocently climbed on board? More like a lifetime. I feel dazed and quickly check the dosimeter, but it shows only background radiation.

'Well, that's unusual,' says Matthew.

'Yes,' says Simon thoughtfully. He turns to the rest of us.

'New anchor at the bow, a modern engine-driven anchor that wasn't there before. Don't usually see that on old boats.'

He thinks for a moment. 'Now we're here I'd like to look the thing over.'

'Should you?' I ask anxiously.

'I want to know why Zukowski lied about sinking it, and I think we should try to figure out what he's planning now.'

'Well, you're not getting on this thing unless I check it for radiation,' I say more bravely than I feel. 'So I'm coming too.'

'And you're not leaving the rest of us behind this time,' says Matthew, tying the tinny to the boat. 'All for one and so on.'

We cautiously climb the ladder and move along the now-clean deck, shining our torches ahead. Simon and I glance at each other when we reach the place where we found that first dreadful corpse. I run the dosimeter along the timbers, the bulwark, the base of the mast.

'How are the readings?' he asks.

'Fine so far.'

I put the dosimeter where the caesium powder was spilling from the cylinder that night. The count rises but not to anywhere near dangerous levels.

'Okay here too. It seems to have been well decontaminated.'

'The cabin,' says Simon. We move down one side of the deck to the open section at the rear. He opens the cabin door and flashes his torch inside.

He glances back at me, surprised. 'That's a change.'

I shine my torch around. 'Certainly much improved by the absence of corpses.'

The previously decrepit cabin is now strikingly clean and tidy. A few dishes and mugs are stacked on a sink to the right beside a small fridge and a sleeping bag is folded along one wall. To the left, there's a table with benches on either side, and several neatly rolled charts on top.

'Looks like that guy on board was a caretaker,' I say.

Towards the front of the cabin a set of steps lead below. Simon and Matthew shine their torches on the steps then warily move downwards. My heart thumps and I wish they'd come back. I check the dosimeter again but it's fine.

Jess shines her torch around. 'Can't see any sensors. Doesn't mean they're not there.' She stands defiantly in the middle of the cabin. 'Hey, Colonel *Creepy*—testing one, two, three.'

'Don't joke, Jess,' whispers Aidan.

'Aidan,' I say, 'are you okay?'

'This boat. This is a *really* bad place, cuz. We should go.'

'In a minute. Sit down with me.'

I pull out a bench and take his hand. It's clammy and cold.

Aidan says, 'Not kidding, Lena. We've gotta get out of here.'

I call out, 'Simon, we should *go*. Who knows what traps—'

From below I hear, 'Okay, just a sec ...'

Then Matthew, '*Shit!*'

Their steps pelt upwards towards us, torch-beams flashing around, and Simon gasps, 'Engine room's locked, don't even have a pen-knife—'

'I do,' says Jess.

'Cables,' says Matthew. 'From the engine room to—'

'– the *bomb!*' yells Simon.

'What?'

'*Come on!*' He grabs my hand and pulls me to my feet.

Suddenly a motor beneath us starts up with a whir and we hear a distant clanking. We listen, stunned, then run out of the cabin.

The noise is coming from the bow and with our torch-beams waving wildly we move to the forward deck. Looking over the side we can see the dripping anchor rising out of the water.

Before anyone has time to react, one of its sharp flukes gets caught in the line to our tinny.

The line parts.

Another engine starts up with a roar and suddenly the boat is moving. We grab the railing and each other to avoid falling, then make our way back to the stern.

I stare aghast at the tinny bobbing in our wake: the now unreachable tinny. And then I see something moving out of the corner of my eye.

My scalp prickles in horror.

The steering wheel is rotating by itself in the moonlight.

21. The Tinny

The blue boat turns in a long, smooth sweep. After a few moments it's no longer facing the way *Jameson* went: it's heading back towards Dampier.

Simon shines his torch over the steering wheel and we see it's being controlled by a metal box. A cable comes out of it and disappears beneath the deck.

'Cut it?' asks Jessie.

Simon shakes his head slowly. 'No. I know these sorts of setups. Certainly booby-trapped.'

We move back into the cabin, shaken, and sit on the benches at the table.

'Jesso,' says Matthew. 'Where are we? Where's this thing heading?'

She gets out her computer. 'Um, just a sec.' Her voice is wobbly. 'Here, Parrot-man. We're off the end of the island, speed six knots, direction about a hundred degrees.'

'Okay,' Simon says slowly. 'Takes us towards Searipple Passage.'

I feel a rush of relief. 'Not the gas plant then.'

I can see the island disappearing behind us. A few moments later the note of the engine changes and I feel the boat turning.

'A hundred and five degrees—' says Jess, and a moment later, 'Oh. Hundred and ten.'

The turning continues.

'One-twenty.'

We're silently staring at the screen, at the innocent grey arrow and the changing numbers.

'One-thirty.'

Simon takes my hand.

'One-forty.'

The turn eases. The boat is now going directly ahead and our destination is obvious. We can see the writhing yellow flares on the horizon.

'How long before we're there?' whispers Aidan.

'Ah, six knots, eleven kilometres an hour,' says Matthew, swallowing. 'And the plant is perhaps thirteen kilometres away.'

'Seventy-odd minutes,' says Simon quietly.

I sit there in shock, my mind reeling. Truly? In a little over an hour this boat will deliver the bomb below to the vulnerable, volatile gas plant?

I shake my head. An explosion would obliterate people, animals, homes. Thousands, perhaps even millions, of beloved existences. How could this happen? I cannot *conceive* ...

The silence seems to last forever. Finally Jessie says, 'This is stupid. If the engine's going we should at least have some electrics.'

She finds a switch near the door and it's a relief when a warm golden light fills the cabin. We turn off the torches and look at each other. I see how tired we are, and how afraid.

Simon rubs his face hard and sighs. He puts his elbows on the table and rests his head in his hands. 'Okay, guys,' he says slowly. 'Options.'

'Bugger-all,' says Aidan.

Matthew simply shrugs in despair.

Jessie says, 'They must have sent a wireless signal to raise the anchors and get the engine going. It's under someone's control, probably someone on *Jameson*.'

'Any chance you could interrupt them?' asks Simon.

She shakes her head. 'Roxy might be able to, but she hasn't got back to me yet. Anyway, even if we could stop the boat I expect the bomb is primed to go off in—what did you say, Simon—seventy-odd minutes?'

He nods. 'And it'll definitely be hard-wired to prevent any electronic tampering.'

'We could ring the plant on shore,' I say. 'Warn them at least.'

'With what?' asks Aidan. 'We left the phones on the lugger.'

'The comcuffs. Simon, what do you think?'

'Worth a try. But the number—'

Aidan reels it off. 'Used to ring there all the time,' he says.

I tap the tiny buttons on the cuff. 'Oh hell, I've forgotten how to get it off my arm. Jessie?'

But she's busy on the computer so Simon laughs briefly and says, 'Give us your wrist, love.'

'I'd like the plant safety officer,' he says, holding my hand and talking into my wrist. 'Off duty? Well, who's in charge tonight? Yes, please put me through to Boffo.'

'Don't think I know Boffo,' says Aidan thoughtfully.

'Yes? Hey, Boffo. This is an emergency. Please listen. I'm in a boat I can't control, can't change speed or direction. It's got a bomb aboard and it's heading for the gas plant. It'll be there in less than seventy minutes—'

A loud guffaw comes out of the comcuff.

'Bloody good, mate, and on time too. But jeez, you're not supposed to ring up and warn us! We've got bets going on which one'll get here first.'

'Which *what*?' asks Simon, his eyebrows fierce.

'Boat. You know. The five attack boats in the exercise.'

'*Exercise?*'

'Great, keep it going! But shouldn't you be putting on a stupid voice, *Me bomb you evil capitalist*, or something?'

'I don't know—' says Simon, incredulous.

'Look, you're doing fine, mate. But we're not supposed to be chatting. We've got to get back to watching for your attack.'

'What—what will you do when we arrive?'

'Tick you off the list and shout you a beer. And tell that wanky Yank colonel we've done our bit towards keeping the Pilbara safe.'

I say desperately, 'This *isn't* a joke, we really do have a bomb on board—'

'And a chick too?' Boffo chuckles. '*Onya*, mate.' He hangs up.

We stare at each other, appalled.

'Zukowski's set up a security exercise?' I say in despair.

Simon nods. 'They're expecting boats to pretend to attack the plant tonight. They won't even try to stop us.'

I cover my face with my hands, and for a moment I'm a child again and I just want Mum to wake me up from these night terrors.

Aidan is the first to recover his wits. 'Gotta get into that engine room. Maybe there's a crowbar, a spanner, something we could use? Even a screwdriver. Come on, check everywhere.'

I'm feeling around the cutlery drawer, wondering if a spoon would be of any use, when my fingers touch something ridged —a key? I pull it out. It has a tag attached reading 'Engine Room'.

'I've got it!'

'That's a crowbar?' asks Aidan.

'A *key*. Come on.'

We dash down the steps to the engine room, which lies beneath the cabin. The steel door is closed with a large padlock. I can see blue cables from under the door snaking in all directions, but most of them run forward and end in a rack beneath the deck hatch that stands as tall as me.

Within the rack is a large metal cylinder with a tapered top, familiar from the gala night. On its side is an instrument panel with lights and a counter. I step towards the rack and stare at the numbers flicker green and crystalline.

'Sixty-two minutes,' I say.

'It looks like a cartoon bomb,' says Jessie dubiously. 'Is it *really*?'

'Yes,' says Simon. 'Really. The door, love—?'

My hand is shaking as I turn and insert the key in the padlock. It doesn't fit at first but I jiggle it and slide it in, then it turns easily. The lock springs open.

'All right, stand back,' says Simon. 'Let me check first. And Jess, I'll need you to try to figure out what's in here.'

Simon unhooks the lock and very slowly opens the door a fraction. He peers inside and opens it a little more and lets out his breath. 'Okay, nothing wired to the door.'

He opens it all the way. The engine thuds rhythmically, and near us, with all the cables running from it, is a rack of electronics.

Jess looks in, her computer under her arm. 'Ah,' she says with satisfaction. 'Power. Switches, router and yes, *server*.' She attaches a small cable between the server and her device, then sits on the floor and starts tapping.

'Can you get into it?' asks Simon.

'Don't know yet,' she says. 'Go away. Make me coffee.'

'Jess, we've only got sixty minutes ...' I say tentatively.

'Yeah. May as well have coffee then.'

Matthew sits down beside Jessie while the rest of us go back to the cabin. To my surprise there's ground beans and milk in the fridge, so we make coffee as instructed.

Before we can take it down to Jess, she and Matthew come back to the cabin looking sombre.

'Well?' asks Simon.

'Firewalled to fuck,' says Jessie.

'Is that a technical term?' asks Aidan.

'Sort of.' She sighs. 'Can't get in. The only traffic it'll let through is mobile IPv6 from a box on *Jameson*.'

Aidan groans. 'Jesus, Jess. We've got barely sixty minutes left. Speak *English*!'

'I'll ring Roxy.' Jessie stands and walks to the front window of the cabin. Over her shoulder I can see gas flaring and swaying from the far-away chimneys.

'Rox, what's happening?' Jess says into her comcuff. 'We're going to be killed! What? Not a game, for real, Rox. And it's so not cool. Okay. The *Jameson* network. Are you in yet?'

Jess walks a little one way, then the other. Finally she nods. 'Yeah. Go for it.' She seems to hold her breath for a moment, then says, '*Whew*. And root too? You're a genius, Okay. I need home agent and mobile node addresses. Check the interfaces then ping6 the link-local multicast and run a sniffer.'

She comes back to the table and sits in front of her computer listening to Roxy, then she comes alert. 'No IPsec? What? *Fantastic*.' Jess starts tapping. 'Uh-huh. Node?' She types and repeats, '2001:db8::dead:beef:6.' She starts grinning. 'And agent?'

She repeats something equally absurd, then can't stop laughing. 'Oh, come *on*, Rox, you're kidding. Documentation prefix and wanky words? *Seriously*?'

I murmur, 'Techies. Unbelievable. Even in mortal danger they still find time to criticise someone else's configuration.'

Jess taps something and waits intently. 'Oh, *yes*,' she says passionately. 'Session duly hijacked. We've done it, Rox. Yeah. Talk to you later.'

She looks up at our circle of startled faces. 'Oh. Well, you see, the bozos didn't use a secure link between this boat and their network. So Roxy and I hijacked the link and now the server below thinks I'm actually the *Jameson*.'

She takes her computer and saunters down the steps to the engine room.

Matthew says, dazed, 'I hope she never expects me to understand that.'

'Hey, look on the bright side. When you have kids you can call them One and Zero,' says Aidan.

Simon clears his throat. 'Guys. Jessie's a genius and if this situation had a digital solution we'd be fine. But it *doesn't*. That's a real bomb. Even experts would need dedicated equipment and many hours to neutralise it.' He shakes his head. 'We don't have the skills, the gear, or the time.'

I grip my warm cup for comfort. I'm slowly realising Jessie and Matthew may never get the chance to have children.

'We're fifty-five minutes out—maybe ten kilometres away from the plant,' Simon continues. 'We can't stop the bomb exploding and we can't change the boat's course.'

He takes a deep breath. 'So we have to decide something. Right now. Do we simply stand by and let the bomb reach the plant and trigger hell for God knows how many people, or ...'

'—or do we try to set it off before we get there?' Aidan says calmly, his eyes on Simon.

Simon nods slowly. 'Yes. And the latest we could leave it before detonation is, say, six kilometres out,' he says sadly.

'We'll reach that point in less than twenty minutes.'

I cover my mouth in shock.

'That's all?' asks Matthew, pale. 'Twenty minutes?'

'I'm sorry, I'm so bloody sorry.' Simon swallows. 'But it's not about us any more.'

'What if we jump overboard?' I ask.

'The boat will just keep going till it hits the plant. We've got to try to detonate it before then.'

'No,' I say. 'Simon, listen, the kids could jump with the table and benches, float in the water till someone rescues them. We could keep going and set off the bomb.'

Aidan shakes his head. 'No, cuz. Remember all those sea-creatures with sharp teeth and bad manners? I'd prefer an explosion.' He looks at us soberly. 'And if you'd ever seen a shark attack, I reckon you would too.'

A few moments of stunned horror pass.

Suddenly we hear a triumphant, 'Oh yes, yes!' from the engine room. Jessie bounds up the stairs with her computer.

'Got control of the server now!' she says, delighted. She looks around. 'Hey, you're pretty glum for people who've just had good news.'

'It's too late, Jess,' I say in despair. 'We can't risk the bomb reaching the gas plant. We've got to detonate it ourselves before we get anywhere near it—and do that in less than twenty minutes!'

'I'm not sure I can figure out how to disarm it inside twenty minutes, Lena,' she says.

'But we can't just let the boat deliver the bomb to the plant.'

Jessie shrugs. 'Well, why not go the other way?'

'How?' says Simon. 'The wheel's locked and booby-trapped.'

Jessie laughs. 'No it's not, guys. It's totally under my control now and working normally. Didn't I just explain that?'

'Not *precisely*, you marvellous woman,' says Matthew as he rushes out to the helm. He takes the wheel and turns it gently, and the boat begins to turn too.

Soon, unbelievably, we're heading away from the yellow flares, back in the direction we came from. I'm shaking with relief but suddenly have a horrible thought.

'But what if the other boats in the exercise have bombs too?'

'Nah,' says Jess. 'I checked earlier and there aren't any other boats heading for the gas plant, none at all. Zukowski was bullshitting. The 'exercise' was just a ploy to confuse site security.'

'All right. So how long do we have now before it explodes?' I ask Simon.

'Fifty minutes.'

'That's better,' says Jess. 'Okay, what sort of bomb is it?'

Simon laughs regretfully. 'Jessie, you didn't hear what I was just telling the others, but there is simply *no* way—'

She looks at him steadily and says, 'I've got to try.'

He's quiet for a moment. 'I'll see what identification it has,' he says and goes below.

A few moments later Jessie is madly searching for information on disarming bombs. Her hands dash and tap and touch and I gaze at her with aching affection. Her long magenta and orange hair, her fine-boned face, her beautiful hands. Oh, my little sister.

Darling Simon comes back up the steps and sits beside Jess and Aidan, a piece of paper in his hands. He reads off letters and numbers, his face drawn. Concentrating fiercely, he runs his finger through his steel-grey hair and I remember caressing his head when we were in bed together.

My eyes sting and I go out to the open space at the stern where Matthew is steering the boat, his eyes on the horizon, his gentle face grim.

After a time I clear my throat and say, 'Aren't we going faster than before?'

'Yes, managed to get some more power out of the engine,' he says. 'We'll be passing the island in five minutes.'

My heart beats in my throat like the throb of the engine and I feel sick with dread. I think of Dad and Mum and Suyin, losing Jessie and me, their only children; a lifetime of grief poised to descend upon them like an avalanche.

I wish I could think clearly. *Oh, Granddad Mike, where are you? You always helped me find the clarity I needed—show me a way out of this nightmare!*

But dear Mike is dead and cannot help me, and soon I too will pass into that abyss. Tears fill my eyes and I shiver uncontrollably.

The low bulk of the island lies ahead. Was it just this afternoon I sat there in such peace, enthralled by the large-eyed quoll? If only we were safe in the tinny, motoring back to my dreaming quoll ...

Safe in the tinny.

'Oh Matthew, what idiots we are! The tinny must still be floating near the island. We can get away and send this bloody boat off to explode somewhere it doesn't matter!'

We stand spaced along the deck as we enter the bay. The barbecue on shore has ended, the distant tent lights are dimmed. Matthew slows the blue boat and we peer into the moonlight, shining our torches, trying to spot the tinny.

'I reckon it'd have drifted towards the rock platform,' says

Aidan and we slowly approach the rocks, then motor back and forth in a grid pattern.

But we can't see anything. I feel sick.

We turn the boat again and I stare and stare till my eyes hurt. 'It's gone,' I say in despair. 'But ... but what about—could we possibly take this boat directly to the lugger instead?'

'That bay's too shallow and this vessel has a much deeper keel than *Sparrow*, love,' says Simon. 'We'd have to swim a long way to reach shore, and if the sea-life didn't get us we'd still be pulverised by the blast. But Christ, if we have to, then—'

'There, over *there*!' Jessie yells, pointing, and suddenly we see it. A dim shape, gently bumping against some rocks. Matthew slows the boat to a halt.

We shine our torches and see the tinny is about fifteen metres away. Without a word Aidan dives over the side and swims towards the tinny.

I gasp and look around for approaching fins. After an endless moment he reaches it and pulls himself smoothly up and in.

After a couple of heart-stopping failures he gets the engine started and brings the tinny slowly alongside. We clamber down the ladder and pile aboard.

'Oh, Aidan,' I say, hugging him. 'That was so brave!'

He laughs weakly. 'Reckon I broke a few speed records there.'

Jessie taps commands into her pink-orange device and the blue boat's engine starts up again with a rumble.

We stare silently as she turns it away and sends it heading out to sea, and watch until we can't see or hear it any more.

Then we start the tinny's engine and motor back to the lugger. I feel like weeping at the sight of *Sparrow*'s sturdy shape outlined by moonlight on the empty beach. We tie up the tinny and climb aboard, half-laughing, half-sobbing with relief and exhaustion.

'Jeez, it's hardly *nine* o'clock,' says Aidan in disbelief. 'Felt like we were stuck on that blue bastard for days.'

'Should we get away on the midnight tide?' Matthew asks.

Simon shakes his head. 'We're too tired, Matty. I'd prefer to stay here a bit longer, it's safer. And we need to find out where *Jameson*'s gone and what happens to the blue boat.'

'I can tell you,' says Jess. 'It's about fifty kays away, heading towards Perth. And the blue boat's five kays off already.'

'How much longer till the timer runs out on the bomb?' asks Matthew.

'Fifteen minutes or so,' says Simon. 'It'll be a good distance away by then.'

'Thank God,' I say, sitting down suddenly on the deckhouse.

'Hey, fellas,' says Aidan, with a tired grin. 'Why don't we have a beer and watch the fireworks?'

'Fantastic!' Jessie and Matthew say together.

Simon and I look at each other and shrug, so the kids drag a few bunk mattresses and pillows up to the deck. Then we all relax in the warm night air, sipping cold beers and waiting.

Simon has his arm around my shoulders and occasionally nuzzles my hair. All the tension in my shoulders starts to ebb and I feel a sense of trust that would have been unimaginable just a few weeks ago.

Fifteen minutes pass, then twenty. Nothing happens.

Aidan is saying, 'After all that, the bloody thing was a *dud*?' when suddenly light erupts on the horizon and starts to expand. We watch for a moment entranced, then throw ourselves flat, hands over our heads. The shock wave rattles and rumbles and passes us by, then we sit up again.

'After a lifetime of peaceful academia,' I say, 'how I have become such an old hand at coping with explosions? I reckon it's my bunch of low-life friends.'

'Too right,' says Aidan.

'That was a smaller explosion than the one at Worm Turning,' Matthew says thoughtfully. 'I expect you don't need as much fire-power to blow up a gas plant.'

'Still think I could have defused it,' says Jess, in Matthew's arms. 'But I'm kinda glad we didn't have to try.'

Simon laughs. 'Oh Jess, I cannot *tell* you how glad I am too.'

The warm air is soft and we're finally comfortable after this dreadful night. Our conversation becomes slow and halting and someone yawns. Silence.

As the others fall asleep Simon and I lie down close together in the moonlight.

'Thank Christ you thought of the tinny, love,' he murmurs, his face against my hair. 'We were all so mesmerised by that bloody bomb but you just went straight for the simplest solution.'

'I met my dreaming today,' I whisper. 'And she helped me think of it.'

I feel his smile against my head. 'Your dreaming?'

'A quoll. A small spotted quoll with clever eyes. She helped me focus.'

'Makes sense.'

'Does it?' I lift my head and gaze at him. 'Well it certainly doesn't to me. But it still happened.' I rest my head on his shoulder again. 'Hey, maybe your dreaming's a male quoll.'

'Hope not. The males die off after mating.'

'Okay, bad idea.'

After a moment he says, 'Something like your quoll happened to me once. Matty and I were camping on a beach near Broome and I was low, working in the Recreation department was killing me. Then a black seabird landed nearby, red beak, a male *Haematopus*. He looked at me and I swear his eyes were just ... so wise.'

I nod. 'Mmm.'

'Suddenly the solution seemed so obvious. I should live near that clever bird, live in this beautiful place. The same day I heard about the lugger, bought it, and everything changed for the better.' He laughs softly. 'And it *really* improved big time when you stepped on board.'

'I felt pretty unwelcome at first.'

'I was a dickhead.'

'You were,' I murmur. 'But I didn't say so.'

'I saw it in your large expressive eyes. Must be the quoll in you.'

We laugh and kiss and fall asleep.

A few hours later I awake, completely at peace. The moon has set and a river of stars streams across the sky. I sit up and sigh in contentment.

Clouds on the inky horizon float dreamily along, hiding the stars as they pass. The night is quiet, the water laps, my loved ones sleep contentedly around me.

I think, astonished, We're safe. We're safe.

22. An Unfortunate Turn of Events

I wake again before dawn, my head clear. I don't feel sleepy so decide to freshen up instead. Gazing towards the east I see the dark sky has hints of pale gold.

Down in the cabin I have a wash and find some clean clothes. The morning air is cool so I pull on a long-sleeved T-shirt. I hear the others moving about on deck and start thinking about when we'll leave the island.

Perhaps we don't have to sail to Exmouth after all. Perhaps after last night the situation has changed and we can go back to Dampier safely. But then ... then what?

Jameson is still out there, and Zukowski and Iceberg are still plotting their ugly conspiracies. I feel suddenly gloomy and wish I could return to the joy of the middle of the night.

I climb the steps to the deck remembering the beautiful stars and how they were blinking out on the horizon like something in an oddly familiar dream.

And suddenly my scalp crawls as I recall the last time I saw a dark form moving quietly and blotting out lights. I step out and there it is: not a dream, but a large grey nightmare moored in the middle of the bay.

And in front of me are three black-uniformed men, brandishing their inevitable loathsome guns and spewing their inevitable spiteful commands. My friends are standing, helpless. One goon points and snarls, '*Now.*'

We climb over the side into the large inflatable and the men follow us.

I press against Simon's side and whisper, 'I didn't see—'

A soldier slams the butt of his gun into my thigh. '*Shut it.*'

I grunt in pain and tears come to my eyes. Jess and Matthew and Aidan are sitting opposite, their faces distressed. I realise Jess is glancing briefly down at my wrist and back to my eyes.

I blink acknowledgement and half-cross my arms and very carefully touch the buttons on my comcuff to start the video camera.

It seems a tiny pointless defiance—I know perfectly well we're being taken to our deaths. Yet the morning is beautiful— the sky a perfect blue-gold, the water crystalline. A lacy wake follows us away from our sanctuary towards the looming grey ugliness ahead.

I see people watching us with curiosity from the flight deck. My throat is dry, my heart is pounding and my bruised thigh aches with every movement.

The inflatable stops beside a ladder and we climb onto a platform. We're herded through a door into a corridor below the deck, then we're taken up some stairs, one gunman ahead of us, two behind.

I realise Jess is murmuring into her cuff but luckily our feet are making too much noise on the metal for the soldiers to notice. Another two flights of stairs, another corridor.

A soldier raps on a door and we enter an office. We're ordered to line up then the soldiers leave. Colonel Zukowski is behind a large desk in front of us. He smiles and says, 'Well, well.' The smile doesn't reach his eyes.

On the left-hand wall three monitors are showing news bulletins, the sound turned down. Beyond them, Max is shuffling files into a cabinet. He stops in surprise.

To the right Alise, composed, sits in an armchair beside a small table with a plate of pastries and an elegant coffee service. She nibbles a croissant.

'Honestly, Lena, you were *told* to mind your own business,' she says. 'Instead you've interfered again. You simply don't seem to have a *scrap* of common sense.'

Zukowski says reflectively, 'That sure was some pathetic little bang last night—thought we'd better come back and check up. Gotta say I was hoping for something more cataclysmic. You fellas know anything about that?'

'*Cataclysmic?*' I say.

Like a kindly headmaster he says, 'Look, I don't know how you got your little dinghy through that cyclone, but I figured you'd learnt—at the very fucking least—to stay outta my way. But you had to go and screw me over again, didn't you?' He shrugs theatrically. 'So what do I do now?'

Simon says steadily, 'Let us go. The authorities know our information is true and they're starting to move. Your bullshit won't work any more.'

'Yeah? But we all know the bigger the lie ...' Zukowski leans back, puts his hands behind his head and gazes at us complacently.

'I'd suggest you get out of here fast and have a chat with your own government,' says Simon. 'They mightn't be as supportive as you imagine.'

'No need to fret, Popeye. They know this plan's for the good of the country.'

Jessie's arm is up, recording everything, rubbing her neck as if she's tired. I'm steadily recording, too. She says insolently, 'So a tsunami's good for America, is it?'

He stares lazily at her. 'Could've settled a few scores, especially with the Chinks. That a problem for ya, Suzie

Wong?'

'Your new military base,' says Aidan calmly. 'Liberty Province? Your bosses must be stoked.'

Zukowski grins smugly. 'Oh pretty boy, they are.'

'And the caesium?' asks Matthew. 'I imagine handling that was something of a challenge.'

'Believe it, curlytop. As your buddies here found out the hard way.' He shrugs. 'Lost a few guys in the process but hey, shit happens.'

He looks at me. 'Got a question for me too, professor?'

'I'm not a—'

'Shut your trap,' he says, sitting forward. He shakes his head. 'Could've played dumb the lot of you, but you talk too much.'

He stands and takes a gun from his holster. 'Okay. Follow me, fuckers. Let's get you locked up and tonight we'll just have to have five tragic eaten-by-a-shark incidents.'

Jessie says, 'Don't think so, Ronald McDonald.'

'*What* did you—'

She smiles. 'Check out what's being broadcast on the global news right now.'

We stare at the monitors, and to my astonishment one of them shows *here*, this office. Zukowski steps forward and adjusts the volume and his TV-figure says '– eaten-by-a-shark incidents.'

'Almost real-time. Good resolution, too,' Jess says in an aside.

Zukowski watches the TV then turns to stare at her, his eyes cold and unblinking. 'How the *fuck*?'

He points his gun at us. 'Hands up. Now.'

We slowly put our hands in the air and he looks at us, one by one, gazing at the angle of view of the broadcast and looking back at us, nodding his head as if agreeing with himself.

'Okay,' he says and suddenly there's a terrible noise.

Jessie screams. She collapses to the floor, clutching the broken red mass of her hand and comcuff, and Matthew falls beside her calling her name, cradling her head.

Aidan drops to his knees too, ripping the hem off his T-shirt and using it to stem the blood gushing from her arm. I'm sobbing, but also keeping my own cuff, half hidden by my long sleeve, trained on the scene.

Alise says, 'Not very *creative* of you, Wayne. In public too.'

Zukowski grins. 'Isn't in public any more, honeybun.'

'I think you may be mistaken, Colonel,' says Alise. 'And as a representative of the government I must express my concern at such an *unfortunate* turn of events.'

Her eyes are on the TV screens. Max is staring too, a stack of files in his hands. Another monitor still shows this room, the Alise-form repeating '– *unfortunate* turn of events.'

Zukowski turns back to us and looks us over, stopping at me, his eyes expressionless.

'Well, well. Come on, professor, show us your hands.'

I reflexively fold my arms.

He shrugs. 'I'll shoot you in the guts, then.'

Simon roars, 'Stop this *now!*'

Zukowski sniggers. Simon tries to step in front of me but I push him back and hold out my arm, saying, 'I'll take it off—'

I see Zukowski calmly lift his gun.

And Max smashes him viciously on the back of his head with the stack of files. Zukowski drops like a puppet.

Max grabs the gun, tosses it into the filing cabinet and quickly locks it. I can't believe my eyes. *Max?*

Alise stands and moves towards us, composed, her platinum hair smooth as a helmet.

'Get away from us, you murdering *bitch*!' I yell.

'Goodness, Lena, I'd just like to offer my condolences on this *tragic* incident. We must send for help. Brigadier, please call an air ambulance immediately.'

Max has a phone to his ear and says, 'I am. Minister.'

Jessie is silent now, lying in a pool of red. Matthew is bent over her whispering her name, Aidan beside them, anguish on his face.

'How long before they get here, Max?' I ask, my voice unsteady. 'How *long*?'

'Soon. The airport's not far and they're always on alert in case of rig accidents.'

'Well,' says Alise calmly. 'I'd better go and discuss this with the captain.'

'Are you out of your *mind*, you fucking cow? You're not going anywhere.'

She sighs and smooths a crease in her skirt. 'Lena, the captain's been getting rather fed up with Wayne treating his ship like a taxi. I'm sure he'll be happy to help.'

'Alise, do you have the *faintest* idea what you're responsible for? Hundreds of people dead at Worm Turning? Trying to bomb a *gas* plant?'

'My goodness, is *that* what Wayne was doing? Oh, I had no idea.' Her ice-blue eyes are pools of professional sympathy. 'He deceived me completely. I thought I was simply acting in the best interests of the people of this great state.'

'Max, phone, please,' says Simon crisply and Max hands it to him. Simon turns away and speaks to someone. As he's doing so we hear a helicopter approaching and I gasp with relief.

There's a knock at the door and a soldier in black open it. My heart thuds, but he can't see Zukowski unconscious on the floor behind the desk, and only a flicker of surprise crosses his face at the sight of Jessie lying in a pool of blood on the floor.

'Ma'am, your 'copter's here,' he says to Alise then leaves.

'Lovely. Well Lena, I *do* hope we meet again in less difficult circumstances.' She picks up her handbag and moves towards the door.

'*Your* 'copter, Alise?' I can hardly speak for incredulity.

'I ordered it before this ... spate of unpleasantness.' She shrugs lightly. 'Sorry I can't help any further but I've got an urgent meeting in Perth.' She turns to Max. 'Brigadier?'

We hear the throbbing of a second helicopter. 'That'll be the air ambulance,' says Alise. 'But if we don't get off the flight deck it can't land. Unfortunately. *Brigadier?*'

She moves towards to the door, stepping disdainfully through Jessie's blood, then stops and stares at me.

'You know, your old boyfriend James thought the world of you—I could never see why, myself. But you're surprisingly *resourceful.*' Her eyes are like knives.

Max, following her, hands me the key to the cabinet with Zukowski's gun, saying, 'Toss it away.'

Then, amazingly, my soon-to-be ex-husband whispers, 'Saw you on the boat that night at Dampier, looking so brave. I'm sorry Lena, sorry for *everything*. She won't get away with this, I swear I won't let her.'

He leaves with Alise.

I'm touched, but think, Oh, *Max*. Don't kid yourself.

Alise's helicopter leaves and another one lands. In just minutes a rush of competent people are clustered around Jessie, bandaging the shattered ruin of her hand, putting a drip in her arm, getting her onto a stretcher and out the door.

Simon says quickly, 'You go with her, love, you and Matty.

Aidan and I'll take the boat back to Dampier and meet you at the Karratha hospital.'

As we leave the office he grabs the key out of the door and locks it from the outside, leaving Zukowski inside, still unconscious. He gives me the key saying, 'You can toss that one too.'

On the deck Simon speaks to the captain, a sunburnt middle-aged man, who nods in agreement. I realise the loathsome gun-wavers are standing in a defeated, weaponless huddle over to one side, and most of the others on deck are sailors, concerned and professional.

One young woman says quickly as she helps me into the helicopter, 'Oh, Ma'am, I'm sorry this happened here on our ship. He's crazy, it's been dreadful the last few weeks. I'm so *sorry*.' There are tears in her eyes.

We take off. I wave to Simon and Aidan below, being assisted into the inflatable to be taken back to the lugger. As we rise I see *Sparrow* herself moored near the beach like a beautiful toy.

We fly over the red rocks of the island's low hills and for a moment I can even see the gully, the home of my quoll.

Jessie moans and I take her slim perfect right hand and press it to my cheek. 'Not far now, darling Jess,' I whisper. 'Not far.' Matthew strokes her head and murmurs to her.

In minutes we're landing at Karratha airport and Jessie's stretcher is loaded into an ambulance. We race along the streets, the siren howling, the lights flashing.

I remember the night Simon and I were in an ambulance too, contaminated and burnt: the start of this desperate adventure. Ending now, with my beautiful sister so mutilated.

At the hospital they rush her into surgery and Matthew and I sit in a waiting room and wait. We get dreadful coffee from a machine. And wait.

Eventually Simon and Aidan arrive. I'm shocked for a moment to see blood on their clothing then realise for the first time we're all covered in it. I feel sick and rest my head against the warmth of Simon's shoulder. We wait.

After a long, long time the door at the end of the corridor opens and the surgeon approaches. We stand up. She's small and fair and looks terribly young. I ache in every muscle. Is she preparing to give us bad news?

'Your sister is alive,' she says. 'She lost a great deal of blood and needed several transfusions.' She looks at me gently. 'I'm very sorry. We couldn't save her hand, it was damaged beyond any hope of repair.'

'She lost her hand?' I ask, dizzy. 'But she's *alive*?'

The surgeon nods. 'You'll be able to see her when she recovers from the anaesthetic.'

We thank her and she leaves. I sit down again shakily, and start to sob.

'She's alive, Lena,' says Matthew, sitting beside me, his eyes passionate. 'That's all that matters. She can get some kind of— hand thing, I don't know. I don't care. She's alive.'

After a time a nurse comes and leads us to a recovery room. Jessie is pale, her hair loose on the pillow, her left arm bandaged, a tangle of drips and feeds running to monitors.

She focuses on us and smiles tremulously. Matthew kisses her and strokes her face and she murmurs, 'Sweet Parrot-man, s'all right. Doesn't hurt.'

We tell her we love her and she nods, tired. 'No more hand,' she says slowly, puzzled, falling asleep. 'Weird ...'

We get a taxi back to the little yacht club at Dampier where *Sparrow* is moored, and take the tinny out to the boat in the warmth of the clear evening. Jess was in surgery half the day and now it's late.

We wash and change our clothes. Simon is busy making endless phone calls. I'm just glad to be back on board again but the lugger seems empty without Jessie's fierce energy.

'Oh God, where's her computer?' I ask, suddenly afraid it's on *Jameson*.

'It's all right,' says Matthew. 'She hid it when the soldiers arrived this morning.' He stops and rubs his curly head. 'I cannot believe it. Just this *morning*.'

Our mattresses are still lying on the deck where we left them and Matthew feels underneath one and pulls out the pink-orange device.

'There we are,' he says. 'She'll be happy about that.'

'But how will she *use* it with ...?'

A terrible vision of a one-handed Jessie trying to work on her computer makes me moan in anguish.

Simon comes over and holds me. 'There, love. It's going to take a bloody lot of getting used to.'

I find the keys in my pocket, one for the filing-cabinet with the gun, the other for the office where I hope Zukowski is still locked up with an aching head. I throw them far away and they fall with a soft splash, ripples spreading on the water.

But it doesn't make me feel any better.

23. Ancient Hands

Next morning I glumly open my laptop to check the news. I'm stunned at the headlines and call out, 'Hey, Alise has been *arrested*!' The others crowd around.

Iceberg is pictured stepping daintily from her helicopter at Perth airport and the caption reads:

> Alise Berg, the ex-Minister for the Industrial Environment, has been taken into custody by Commonwealth police. This afternoon they stated she'll be facing charges of treason.

'Treason? Is that even a thing nowadays?' I say.

Simon nods. He recites, '*A person commits an offence called treason if the person instigates a person who is not an Australian citizen to make an armed invasion of the Commonwealth.*'

'Armed invasion?' asks Matthew. 'But I thought the Americans were obliged to take over during security incidents.'

'Ah, but it turns out the famous Dampier Peninsula Pollution and Protection Agreement doesn't say that at all,' says Simon. 'Zukowski was bullshitting with guns, and Berg and her fellow secessionist psychos were backing him up. They thought the chaos would make it a done deal once the gas plant exploded.'

'Is that why you've been on the phone so much?' I ask.

He nods. 'Seems your old mate Max was just playing along with them. He's been passing information to the Commonwealth authorities ever since the Worm Turning bombing.'

'Do you reckon there'll be enough evidence to put her away?' asks Aidan.

'With our reports and all the intelligence Max sent them, they've got more than enough to justify both arresting and prosecuting her.'

'All right. Max is still a bastard,' I say. 'But maybe not as much as I thought.'

Aidan sits in the sunlight beside me on the deckhouse. He's wearing a new T-shirt, and I remember him ripping the hem off the old one and carefully applying pressure at all the right places to stem Jessie's gushing blood.

'Thank God you were there for Jess yesterday and knew what to do,' I say, still shaken at what might have been.

'Hey, ship's ambo, remember,' he says. 'Got to come in handy sometime or other.'

'And ship's retriever of tinnies too, don't forget,' I say. 'What if you'd been taken by a shark that night?'

'Nah, they'd never bother me. My dreaming, you see. We understand each other.'

'I didn't see such fabulous confidence just after your swim.'

He grins. 'Well, not at the time, no.'

'*And* you brought us to Murujuga, got us fuel from the magnificent Dreads, and introduced me to my quoll,' I say. 'We'd have been stuffed without you, cuz.'

He looks down and says, 'Figured out a few things too. Going to keep on fighting for Murujuga for a start. Heading back to Broome pretty soon as well.'

He gazes along the deck. 'And after all this I'm not going to mess around. Not going to let someone drift out of my life ...'

'Oh, *go* for it! Cath's gorgeous—'

'Um. Not Cath, love her like a sister, but ... well, Russell.'

'Oh. Okay, he's gorgeous too.'

Amber eyes affectionate he says, 'Assumptions, Lena. Got to watch those assumptions.'

Aidan flies home to Broome and a week later I get an email with a picture of a shark, and underneath it just says, 'Deadly.'

I don't think he means the shark.

I contact my university and take three months' long service leave. Matthew rents a small apartment near the hospital and when Jessie is discharged she moves in with him and starts therapy, learning how to cope with only one hand.

After six weeks or so moored at Dampier, Simon and I make plans to sail *Sparrow* home to Broome. The evening before we're due to leave we visit Jess and Matthew.

Jessie looks tired. The sight of her slim left arm terminating in a bandage still tightens my chest in distress, but she says she's started researching the latest in electronic prostheses.

She shows me some of the papers she's studying and I murmur encouragement. But I worry she's deceiving herself and the reality hasn't sunk in yet.

We've brought them some good champagne—Simon says he owes me some since we had to leave the gala so abruptly that evening. He pours it and hands the glasses around.

'Didn't tell Lena this earlier, I was saving it for all of you,' he says. 'But I've just had some great news. Remember Jumbo, the treacherous bastard? Betrayed us all to Zukowski?'

'Who could forget good old Jumbo?' I say. 'Last we saw of him he was scuttling away in Broome like a woodlouse. Didn't I always say you couldn't trust ex-army men?'

'Except for coastal ecologists, I hope,' says Matthew.

'Oh, all right. Sole exception.'

'Well,' continues Simon, grinning, 'I thought Jumbo was breeding endangered marsupials. Gave him a lot of leeway because I respected that.'

'And was he?' asks Jessie in an armchair, her head on a cushion.

'No way. He was *smuggling* them! So now he's going to be prosecuted. Asked me for a reference, cheeky bastard. He'll get a reference all right.'

'So perhaps there's a little justice in the world,' says Matthew, but I can hear in his voice he doesn't quite believe it, not after what happened to Jess.

'Yes,' says Simon. He hesitates and says gently, 'Let's hope there's more coming up. I was also told today they've had some progress in setting a date for Iceberg's trial.'

I look at Jessie wondering how she'll take it, but she says 'Cheers,' and holds her glass out. We all clink in celebration.

'That reminds me, Jess,' I say. 'The prosecutors got in touch with me the other day for a statement about my comcuff data. But they don't have a clip of that broadcast of Zukowski admitting everything. I can't figure out why, when it was all over the news. So have you got a copy?'

Jessie laughs. 'Oh, yeah. Meant to explain at the time but I guess events overtook me.'

She takes a sip of champagne. 'It wasn't a real broadcast at all. I told Roxy to transmit the images straight into *Jameson*'s network, so Zukowski'd think everyone was watching him and not do anything too drastic. Didn't quite work out as I'd hoped, though.'

Simon shakes his head and says, 'Did I ever mention how much I admire your deviousness, Jess?'

She smiles. 'Hey, Roxy and I got a great conference paper out of their lame set-up. *Stupidest Network Ever* we're calling it.'

We laugh and chat some more but it's clear she's in some pain, so we get ready to leave. As we walk to the door I say quietly to her, 'Darling Jess, I'm so sorry it came to this—'

She hugs me fiercely. 'Don't you *dare* be sorry, Lena. We had an adventure and I met my psychedelic Parrot-man and we stopped those stupid bozos in their tracks. We did good.'

Next morning Simon and I leave Dampier to sail *Sparrow* back to Broome. Now it's just me as first mate and deckhand, I'm amazed to discover there are sensible reasons for salty jargon after all—it's not simply a ploy to confuse the non-maritime-minded.

After several episodes of me yelling—*Do I pull on this thingy or that? Oh, sorry, are you all right? Let me get you a band-aid!*—Simon and I sit down to define a few terms. I find out it's rather useful to be able to speak of sheets, halyards, luffs, leeches and topping lifts, although when vangs are mentioned I really have to wonder if he's teasing me.

We take a leisurely two weeks on the passage, a time of beautiful weather and great peace. We moor the lugger near Minyirr again and find Simon's salt-encrusted ute sitting on the beach just where we left it.

My hire car is still at the hotel too and I return it to the depot and apologetically pay the enormous overdue fine. 'You said we'd only be two weeks,' I grumble to Simon. 'Try two months, mate.'

He laughs and says he won't charge me for the 'luxury cruise' on the lugger then. I throw a cushion at him and it all ends as delightfully as you'd expect.

It's winter now in Broome—warm, beautiful blue-sky winter —and at Simon's house we relish the space and showers and big comfortable bed, heaven after so long on a boat.

But all too soon my leave is nearly up and I start to wonder what lies ahead. As he promised on the night of the gala, Simon takes me out on our 'third date' and I wear my lovely long dress of Walmadan copper and rose.

We talk about the future, and next day I fly to Sydney, resign from my job and start packing for Broome.

Jessie and Matthew come home and settle in a place not far from us, but I'm still worried for her. One weekend we go to a barbecue at Maggie's house.

While Simon and Matthew and Paddy Bull tackle the men's business of the barbecue, Maggie, Jess and I sit on the back veranda. Jess is pale and quiet, and Maggie tucks her streak of silver hair behind an ear and very gently touches Jessie's' wrist. Her stump.

I'm surprised to hear her say, 'I know where there's another hand for you.'

Jess gazes at her. 'Do you?'

'I'll take you there,' says Maggie, and to my amazement Jessie nods.

A few days later the three of us go out into the countryside. It's a long way in the bouncing four-wheel-drive and Jess is silent, clearly in discomfort.

Maggie takes us to a place of gorges cut by a narrow river, and we sit under a tree on the bank and drink tea from a flask.

Then Jess says quietly, 'Maggie. Show me.'

Maggie leads us along the river to a place where the sides of the gorge hold shallow sandstone caves. I see paintings, animal figures and complex forms. There are dancing women like those I saw on the island and a familiar spotted shape with a pointed nose.

Finally we reach a curved wall covered in prints of hands, red and white, large and small. My heart sinks. Is this it? Just hand prints?

Jess sits down calmly on a boulder and Maggie beside her murmurs to her. Jessie nods then Maggie rises and says, 'Leave her now.'

She sees I'm worried and takes my arm. 'We'll go now, Lena,' she says firmly, and I follow her back to where we had tea. I don't know what to say. Maggie's comfortable sitting in the shade, watching the river, humming quietly to herself.

I'm anxious, worried Jess will become upset, or perhaps slip and fall on the way back from the wall of hand prints. From the corner of my eye something flickers, like a small spotted rump disappearing behind a rock. All right, Lena, just relax.

After a long time Jess comes towards us along the river bank, smiling and flushed. She kisses Maggie—undemonstrative Jess! —and sits and pours herself a cup of tea, and says, 'Wow.'

'Wow?' I ask.

'*Wow.*' She turns to Maggie. 'You made me cry.'

Maggie grins. 'Yeah. And?'

Jess takes a long breath. 'So many hands. So many ancient hands—what, forty thousand years?'

'At least,' says Maggie. 'Maybe more.'

'I just ... first of all, I just felt bitter. Then I felt a complete fool for feeling bitter. I'm alive and all those lovely people who put their hands there so long ago aren't. They don't have what I have. I'm so *lucky.*'

'Oh, Jess,' I say, my throat tight.

'Then a big lizard appeared, absolutely the coolest lizard ever. He swaggered out and gave me this "Hey, man" look, like he was simply the best and he knew it.' She laughs. 'And I couldn't stop staring at his amazing fingers ... so flexible, so different from ours, so—*articulated*.'

She gazes at me, delighted. 'Lena, I've had this explosion of ideas. The people building prostheses are doing it all wrong, there are much better ways. Can we go home now, Maggie? I've got work to do.'

Of course, Jess is famous now for the hand she designed to replace her own. She never pretends it can replace what she's lost, but the refining of its delicate functioning fascinates her.

Hailed as a breakthrough in human prosthetics, it has the all functions of a comcuff with her own particular touch: a layer of brilliant enamels and gemstones.

The newspapers call it a jewelhand. Jessie calls it her lizard paw.

For all my newfound peace, I'm still haunted a little by the loss of my granddad Mike. Of course Simon is part of my life now but that's different, with its own adult joys and complexities.

My bond with Mike was simpler, more fundamental. I'm intellectually aware it helped *grow me up*, as Maggie says—but I still can't recall him emotionally.

I think, if I could just imagine him here in Broome, the place he loved so well, I might regain that sense of his essence. Or if I could just feel he's somewhere, *anywhere*, at all. But the only thing I can feel is his absence.

Simon and I visit my great-aunt in Perth, Mike's sister Anna, whom I haven't seen for years. She's an elegant, witty woman in her nineties who tells us about Mike's childhood in Broome and their mother Lucy's life with Simon's beloved *Sparrow*.

It gives me joy to expand my sense of belonging through Mike's family—from Liam to my Indigenous cousins and from Anna to her own friendly brood.

But in the end it makes no difference. I cannot feel my granddad in the memories of my life and I cannot feel him in this place that was once his home.

Early one morning I wake up with a strange conviction: the time has come to forget this pointless quest.

I take a walk and sit down at the end of the small jetty on the bay. The day is glorious, a clear blue sky with the promise of heat to come.

Water ripples around the roots of the mangroves, golden whistlers and red-headed honeyeaters flitter from branch to branch and a pair of kestrels hover, quivering, high above.

Time to let it go, I think. I'm sorry, Mike. That wonderful day on the island at Murujuga brought me so much I'm grateful for, but it was foolish to hope for more. To hope it might bring back some awareness of you.

I close my eyes and feel the familiar sweet descent into the life teeming around me, such an easy thing to do now. I think about my dreaming, my quoll. She's not something I actually see, of course, she's a flickering at the edges of my perception, a *clarity* that comes when I need it most.

Yet, I wonder idly, why have I never again met that great breathing presence from the island? So gentle and vast and strange at first, then less vast and less strange until it was something almost familiar, though I couldn't give a name to it.

But then, why imagine I could? Surely nothing in that extraordinary place would be familiar to me.

Assumptions, Lena, whispers my quoll.

I seem as light as air in this serene morning world. Leaves rustle, birds call, water laps, and even if I wanted to I cannot move a muscle for the peace of it. And softly, slowly, I sense that distant rhythm once more. The hair on my head prickles with awe.

But this breathing is slow and comforting. This presence is kind and wry and perceptive and of course, this presence is utterly familiar. Feelings flow back to me like waves of long-forgotten music: and at last I remember.

Much later—when the world has become ordinary again—I think, that wasn't *really* Mike. It was just some psychological barrier lifting and letting suppressed emotions rise once more into my consciousness.

Nothing mysterious about it. I'm a scientist, for heaven's sake.

My quoll laughs.

24. Reality

Alise Berg finally goes to trial, and the comcuff images, Max's testimony and our reports make up an overwhelming body of evidence. She's convicted and will end her days in prison.

Sometimes I almost feel sorry for her, but then I think of Glenn Garrod and his friendly yacht crew, the happy guests, the young Aboriginal waiter, even the hapless ambassador—and I think, yes. Rot in gaol, Alise.

Colonel Zukowski gets away of course, safe from prosecution, and takes *Jameson* back to the US, where his masters flatly reject any responsibility for the Dampier Peninsula contamination. But the revelation of their role in the Worm Turning tragedy is a tipping point in credibility.

Already over-extended, the empire is hit by an economic crisis. I pray this might mean the spiteful little wars in the poorest places on earth, spurred on like so many cock-fights, will fade away without the constant, cynical goading of the arms industry.

Or perhaps the thousand-plus bases in other peoples' countries will close down, and the men in armour and the destroyers and carriers will sail for home. And all that brutal, bristling power will be revealed as the childish masquerade it's always been.

It hasn't happened yet.

And some things never change.

Zukowski is decorated, leaves the army and goes into politics: he's tipped as a future presidential contender.

The Geo-Garrod company has plans to build another plant near the old test grounds at Maralinga in cooperation, at last, with the local custodians. It will begin the vital task of dealing with the world's grim mountains of nuclear waste.

Still, I'll never forget small Irina, or the Chernobyl children with scars at their throats, or the hells of Hiroshima and Nagasaki, or brave Gabriela and the blue sparkling powder of Goiânia.

I think of the hafnium lying in the Nevada desert, and wonder if sometime, somewhere, a passionate scientist will unlock its secrets and we will all come to rue the day.

Yet for now, I tell myself, we are safe. For now, those I love are living their quiet, creative lives.

I love to sail on the lugger once owned by my great-grandmother, but whenever we're off the long beach in the sunlight, I recall the dark and the rain and the fear. I shiver when I see a small boat in the distance and think for a moment it's an old blue fishing vessel.

Then I gaze at Simon, my love, at the tiller, and remember what he told me in hospital. Sometimes, he said, when the company's good and the wind's just right, I reckon it's got to be worth it.

A year after the bombing at Worm Turning, the politicians still can't come to grips with the concept of decontamination, so they pull what they fondly believe is a fast one. They offer to return the land of the Dampier Peninsula to its original custodians, forever. Paddy Bull and Maggie Everett lead the delegation to the handover, and sign the unbreakable commitment into national and international law.

Discarded by the invaders of two centuries before, Walmadan once again becomes Aboriginal country. Despoiled, radioactive, Aboriginal country.

So we clean it up.

I go back to the ruined plant with specialists and we're amazed to discover the explosion broke open only three of the caesium assemblies—the other tough little containers are intact and we carefully (*very* carefully) retrieve them.

We measure and record radiation levels and bury the surface contamination with bulldozers and set up fences. Other workers uncover the remains of those killed at the gala and we soberly watch the trucks taking them away.

Together with the local mobs we work on stories and songs for the children who must be the guardians of this place for generations to come. Slowly we bring order to the chaos, and we find an unexpected consolation.

The smallest worm will turn being trodden on, and doves will peck in safeguard of their brood. Just as foreshadowed, the serpent of Walmadan finally turned.

The Law men of Minyirr sang their songs to the cyclone, and Cyril's torrents poured into the open wound of the Wormhole, gathering sand and soil and filling it almost completely. Now it's just a hollow in the earth marked by a tangle of rusty rail-lines. The serpent aquifer is safe once more.

The rains, too, dissolved much of the caesium and washed it beneath the ground. It's still lethal to living things but over the years it will move deeper and deeper and one day become unreachable. Country is healing itself.

And we discover another small miracle: the low hills around

Walmadan contained most of the blast, so the rest of the peninsula is clean.

But of course we keep bloody quiet about that. As Paddy Bull says, 'Wouldn't want the pollies getting sellers' remorse.'

Beside the flickering fire at our Walmadan work camp late one night I ask, 'Do you honestly believe there's a serpent underneath here, Paddy?'

He strokes his white beard. 'It's as real as your quoll, Lena.'

'But she's just something in my mind,' I say. 'An inspiration, an image that helps me focus. How can you call that real?'

'Why not? Even scientists say there's no such thing as objective reality. All we can ever know about the world is just a mental construct.'

'That's true,' I admit.

'So you've gotta laugh at the blokes convinced all the bad stuff in the universe is real, the death and chaos and emptiness, but somehow all the good stuff—the life and love and meaning—isn't.'

He pokes at the fire with a stick. 'It's our choice what reality we see, cuz. I see a serpent. You see a quoll.'

'Well, given the latest theories of consciousness and quantum physics, I suppose there may be something to it,' I say. 'But it's very early days.'

Paddy grins. 'Hey, if you scientists understood it now you'd have nothing to do for the next century. Got to keep you busy while you're figuring out what the rest of us already know.'

He adds a small branch to the irrational glory of the flames, and flurries of sparks fly up to the stars.

Thank You, Readers

Thank you for reading *Atomic Sea*, book 2 in the Radiation series. If you've enjoyed it, please recommend it to your friends and give it a review or rating on your favourite book site.

You may also enjoy Radiation book 1, *The Turning Tide*, which tells of Lena as a young woman and her friendship with bitter, broken-hearted ex-commando Mike Whalen. And if you'd like to know more about pearling luggers and Broome history, try award-winning *Redbill: From Pearls to Peace*.

The cover image is taken from a photo by Yousef Espanioly on Unsplash. An earlier cover was derived from an image of *Redbill* in 1989, courtesy of Peter Malcolm.

Go to seabooks.net for links to the books, reviews, extracts, images and background information. On the website I offer a free ebook copy of *Silver Highways*, the foundation of all my novels, to anyone who subscribes to my mailing-list (and you can unsubscribe at any time).

About the Author

I grew up at Speers Point on Lake Macquarie, NSW. My background is in science and Internet technology, but in 2000 I ran across the story of the charmed life of an old Broome pearling lugger, and discovered the joys of historical research and writing.

My first book, *Redbill: From Pearls to Peace,* won the Western Australian Premier's Book Award for Non-Fiction, and the second, *Alan Villiers: Voyager of the Winds,* won the Mountbatten Maritime Award. My novels include *Harbour of Secrets, Embers at Midnight, Testing the Limits, Silver Highways, Atomic Sea* and *The Turning Tide.*

I'm mother to two sons and live in the rolling hills of green South Gippsland, Victoria, with an elderly whippet. I make no apologies for my passion for K-Pop and Korean TV.

I post on Twitter as @katelance6 (warning: swearing, birds, art, trees, Green and Australian politics). You may also find me on https://seabooks.net, where there are extracts, images and reviews of my books. [Image above by Alex Lance.]

Acknowledgements

With appreciation to my mother Margaret Lance, and to the Woflers —Alison Shields, Gillian Clarke, Ruth Carson—who helped clarify drafts of the manuscript with wit and perception.

My thanks to Tony Larard, Dick Sonners, and all those who helped me with research for *Redbill* and made me feel welcome in magical Broome, and to Robert Bednarik for his years of work on the rock art of Murujuga.

And my gratitude to sons Joe Rowley and Alex Lance, brothers David and Peter Lance and, as always, whippets Polly and Mickey.

Other Books

FICTION

THE TURNING TIDE — CM Lance, Seabooks Press, 2022

"It took me about two pages to fall in love with this beautiful Australian book."
Commandos in Timor 1942. Love in postwar Hiroshima. Promises made and forgotten.

In 1982 Mike Whalen reluctantly visits his wartime commando base at rugged Wilsons Promontory, and is shocked to meet Lena, the granddaughter of his glamorous old friends, Helen and Johnny.

When Johnny died he left behind a burden of secrets, and as Mike is drawn back into Lena's family he's overwhelmed by his past: growing up in wild Broome, tragic guerilla missions in Timor, desire in devastated Hiroshima, betrayal in the jazzy fifties. Before Mike can turn the bitter tides of memory he must rebuild his bonds with wartime mates and confront Helen, and himself, with the truth.

HARBOUR OF SECRETS — CM Lance, Seabooks Press, 2022

The war is over. The reckoning is not.

It's the hip 1950s on Sydney's shimmering harbour, but how do you reconcile a past that gave — and stole — so much? Tina runs Tempo jazz club at shady Kings Cross, keeping secrets with, and from, her beguiling boss Jimmy. And from her lonely husband.

Harry yearns to forget his days in a Singapore prison camp, yet his friends won't let him. Nor will his conscience. Ex-pilot Billie now works at the flying-boat base. When her old lover Pete turns up with a new wife there's a lot she prefers to conceal. Even from herself.

Yvonne rebuilds a life by the harbour with her beloved Klara. But secrets emerge when she publishes Harry's war memoir, and then no one can postpone the reckoning.

EMBERS AT MIDNIGHT — Kate Lance, Seabooks Press, 2021

"The writing is beautiful and haunting. The characters are drawn with razor-sharp precision. It's compelling reading of the highest standard, full of evocative triumph and tragedy."

In the late 1930s, a group of old friends at a sunny wedding could not imagine what storms are about to engulf them.

Fierce pilot Billie is glad she's got a job at last — only trouble is it's in some little dust-up in Spain. Secretive Toby has no wish to volunteer for anything. Till he finds out for himself what blitzkrieg means.

Newlywed Eliza is posted to Intelligence at Singapore — safer than London, she thinks. But when fortress Singapore is reduced to embers, it is actress Izabel who is forced to play the role of her life.

TESTING THE LIMITS – Kate Lance, Seabooks Press, 2020

"I can't recommend this series highly enough: the writing is brilliant, the story wonderful, and you can't help but fall in love with the characters."

1930s England: will the sunny days of ships, flying and love ever end? Eliza McKee sails away to a new life in London, where her glamorous aunt Izabel is a star with a secret to hide. Her brother Pete yearns to fly, but he has no idea how much he needs to learn from fierce pilot Billie Quinn. Eliza's friend Harry loves golden Charlotte, but Charlotte just loves gambling with flyboy Pete's heart. And when a great white barque encounters the coast one foggy night, more than an era of sail finds itself tested to the limits.

SILVER HIGHWAYS — Kate Lance, Seabooks Press, 2018

"A beautiful and poignant coming of age romantic tale that kept me reading from start to finish."

Lucy Fox is sailing to Melbourne in 1906 with her sister Rosa, when a tragic landfall leaves her life entangled with three seamen: gentle Sam, cynical Danny and beautiful Gideon. After Rosa's scandalous elopement, trader Min-lu shows Lucy a new world of silks, spices and the silvery pearlshell of Broome: a place where breaking the rules is a way of life. The Great War begins, and Lucy's beloved must go to sea, where ruthless U-boats stalk the last of the old sailing ships. But when peace returns the influenza pandemic comes too—and Lucy, far from home, discovers how cruelly she has been betrayed.

NON-FICTION

ALAN VILLIERS: VOYAGER OF THE WINDS
2nd Edition, Seabooks Press, 2020. Fully revised and with over 100 photos. **Won the Mountbatten Maritime Award 2009.**

> *"Outstandingly researched and beautifully written."*

When Australian journalist Alan Villiers sailed on the last of the giant merchant windjammers in the 1920s and '30s, his writings and photos made him famous.

Villiers crewed on beautiful *Herzogin Cecilie* and tragic *Grace Harwar*, took tiny *Joseph Conrad* around the globe, sailed on Arabian dhows, led wartime landing craft, captained *Mayflower* II across the Atlantic, and inspired sail training and ship restoration projects.

Drawn from his personal diaries, this award-winning biography of the author-adventurer reveals both his mythmaking and his achievements. It is a tribute to the greatest sailing ships ever launched—and to the extraordinary man who loved them.

REDBILL: FROM PEARLS TO PEACE
Fremantle Press, 2004. **Won the Western Australian Premier's Book Award 2004 for Non-Fiction.**

> *"Lance has presented the biography of Redbill with quiet passion and exquisite detail."*

Redbill is the true story of a sailing boat's voyage through a century of history. She began life as a Broome pearlshell lugger owned by the buccaneering Captain Gregory, then became naval vessel HMAS *Redbill*, bombed in Darwin during WW2. After the war *Redbill* went pearling in Papua, then worked for Greenpeace in Tahiti, and raised funds for refugees.

Redbill also filmed a Bass Strait voyage, *If It Doesn't Kill You* and reunited a young Aboriginal man with his long-lost family. Finally she took on an epic voyage around the coast of Australia, to return to the North-West to face her greatest challenge yet: Rosita, the most powerful tropical cyclone to strike Broome in ninety years.